FATEFULLY

Elle DeMarco

CHAPTER 1

The anticipation for my final year of high school has my hand shaking as I apply mascara to my lashes, careful not to smudge it. I've been up since 4:30, but I still feel jittery as I wait for my best friend, Selena, to pick me up.

The stairs creak as my dad comes running down. He works an hour away in Meadowbrook, the nearest large city. His weary eyes crinkle as he smiles robotically at me and grabs the paper sack lunch that I packed for him.

"Senior year, it sure goes fast," His dark brows are arched as he takes in my outfit, and I know he wants to say more, but he's too task-oriented to offer me any sympathy for my nerves, let alone to notice.

He checks his thick gold wristwatch and frowns when he sees the time. "Is Selena on her way?"

Selena is habitually late, even though everything in our town, Harmony Falls is so close together.

"Yes," I assure him. "Now get on the road before the traffic gets too bad."

"Have a good day," he says, adjusting his rectangular glasses and smoothing out his crepey dress shirt. Despite working in surgery, my dad still wears a linen dress shirt every day until he changes into scrubs.

My voice catches the way it always does as I say, "Drive safe,"

Sometimes uttering those words feels taboo as if I'm tempting fate again, but saying them is a habit at this point.

As if somehow taken over by the man he used to be, he gives me a stiff embrace before saying goodbye. I want to hold on a second longer, just to take in this moment, but I know he's in a rush so I step back after he swiftly releases the hug.

Dad's voice is almost robotic. "Love you, kiddo,"

I find myself staring into his faraway eyes, lined with the dullness of grief. I'm still wondering if the man my dad used to be is ever going to come back. "Love you too,"

He scrambles out the door, rushing as always. I'm putting my coffee into my thermos when I hear Selena's familiar two honks, signifying to me she's here.

"Hi!" Selena yells over the country music blaring on the speakers of her black sedan, a hand-me-down car from her grandparents. "We have a guest today!"

She gestures to the row behind her, revealing Carlos, her younger brother. Despite sitting in the cramped back of the car, which is filled with half-finished canvas art projects, outfit changes, and the smell of Selena's floral perfume, Carlos wears a big grin.

"He's outgrown the bus," Selena chuckles as she pulls onto the main road. I grip the door handle tightly as the vehicle swerves with her quick movement.

"You've made it to the big leagues, huh? Are you looking forward to your first day of middle school?" I crane my neck to turn back to him.

His dark curls are slicked back and his button-up shirt, no doubt a hand-me-down from his dad, is practically hanging off him.

"Yes, I'm more excited for high school though," Carlos replies.

Once we're at the crosswalk for the middle school, Carlos waves as he walks out of the car, his heavy backpack almost pulling him backward. He has to adjust the straps several times before he finds his rhythm. Even though we're not related by blood, he's practically my little brother at this point since I've known Selena and her family for six years, since the first day of sixth grade.

As if out of instinct, I cling to the inside handle by the

passenger door as Selena's car lurches to a halt. She gives me an apologetic smile as her eyes trail to my death grip. I immediately release my fingers and clasp them in my lap instead.

A group of guys huddled by their lockers pause their conversation as Selena and I walk by. In the corner of my eye, I can see Selena trying her best to hold her tongue, but the widening of her dark eyes tells me I have about thirty seconds before she goes off on them. I gently tug her arm and pull her towards another hallway. I was hoping to fly under the radar this year, but the group's blatant stares tell me that people still haven't forgotten what happened over the summer.

I almost bend into the background a little too well the rest of the day. Selena arrives fifteen minutes late to lunch, trailed by a clique of girls she waves goodbye to before joining me in my spot on a hidden bench. I don't know why I thought making more friends would be easier this year, but I'm learning it's not. I give Selena a convincing smile after the lunch bell rings before I rush toward my next class, doing my best not to let it show just how much I feel like a social dud sometimes.

In AP Chemistry, I'm walking toward an empty table at the back of the room when Mr. Hughes, my teacher says, "Adele, the seats are assigned already. You're with Hunter." He gestures toward where Hunter Watts, otherwise known as "Mega Watts" to the football boys, sits wearing a smug grin.

Just the sight of him has electricity pulsing through my body; it evokes memories I don't want to think about. It's too much too soon. I was planning on avoiding him at all costs this year.

Act natural, I remind myself. Pretend like he isn't the only person who's seen you completely fall apart.

"Hey, Adele. Long time no see," His voice is smooth as he gives me a once-over. "Now that I've made it to AP and am one of your people, am I worthy of a response?"

I grit my teeth at him. This is going to be a long year.

I'm standing in place, so Mr. Hughes, softly says, "Don't worry, Adele, He doesn't bite."

I cautiously set my bag down, scooching my uncomfortable, backless chair as far from Hunter as possible, a difficult feat since the table must be three feet wide, so it's hardly enough for two chairs, let alone with space between us.

I ignore the wooden, amber smell of his cologne, which is a nice contrast to the guys at school who constantly smell like they took an Axe shower.

"Hi, Hunter. Nice to see you again," I say, my lips turning up in a forced smile.

I kept my head stiff and leaned in toward the screen the entire class. My chair screeches as I grab my belongings and rush toward the gymnasium for P.E.

I thought by getting to class early, I could get an early head start on changing but I have had no such luck. The girl's locker room, which smells like a combination of floral perfume, mint gum, and hazy hairspray, is complete chaos. There must be fifty girls in a space that is meant for ten. My eyes are completely surprised as girls casually chat with their best friends while simultaneously haphazardly shoving their clothes into lockers, revealing lingerie that can only be described as "date night ready".

"Anderson? I didn't know you were retaking PE," Hunter Watts wears the same cheesy smile on his face as he effortlessly jogs toward me. Since I spent so long changing, I was late to class and am stuck walking laps as my punishment. The sunlight brings out the green flecks in his piercing teal blue eyes, and the light brown freckles lining his golden tan skin. With sandy blonde hair, he's the definition of a California boy. Well, the kind who probably pumps iron for two hours a day.

"I'm not retaking it," I say matter-of-factly, "I just wanted to wait to take it,"

He places his hand on his chest in faux concern. "Worried it would mess up your makeup

To my surprise, he walks in step alongside me and matches my pace.

"No, I just have different priorities than getting sweaty in front of a bunch of my classmates," I wave my hands around. "You wouldn't understand."

Hunter has always brought out the worst in me. While I don't think of myself as a sugary-sweet person, there's just something about him that has always driven me nuts. Maybe it's the way he's always poking into people's business. Like mine, for instance. I can think of a couple of scenarios, but one comes to mind the most.

I could even argue that his big mouth, beautiful as it is, is the reason why I'm such an outcast this year.

"Ah, I wouldn't normally," Hunter's eyes dance with mischief as they meet mine. "But I'm a scholar this year. I'm sophisticated now."

I chuckle. "Whatever you say, Hunter,"

"Adele! Hunter! It's been ten laps! Quit screwing around!" Coach Z's loud voice startles me out of my daze.

"I'll race you there," Hunter turns to me. "Unless you think you can't win."

I gesture between us. "Trust me, I know you'll win,"

"What if I give you a three-second head start?" Hunter challenges.

My lips tilt up. "What do I win?"

Even though I'm sweating just from being outside, Hunter looks right in his element as we walk together. His bright smile is nearly blinding under the sun's beams.

Hunter shrugs. "Bragging rights of course,"

"I guess it'll make me cool by association," I say in a teasing tone.

We're halfway through this lap, about two hundred yards from the finish line. Hunter counts to three, and I sprint with all my strength. I run so fast it feels like my legs will give out. I tilt my head back and sprint, full speed ahead, smiling smugly as I realize I have a lead on him. At the last stretch, though, Hunter comes out of nowhere and flies ahead of me. The way his strong legs move is so effortless, it makes me have a new appreciation for sports.

"Well, I guess you won fair and square," I say, putting my hands on my knees as I catch my breath.

"Well, I mean, I did have an advantage," Hunter says.

"Being the football captain?" I ask.

"Well, that too," Hunter's eyes roam over my makeshift gym outfit. "I think wearing sweatpants in August may have lost you a couple of seconds."

"Nobody likes a sore winner," I say, throwing my hands up and smiling as I walk away.

"You butchered that phrase, but I'll give you a pass," Hunter grins as he waves goodbye. "See you around, Anderson."

After school, Selena sent me an apologetic text, saying that she was not able to drive me home because she had to run an errand with Carlos. I reassured her that I would get a ride from my dad.

I tilt my head up at the blue sky; it's a perfect day outside, and besides, my dad won't be home for hours anyway. I ignore the racing in my chest as I make my way through the school parking lot toward the main road, where I can take the sidewalk home.

I keep my head down as I pass a group of guys. The only one whose name I know is Sean, but I'm not about to say hello to him. I feel his eyes on me before I glance up and make eye contact with him. Recognition dawns on his features; he recognizes me from this summer. I hate the way his face twists into an expression of pity as if he has to apologize for something that he didn't even do. I quickly look away, picking up the pace. My legs burn as I make my way to the edge of the parking lot, and I can't stop the need to look back one last time, just to make sure that no one else is here.

I exhale a shaky breath once I'm back to the main road again, but I don't feel like going home anymore, where I'll inevitably be alone for a few hours.

Instead, I walk toward the Coves with my head in the clouds as the sidewalk becomes a gravelly path. As the incline becomes steeper, I take a break and look around at the shiny, dark rocks where the crisp white water breaks so strongly that it sends a mist of salt spray that fills the air around it. I nestle into a snug spot in a little dark cave overlooking the ocean and let my legs dangle over as I listen to the rhythm of the roaring waves for hours on end. The wind tickles my hair and the chilly breeze picks up while the sunset begins to unfold. As much as I want to see all of the vibrant colors unfold, I gather my things and begin to walk home.

I feel a pang of sadness when I finally arrive after dark to find that all the lights in my home are still off. The house feels drafty because we forgot to close the windows. My dad's single text illuminates my phone screen: Going to have to stay the night; the surgery is taking longer than expected. Have fun at dinner at Selena's!

I'm too disgruntled to reply, knowing he won't read my response anyway. I set my phone across the room and turn my music to full volume. I sing at the top of my lungs and let the lyrics numb me down until the song drowns out all my thoughts. Then, I re-read the book I've read twice this month already, and wait with anticipation for the sleep that rarely comes. Sweat forms on my forehead as the music I've been playing does little to help me relax. I check the clock: 1 am. Four more hours until I wake up for school tomorrow. When sleep does wash over me, though, I wish it hadn't, because all it does is remind me of the day everything changed.

CHAPTER 2

It's the first pep rally of the year, and I'm looking around for Selena when the music begins blaring as the marching band plays brass music.

In the bustle of everyone taking their seats, I feel backpacks whipping against me as throngs of people squeeze past me in the narrow row of bleachers. The sound of cheering echoes throughout the auditorium. I see a girl waving at me with a shy smile.

"Everyone, please be seated," The shrill microphone blares as the school principal, Ms. Walker, our principal, says, her tight fingers gripping the microphone.

I weave my way through the crowd toward the open seat next to the girl, who waves me over.

"Hi," she says.

I give her a hesitant smile. "Hi,"

"I'm Jackie, we're in Study Hall together," she explains.

It's then that I place her familiar curly brown hair and mocha eyes.

My voice softens a little. "I'm Adele,"

Before we can make small talk, the assembly begins with the Dance Team twirling in their red and white skirts. A peppy pop tune plays as they sway their hips. The crowd goes wild as the football team comes charging through the side entrance of the gymnasium. Several of the guys on the team pull on their red jerseys, chanting and yelling as they pat their shoulders to point to their numbers on the back.

I stifle an eye roll as I hear a guy a couple of seats away yell, "Megawatts! He's the one to call the shots!"

Surely enough, Hunter is front and center, surrounded by

his pack of football buddies. The song changes, and the football team joins the cheerleaders in a dance that can only be described as hypnotic. Even I can't look away as the football team stumbles around the choreography while the Dance Team gracefully turns around them, trying to lead them through the movements. As they all move in sync with one another, I feel a pang of jealousy, because I could never do that. I don't know how to let loose in a crowd like that. Instead, I'm sitting in one of the back rows.

The rest of the assembly goes by in a blink. Usually, everyone makes small talk with their friends, grateful to have an excuse for being late to their next class. I slip by the crowds of people and out into the fresh air outside. Today though, Jackie's voice struggles to match the clamoring and yelling in the gymnasium. I lean in and faintly recognize her asking me which class I have next.

"Calculus," I say.

"I'm in Trig, so we're in the same building," Jackie faces me. "Do you want to walk together?"

It takes us a while to navigate through the crowd, who are being ushered by the teachers out of the gymnasium.

After Jackie and I part ways, I pause when I see Hunter. He has his cell phone to his ear, and his expression is downcast. I can't make out what he's saying, but the hushed tone he's speaking in surprises me. Not wanting him to see me, I tilt my head down and rush toward the school library.

I don't see Hunter again until AP Chemistry, where he wears a smile that appears ingenuine. He doesn't even greet me with a snarky comment, and I almost wish he did, because seeing him like this is weird. It feels too vulnerable, and it takes me back to the one time I let him see me a different way, only to be humiliated.

The table feels even smaller today as we fight for space for our bulky textbooks and notebooks. I feel my mind going somewhere else as Mr. Hughes begins droning on about the history of the periodic table.

I sneak a glance at Hunter, whose eyes are as focused as

laser beams on the screen at the front of the room. Hunter gives me a questioning glance, a smile on the edge of his lips, causing me to immediately regret my choice to look at him. It's not my job to see if he's okay. Hunter knows he's devastatingly attractive, so me looking at him will only make things awkward. The last thing I need is to appear to be interested in him, in any shape or form of the word.

I pretend I have blinders on, and try to take interest in what Mr. Hughes is saying, but it's difficult when I'm essentially taking Chemistry for the second time. I've lived and breathed science for the last three years, and I'm ready for a change.

"All right, class, Today is our first pop quiz," Mr. Hughes announces, "it's time to see who did the textbook reading last night. This class is college credit, so the rigor and pace will reflect that."

Next to me, in my peripheral vision, I see Hunter's shoulders tense as he sits upright, his leg bouncing up and down.

I hunch my shoulders, putting my head down as I quickly jot down my answers, feeling my face flush at how swiftly I completed the quiz. I'm trying to be different this year, and this isn't helping to fix my reputation. Blood rushes to my head as I tilt it down again, pretending to check over my answers. Once I see someone else turn their quiz in, I cautiously walk toward the front of the room to submit mine, feeling my heart race. Mr. Hughes has a weird rule where everyone has to put their heads down after finishing the quiz. He calls it a "brain break", but I know it's to prevent cheating, or taking pictures of the quiz to show the next class. I feel a sense of dread wash over me as I realize that I will be going to Physical Education class next. I'd rather take ten more quizzes than have to publicly run laps again. As soon as the bell rings, Hunter's voice startles me. "Hey, Anderson? Are there quizzes every day?"

His aquamarine eyes look discouraged, and I find myself wanting to extend an olive branch, just this once.

"This first one's just to weed people out," I explain, "but

yes, the reading does need to be done every night, just in case. He usually gives a quiz every Tuesday and Thursday."

"Twice a week?" Hunter groans as he tries to shove his bulky textbook into his backpack. "What about those of us who have lives outside of school?"

I know he probably means nothing personal with his words, but I feel a knot in my stomach as soon as they sink in because his message is clear and received. His words sting, even though I know they shouldn't.

My voice is seething. "Maybe you should go join another class, the one meant for people who have lives." I don't even bother to look back as I race out into the hallway and straight towards PE. In the locker room, I quickly change into my sweatpants. My face flushes as I take my clothes off as fast as humanly possible. I join the group on the field as they go through the stretch.

Coach Z gives me a small nod of recognition as he tells us to do jumping jacks. After we go through the warmup, Coach Z says, "Two laps, everybody!"

I'm walking toward the track when Coach Z calls my name. "Adele! Hang back!"

His voice is so gruff it jolts me awake.

"Yes, coach?" I ask.

"Where is your uniform?" Coach Z asks.

"Uniform?" I ask, trying to play dumb. There is no way I am wearing those tiny shorts in front of everyone.

Coach Z gives me a pointed look. "Adele, the only reason why I'm fine with you neglecting to wear the uniform is because so far, you have been following the school's dress code. But, with how hot the weather has been this week, sweatpants are a safety issue. You could get a heat stroke,"

"I'll lie down if I catch heat stroke," I respond.

"Very funny," he continues, "I know you wanted to pass on Physical Education, but I think it will be good for you. You might even make a few new friends."

Over the summer, I begged the school administration to

make an exception for me to not take P.E. I pleaded my case on three different occasions and was rejected every time. Coach Z is now dead set on me becoming some sort of fitness protégé. The idea of having to do all of these games in front of my classmates terrifies me though.

I'm about to respond to Coach Z when I hear a voice say, "Hi, Anderson."

I look over and see none other than Hunter, who wears a big, smug smile on his face. I'm glad to see he's enjoying this. Great.

"See, Adele? You're already making friends," Coach Z says in a kind tone.

"Us, friends? Nope, he only is friends with people who have *lives*," I reply.

Coach Z just looks at Hunter. "Hunter, buddy up with this one, will you? Show her that exercise can be fun. I'm going to go collect the rest of the class." He trots toward the group gathered in the center of the grassy field.

As soon as Coach Z leaves, Hunter smirks. "It looks like I found your weak spot,"

My voice is as cold as ice. "Great,"

"It is a graduation requirement," Hunter says matter-of-factly.

I make no effort to keep the edge out of my voice. "I know, that's why I'm here,"

"I thought you were here because you love running in sweatpants," Hunter says.

I'm surprised to find myself grinning.

"I know, I know. I'm atrocious at exercising. Believe me, I know," I put my hand on my forehead to shield my eyes from the sun, and my embarrassment. "Why do you think I waited so long to take this class?" I ask, surprised to see his smile matches my own.

"I take it you don't do a lot of sports?" Hunter asks.

The look I give him makes him chuckle.

"I don't do much outside of school," I explain, "I'm sorry

for biting your head off about it though. I was more frustrated than anything."

"I'm sorry too. It was wrong of me to say that," Hunter says, "I was frustrated too. I know for certain that I failed that quiz."

I offer him a reassuring smile. "If it helps, his class gets easier."

Hunter sighs. "I wish it did, but I'm retaking chemistry,"

"What do you mean? You didn't take Chemistry 1?" I ask.

"I did, but I failed it," Hunter says quietly, "if I retake Chemistry 1, I'd have to graduate late, so I have to take AP to stay on track."

"That's rough," I reply.

I follow him to the school's track and begin fast walking alongside him. He turns around and walks backward, facing me, still somehow walking faster than me. Since he has a few inches of height on me, I find myself struggling to catch up.

"You could say my entire future is counting on passing that class," His tone is light, but his facial expression is tense.

"I'm sure you'll do just fine," I shrug. "You have me as a lab partner, remember? At least you have the guarantee of acing every lab."

"You're quite confident in that class," Hunter says.

My smile tightens. "Well, I'm Pre-Med, so my entire future is dependent on it too,"

"So, you understand then," he replies.

I know the feeling all too well. "I do,"

Coach Z tells me to pick up the pace, so I switch into a slow jog. It's a baby step, and I'm running as slow as walking, but it's a start. My breath shakes as I kick it into gear, challenging my legs to move swiftly as Hunter and I round the corner. While I'm working up a sweat, Hunter is nonchalantly running backward. He quietly cheers me on, chanting my last name while I run to the end of the track. I laugh hysterically as I struggle to match Hunter's pace, trying to beat him at the last second, and still somehow get left in the dust by him although he's running backward.

Exhilaration flows through my body even though my legs ache and my forehead drips with sweat. And for the first time in a long time, I feel proud of myself. The buzzing feeling follows me for the rest of the day.

"How are the college applications coming along? Do you need to add any more extracurriculars?" my dad asks over dinner.

I set down my water glass, wishing for a change in subject. Anything. Even talking about the weather would be better than this. "Everything looks good so far,"

"I can't believe everything we've been working toward is almost here," He remarks.

His use of "we" is completely warranted, evidenced by the dark circles that rim his soulful brown eyes, which mirror my own. One of my least favorite aspects of his job is the lack of balance he has. Even when he's not at work, it's all that occupies his mind. He works so hard so that I can have a good future, but I have a different understanding of what that looks like. Right now, I wish we could have more time in the present.

"Me too," I say, "I'm still narrowing down my options."

"You don't need to narrow anything down, sweetheart," His tone is adamant. "I want you to have all the options. Keep applying, and we'll send you to the best pre-med program you get into."

I try to smile, but it looks forced. "Thanks, Dad."

He pauses. "We might even be able to get you an internship at the hospital."

I search for an excuse. "Thank you, but I know I need to focus on my grades this year,"

"Good point," He says, "We'll circle back to it next semester."

The rest of the dinner is deafeningly silent until we go to our separate rooms.

"Goodnight!" my dad hollers as he walks to his room.

While my dad sleeps, I read every book I can get my hands

on. While I love the thrill of fantasy books, I mostly prefer books that make me feel something, anything. When I first started to read, I'd read the trashiest books I could find, just to see if they'd evoke some kind of response. Now, I lean towards gooey romance or heart-touching drama. At eighteen years old, I struggle to feel anything. Selena, who feels more strongly than anyone I know, claims it's because everything is bottled up.

My favorite part of reading, though, is the way I don't have to overthink anything when it comes to the ending. Things usually work out, for the most part at least. Only in books though, of course. Not in my life. Which is what makes reading so much better.

CHAPTER 3

At lunch, Selena and I jam out to country music that drowns out the elephant in the car: the inevitable goodbye we'll have to say at the end of this school year as we go our separate ways. Her, to wherever the wind carries her, most likely an art school in New York, if I were to guess. And I, to whichever prestigious school my dad deems the best fit for "our" plan. My heart stirs to stay in this town, but my dad would never approve. According to him, there's no opportunity here; Harmony Falls is simply a place where people get stuck.

While we have no major outlet malls or fancy hotels, Harmony Falls has its appeal. The charm of my hometown lies in the coastal architecture and the ocean views.

"I've been meaning to ask you," Selena turns down the music. "Would you want to come with me to Mario's party on Friday?"

My answer is an immediate resounding no, but I pause and pretend to think about it a little.

"Maybe next time? I have to study," I reply, trying to sound convincing about wanting to go next time. The study part is sincere, though. My Friday nights during the school year often consist of textbooks and teen dramas.

Selena tilts her head. "Come on, just this once? Before the semester gets harder?"

"I would, but I'm already swimming in papers I have to write," I say, "and besides, I don't want to miss Game Night."

On the first Saturday of every month, Selena's family has a game night. It's a tradition her family has been doing for her entire life, and one that became a special part of my life when I met Selena on the first day of middle school.

"I guess that is a pretty good reason," Selena sighs. "I'll let it slide this time."

My tone is light as I hold back a laugh. "Thank you,"

"It's nice seeing you so happy." She gives me a knowing smile. There's an unspoken message behind her words, but I don't respond to it. Instead, I ask her if she has her eye on anyone this year.

"I don't even know if it will turn into something, but I want it to." She looks down at her cherry-red acrylic nails.

"Well, it sounds like there's chemistry there," I offer.

Selena arches a brow. "Speaking of chemistry and cute boys, why didn't you tell me that Hunter Watts is your lab partner?"

"Because I knew you'd respond like this," I gesture to her, giggling.

Selena's voice is an octave higher than usual. "Is he already driving you nuts? Because I can think of ten girls off the top of my head that would be more than happy to take your place,"

"I'm sitting next to him in class, that's it," I shrug. "It's not like I'm dance partners with him or something."

"Please tell me, that even in your unfeeling heart, you can acknowledge that he's dreamy." Selena's witty sarcasm soothes me like it always does because she's not afraid to put the truth out there.

"I hadn't noticed." I try to hide my smile, but it's pointless. Selena can read me.

"Liar!" Selena says, and I begin laughing.

"I can't get distracted," I say, "books before boys."

"I've never heard that one before," Selena's brows furrowed. "But then again, with the books you read, I could see how they'd closely compared."

Selena often asks me about the stories I'm reading, listening with the same attention someone would give to a story about real-life experiences, like crushes and relationship drama. Instead, my knowledge of most of those things is between the pages of a book.

"I've been thinking," I pause "and, I want to start putting myself out there a little more with the whole dating thing."

"Finally! I've been waiting for this moment! I love this for you," Selena gushes. "I already have so many ideas!"

I hold up a hand and grin. "Let's not get too ahead of ourselves,"

"I haven't even shared yet," Selena says, the reddish tint of her dark hair glistening in the sun as she wears a huge smile. I can see her brain racing with a million ideas, and I love it because I'm not even sure where to start.

"Let me guess, you want me to get a boyfriend right away?" I ask, arching a brow.

The way her smile gets even wider tells me I'm right, but she'll never admit it. "Well, maybe just a date to the Homecoming dance,"

"Who? I wouldn't even know how to get asked,"

"Greg!" Selena notices my blank stare. "Come on, he's cute, smart, and funny."

I sigh. "It wouldn't be right, I don't see him that way,"

"How you don't see him that way is shocking, I mean he has the whole Oxford scholar thing going on, and you have the whole doctor vibe going for you. It just makes sense," Selena continues, "maybe if you spend some time with him, like dancing with him, you'll see him differently. I mean, have you ever seen him let loose outside of school?"

I'm still skeptical, but she might be right. "That's a good point,"

"You sound surprised," Selena says.

"Then, what is your plan for your date? For Homecoming?" I ask.

Selena's eyes widen. "I have someone in mind,"

"Does he have a name?" I ask.

Selena wears a mischievous smile. "Stay tuned for more details,"

I don't want her to feel like she has to get me up with someone just so she can start with a guy. Given my luck in the past, I know that it's unlikely I'll have a date this year. "Well, either way, you're going with him, whether or not I have a date," I say.

Selena's eyes meet mine. "You'll have a date,"

"We'll see," I hesitate, "but either way, I won't hold you back."

"We'll coordinate our dresses," Selena says, pausing, " I'm thinking red, like burgundy, to match my hair,"

"Of course, you are," I say, smiling, "maybe we can choose colors that complement each other. Because we both know red will look weird on my skin tone."

"Speaking of red, have you given any more thought to my hair idea?" Selena asks.

Selena, who impulsively dyed her hair at 2 a.m. a couple of months ago, has been trying to convince me to let her put subtle, honey-brown highlights in my wavy dark brown hair.

Feeling a rush of excitement at the possibility of walking into school feeling brand new, I reply, "I have, and I'm leaning towards yes. Maybe after I get a date to the dance, we'll talk about it."

She claps her hands together, and the car fills with her harmonious laughter. And I realize once again that it feels good to be feeling things again.

~

I wait until my dad's sound asleep and do something I've only done one other time: I sneak out. The fact that I'm just only going for a walk, not doing anything scandalous, should ease my guilt, but it doesn't. Having to sit through another dinner with my dad and talk about medical school was unnerving.

Now that the sun has long since set, the chilly air whips at my hair. I pull my hoodie tighter around me to ward off the relentless ocean breeze. My house is only a ten-minute walk from the ocean, but it feels longer tonight as I wander alone. Even though Harmony Falls is as safe as can be, it still feels unnerving when the sky is completely pitched, the dim street lights fail to offer me any leeway with my vision, only allowing me to see a few feet in front of me.

As I get closer to the beach, the rushing of the ocean grows louder in volume. The waves crash on the shore in a soothing rhythm as the water lightly mists the sand. The moon illuminates the glassy dark water, which has a gray glow tonight.

I'm about to set up a spot on the sand when the idea of sitting alone out here, unable to see if someone is behind me, has me feeling spooked. Instead, I walk right to the water's edge, taking my shoes off and allowing the cold water to brush against my feet. I lean forward, and hesitate, wanting to test the limits and reach further into the water. Since I'm by myself, though, I settle for the water hitting my calves; it's been years since I've swam, and I don't even think I remember how to. I stay there for several minutes, enjoying my solitude until the faint sound of people in the distance disrupts me.

I can't make out the faces in the dark, but I recognize some of their voices from school as they come closer to me. I'm still putting my toes in the water, and I feel myself freeze, unsure about what to do. How do I slip away unnoticed?

I put my hoodie over my head, hopeful that I can rely on the darkness to help me blend in. I tiptoe past the group of people on the beach, surprised to see people from my school out so late. There are only eight or so people, and they're all too occupied with talking to each other while they lay out wood for a bonfire to notice me creep past them. My eyes linger for a second, and I wonder what it would be like to be a part of something like that.

I'm walking back towards the road and feel grateful for the return of some light, albeit dim. The glow of the faded streetlight keeps me from falling into the rocky part of the path. I suddenly feel off-kilter, and glance up to come face-to-face with Hunter.

"Adele?" He asks.

I was shocked that he would recognize me with my hoodie up, but then again, I immediately recognized him. He's hard to forget though. Even in a bulky jacket, he stands out. It's no wonder that he was unanimously selected to be the captain of our football team.

"Hi, Hunter." I try to hide my surprise, but it's to no avail.

His lips curve in a smile that I can barely make out in the dark. "I didn't know you were coming tonight,"

"Oh, I'm not," I dismissively wave my hand toward the road. "I was just heading home."

"Oh," He meets my gaze head-on. "Late night swim?"

"Something like that," I explain, "well, it was more of a late-night walk."

I hug my arms around myself as he stares at me.

"By yourself?" Hunter asks.

"Yes," I say softly, acting as if taking a walk on the beach while it's pitch outside is a thing I regularly do.

Hunter takes a step closer to me. "Where's your car? I can walk you."

I shake my head. "I walked here,"

"I'll drive you home then," Hunter says.

Before I can object, he leads me to his black pickup truck and opens the door for me. Our hands brush against one another as they reach for the door handle simultaneously, and I find myself pulling my hand away while he chuckles.

"Thank you," I say before he gently closes the door.

We sit in comfortable silence during the short drive from the beach to my house. As soon as we pull up to my house, Hunter murmurs, "Well, here we are, home safe,"

His awkwardness catches me off guard. Maybe he's thinking about the last time I was in his car.

"Thank you for the ride," I whisper.

As I open my car door, Hunter hesitates. "Adele, wait,"

"Yes?" I ask, turning to face him, trying to identify why I see protectiveness in his eyes.

"Be safe out there," Hunter says, reinforcing yet again how we're leading lives that are going in completely different directions.

"I will, thank you," I reply

"I mean it, Adele. No more walking alone in the dark," Hunter says, his eyes locked on mine. His eyes darken as he meets my gaze, relentless in making his point. His protectiveness catches me completely off guard and sends a small shiver of goosebumps down my arm. His intensity surprises me and scares me a little.

My breath hitches in my throat. "Understood,"

His words are starkly different from our usual snarky banter, and end the night on a weird note, because they bring me back to the night when I stopped being invisible, and I'm not sure how I feel about it.

CHAPTER 4

It feels like my entire body is on fire as I snake my way through the cafeteria in an attempt to find Selena. My hands tremble as I glance around; no sign of her. I almost drop my lunch tray as I try to look for someone, anyone I can sit with. Jackie, the girl from my study hall class, offers me a polite wave. She seems nice enough, and I'm sure she'd let me sit with her, but panic rises in my chest at the idea of sitting with a group of people I don't know. There's a small spot next to her at a jam-packed table with a bunch of juniors. I give her a hesitant wave back and then make my way through the heavy metal doors leading to the outdoor courtyard. I don't miss the way her face falls as I walk in the opposite direction, and I hate being the cause.

As I walk through the lawn area, I see Greg, surrounded by a couple of other guys and girls on a giant blanket in the grass. His head is in a book, one for an assignment that's due a month from now. His dark glasses are perched on his nose as he leans in, thumbing the pages to go to the next one. I try to scramble away with my head down before he can see me, but his voice calls me over.

"Adele, I've been meaning to catch up with you," We've gone to school together since kindergarten, and always seem to have at least one class together every semester. He's very invested in his academics, and dresses for the part, looking as if he's ready for Oxford every day instead of our average public high school, which is more known for sports than anything else.

Today he's dressed in a dark green polo shirt that brings out his olive skin. His black Ray-Ban glasses frame his green eyes. He looks handsome, and the smile on his face today shows me he knows it. And yet, I don't feel any butterflies, which is why I usually keep a little distance from Greg.

"Hi," I offer him a polite smile. "How was your summer?"

Greg's voice is enthusiastic as if he were talking about a tropical vacation instead of studying. "Oh, you know, lots of tutoring and test prep. Nothing too exciting."

"We both know you love that. You live for it," I say and he chuckles.

He shrugs and gestures to me. "I guess you get it,"

Only I don't. I'm on the pre-med track, but I don't enjoy it the way that Greg, the captain of the speech and debate, does. He's meant to become a professor and has his eye on every Ivy League university. While I'm "meant" for pre-med, it's only because of my dad, who wants me to follow in his footsteps.

I'm frozen in place, towering over him and his spot in the grass. "It's nice to relate to someone," It's a half-truth, at least. I feel myself flush as some of the people in his group begin to stare at me. "I'll see you in AP Lit, Greg."

Greg hesitates, and I can see him scooching in his place to make room for me, but my heart is already racing under the gaze of his friends.

He gives me an understanding smile, but his eyes don't look as bright as they did a couple of minutes ago. "See you then, Adele."

I ended up making my way toward AP Chem, even though there were still twenty minutes of lunch left. Mr. Hughes keeps his classroom unlocked at lunch for people like me who have nowhere to sit when our only friend is M.I.A.

I put my earbuds in and turn the volume all the way up as I finish homework in the empty room.

Before I know it, the clatter of people coming into the classroom startles me out of my trance.

Today is our first lab, and Mr. Hughes encouraged us to "collaborate", which is why I'm currently watching Hunter incorrectly mix the substances.

"Relax, Anderson. I've got this," Hunter says, his voice as

charismatic as ever.

The thick plastic lab glasses line his eyes as he carefully stirs the sulfuric acid and vinegar in the large glass beaker.

I'm so distracted by the way his arms strain against the lab coat that I completely zone out. My heart races as I notice that the mixture is steamy-looking, rising above the beaker, at risk of bubbling over.

I grab Hunter's hand, shocked by how callused his large palm is, and tug him, trying to pull his body down with me, hidden by the table, but he stays put, feet planted in the ground as he arches a brow and asks, "What are you doing?"

"Get down!" I say, tugging on his arm. My fingers dig into his skin as I attempt to prevent him from getting splashed by the dangerous concoction we just made.

He finally joins me, followed by Mr. Hughes, who wears a disapproving scowl as he comes running over with some liquid that helps to dissipate the gaseous spray that is being released into the air. I sputter and cough until the nauseating smell fades a little. Hunter's hand is still in mine, our fingers interlaced. His hand is shaking slightly, gripping mine for dear life.

"That was a close call," Mr. Hughes says, his tone stern. The rest of the class has their eyes locked on us. The room falls into a hushed silence, with neither of us saying a word as we break apart.

Hunter stumbles as he gets up, and it's the first time I've seen him not be so self-assured. Is it because he's out of place for maybe the first time? I think back to how he gave me a ride home last night and blurt, "I must've given him the wrong measurements, my mistake,"

"Whatever happened today, I do not want it happening again," Mr. Hughes' voice is firm as he adjusts his glasses and pulls them down to the tip of his nose. "You both could have gotten injured. I need you to follow directions to the exact amount next time. Do you understand?"

"Yes," I reply as Hunter simply nods in response.

We work in silence until the bell rings.

"Adele, I'd like to speak with you for a moment," Mr. Hughes says.

My back stiffens as I walk towards his table, which is scattered with diagrams, photos, and notebooks.

As everyone clears out of the room, he looks up from his desk. "Have you thought any more about your next step? Now is the time to start narrowing down internship options for your college applications,"

"Yes," My voice falters as I lie. I decided to focus on appealing to his expertise. "What do you recommend?"

"Any medical experience is beneficial," He sorts through the mound of papers on his desk. "Do you have a specific area that interests you?"

When I stare blankly at him, he clears his throat. "It can be difficult to choose from so many different avenues, but it's very important to dip your toe in,"

"Thank you for the advice," I say as I collect my things,

"Anytime," Mr. Hughes' eyes meet mine. "You'll need to decide soon."

I nod as I walk out of the classroom, thrown into the crowd of people rushing toward their next class.

I fast walk toward the gymnasium, determined to start P.E. on a better note this time.

I'm walking around the track, at the tail end of the entire group, when I hear Hunter behind me. "Adele! Just the girl I was looking for,"

I smile smugly at him. "You just saw me,"

I can see the hesitation in his eyes as he walks into step beside me.

He pushes his hair back. "Did Mr. Hughes bite your head off?"

The sun beams off his sandy hair, and I think about how unfair it is that he looks so handsome in athletic clothes. As much as I want to milk it a little and have him feel a little guilty for almost exploding toxic chemicals on us, I give in.

"Surprisingly not." I slow my pace.

"That's good," His eyes meet mine. "Thank you for covering for me."

"You're welcome," I nod my head. "We are partners after all."

He gives me a cheeky smile, and says, "Anderson, you're pretty cool, you know that?"

"That's an honor coming from you," I say in a teasing voice.

His eyes light up. "I've been thinking, and I think we can help each other,"

In the distance, I can see Coach Z gesturing for my classmates and me to hurry up on the track. A group of my peers are already crowded on the field, huddling in for the next game. I see rubber balls lined up on the field and immediately feel dread.

I know I should sprint over, especially since I do need a good grade in this class, but something about the smile Hunter is wearing causes me to linger.

"How so?" I ask.

"Well, I need to pass AP Chem to graduate," Hunter drawls.

"And?" I ask.

"Maybe we could help each other," Hunter lowers his voice, prompting me to lean in. "You could tutor me."

"Hunter," I say, pausing my walk because my sweats are sticking to my skin, "I'm sorry, I don't have time to help you. I have to find an internship. I know you have a lot going on outside of school, and while I don't, school is my life, and I need to start taking steps toward my future."

"But what if I helped you?" Hunter asks.

"With what?" My voice is frustrated. "And don't say P.E., because I know I can fake it and still do okay in this class. I'm not trying to become a track star or anything."

His shoulders slump, and I instantly feel apologetic because I know he needs it, but I can't help anyone right now, not with all those application deadlines looming over my head. And especially not him.

I open my mouth to respond, to try to reword everything,

but Coach Z yells my name. I give Hunter a small smile as I sprint towards the field. The sad look in Hunter's eyes stays with me for the rest of class.

~

I'm walking towards Selena's car when she exclaims, "I'll see you tomorrow!" Her voice is sugary sweet.

"What?" I ask as I get closer.

She has a mischievous glint in her eyes as she leans in. "I can't believe you didn't tell me that Hunter is taking you home today. I thought you hated him."

She hops into her car at record speed, and I don't have enough time to react.

I'm about to question her when I hear Hunter behind me. "Hate is kind of a harsh word, don't you think?"

I give him a playful smile. "I know you're used to everyone rolling out the red carpet for you, Hunter, so it might be a shock,"

He smirks at me. "You'll come around soon enough,"

Hunter walks closer to Selena, who's rolling her window down in her car, ready to pick her brother Carlos up. I'm frozen between them wondering what on earth is happening.

"We worked through our differences," Hunter offers her an award-winning smile. "I forgave her."

"Well, that's a new development, but I'm here for it. Tell me everything later," Selena says, rolling her window up and backing out.

I turn toward Hunter. "What was all that about? Why does she think that you're driving me home?" My voice is shaking.

"Because I told her," Hunter says nonchalantly.

"Why would you do that?" I ask.

"Because our conversation was interrupted earlier," Hunter gestures to his truck pulled a few spaces away. "Come on, Anderson, I'll buy you a coffee."

"Fine," I huff. "Thank you," I murmur while he closes my door.

As we leave the parking lot, I see plenty of people staring at us, so I tilt my head down.

"Do you really hate me?" Hunter asks as he pulls up to the Java Shoppe.

"I used to," I say.

He doesn't say anything back, and I'm grateful, not wanting to take a turn down embarrassing memory lane with him.

After we receive our drinks, Hunter breaks the silence. "So...I came up with a plan,"

His eyes gleam with excitement as he leans in, and I can't look away.

"Let me guess," I tease. "You're going to drop AP Chemistry."

His voice is dripping with charm. "Anderson, you're kind of stuck with me,"

"Well," I quip, "I think the lab was a sign for you to stick to doing what you do best instead of Chemistry. I'm sure you can finagle your way into convincing the school to let you take a regular Chem class and still graduate."

His lips tilt into a smile. "I already tried that,"

I set my drink down. "Of course you did,"

His rich laugh takes over. "Which brings me to my new plan. You could help me, and I could help you,"

"How?" I ask.

"I'm glad you asked," Hunter says in a salesman's voice, causing me to chuckle. My entire face flushes as he gives me his undivided attention, his eyes directly on mine, and I can see once again why he's the talk of the school. If this is how it feels to be under his gaze in this setting, I can't even imagine how it would feel to date him. I've never met someone as attentive as him before. I immediately shake the thought away, disregarding it as having a soft spot for athletes in general.

"You can tutor me for the next two months until football season is over, and I can help you get out of your shell more," Hunter explains.

"And what makes you think I want to do that?" I ask. The smile on his face lets me know that I've taken the bait, but curiosity did get the best of me.

His face softens. "I saw you wandering around at lunch the other day. Something tells me you don't want being alone to be a regular part of my Senior year."

I officially want to sink into my chair right now.

I try and fail, to keep the edge out of my voice. "Yes, well, not all of us were born to be in the spotlight like you,"

His voice is gentle, a change from his usually playful tone. "I noticed the panic in your eyes. I would have said hi, but I know I'm probably not your first choice,"

I chuckle. "That drives you nuts, doesn't it?"

He tilts his head toward me. "What does?"

"Me not immediately giving you your way,"

It's then that I realize I've taken the teasing too far. Something flashes in his eyes, but he quickly recovers with a dazzling smile once again. "I can be patient when I need to be. If you let me help you, you could see."

Curiosity gets the best of me. "Say I do agree to this plan of yours, what exactly can you do to help me?"

"Well," He glances around us as if he's about to reveal some top-secret information. "I'm glad you asked because I think I might be just what you need," He lowers his voice a little. "Think whatever you want about me, but even you have to admit that I'm pretty good at making connections, something you seem to be lacking, if I may add."

"So," I arch a brow, "You're going to try to make me fit into your group? I'm confused."

He shakes his head, a grin tugging at his lips. "Not at all," He pauses, meeting my gaze head-on. "What do you want out of Senior year?"

I think back to the way I've been keeping my head down so much already, just like how I always have. "Something different," I murmur.

He gives me an encouraging smile. "Be a little more specific."

I let my shoulders relax a little as I moved a little closer to him. "I'd like to live more."

His eyes glint with an emotion I can't quite place, and I wonder if he's thinking about what happened this summer. I hope he's not connecting the dots between the change in me. "I can help you with that?"

"I don't know, Hunter," I breathe, feeling exposed all of a sudden.

It feels as if this conversation alone is something that could be used against me. Not by Hunter, necessarily, but his place in the social circle at school has only been a negative influence on every interaction we've had. Especially since we have opposite goals. He's the shiny star of the school, and I'm the girl who's just trying to make it through school unscathed.

It's a nice thought, trying to branch out more this year, but the last time I tried to do just that, it ended in disaster. Hunter was there then, too, so I'm surprised he'd even suggest that we work together. Simply being lab partners is more than enough public social interaction with him. Although, I do like our banter in P.E., where it doesn't feel like all eyes are on us.

"Come on, Anderson," He glances at the cup I'm clutching for dear life as if he knows this decision is bigger than just tutoring. Understanding settles into his features. "I have an idea. Trust me on this one."

I hesitantly follow him to his truck, feeling anticipation make its way from my head to my toes as he drives us in complete silence.

Once he pulls over at a lookout spot, he murmurs, "All right, we're here."

I numbly get out of the car, nearly tripping as his hand clasps mine to help me out. I glance around, and the strangest sense of bittersweet peace washes over me. I haven't been here in years, but this was one of my mom's favorite lookout spots. It's one of the few touristy things in Harmony Falls, which is sort of tucked away by the hills that surround the town.

The hilly clearing offers the perfect vantage point to see the sprawling town below. The sunshine casts an ethereal shine on the pastel buildings. If I squint, I can even see my house, a little cottage-style house a few streets behind Main Street, nestled into the steep high ground closer to the ocean.

"I love it here," I muse.

Hunter arches a brow. "So, your dislike doesn't extend to the whole town, but just to me then?"

I grin at him. "Guilty as charged. I like living in Harmony Falls."

Hunter gives me a perplexed smile "I never would have expected that."

"Well, don't broadcast it."

"I wouldn't dare," He pulls out a pen and a piece of paper. "What are some things you want to do from now until October? For each week you help me, I'll help you cross one thing off your list. It would only be until Homecoming, so you'd still have plenty of time for your internships,"

"But I'm not even sure I have enough things I want to do," I say shyly.

"Try it right now," Hunter instructs me, handing me the paper.

Goosebumps cover my arms as our hands connect while I grab it.

I cover the paper with my hand as I think, but he prompts me. "Don't be shy. I'm the one who will be helping you, remember?"

"Okay." I think about the experiences I want to have, but I come up short. I want to groan. I do so little that I don't even know what I'm missing out on.

His voice is gentle. "Adele, they can be small things,"

I think back to how school has been going so far, and the first thing that comes to mind is just how much of an outsider I am. Without Selena, I just blur into the background. Even by her side, I'm just invisible. And after what happened over the summer, it almost feels easier that way, as if everything will come bubbling to the surface if I don't fly under the radar.

Mostly, though, I want to be able to do some of the things I haven't been able to do because of anxiety.

"Okay," I say, my hands shaking as I hand him my list.

Senior Year:
Watch a sunrise
Drive down Main Street
Learn to surf
Go to a football game

Hunter wears a knowing smile as he reads the list. "Interesting that none of this has to do with P.E. I don't know if Coach Z would approve."

I chuckle and swat his hand away from the paper, but he keeps his grip firm.

"All of these are doable," Hunter's eyes skim my writing once again. "Which one do you want to start with?"

"I don't know," I look down at the list another time. "All of them are equally scary, except for the sunrise, so that one I guess."

"I feel bad cutting out early, but I have to be somewhere," Hunter says, "I can still give you a ride home though."

"No worries," I tap my fingers along my seatbelt. It's strange to feel so at peace in a car. "Thank you."

As we pull up to my house, I'm reminded that I'll be home alone for the next couple of days.

"Home safe," Hunter murmurs, moving around to open my door.

I keep my gaze on my feet as I climb out of his truck. "Thank you for the ride home,"

"Anytime. And Adele?" Hunter gives me a knowing smile. "This will be good for you."

My voice is teasing. "If you say so,"

"What are you doing tomorrow?" Hunter's voice sounds as smooth as honey. With his charisma, he should consider trying out for speech and debate.

As he gazes at me with gratitude, I scramble for an excuse,

afraid to let him in so soon.

I blush. "Just school,"

"Perfect, we'll start with tutoring tomorrow, after school," Hunter says, "I'll give you a ride home too."

"Thank you so much," I'm hoping my voice doesn't sound as flustered as I feel.

"Of course," Hunter's kind eyes stir something in me.

He watches me as I walk to my front door, not pulling onto the road until he sees me inside. And for the second time this week, I'm feeling things again. It's exhilarating and terrifying at the same time because I'm scared that now that all the good feelings are coming up again, the bad feelings will follow.

CHAPTER 5

"Hi," Hunter says, slightly out of breath, "today has been a crazy day. I'm excited for a change of pace."

I nod, completely oblivious to most of the details of his life, and climb into his truck as he opens the door for me. The smell of his cologne catches me off guard, and I climb in as quickly as possible, eager to shut any weird ideas out of my head. The last thing I need is to screw this up with awkwardness.

The scenery shifts from the white and seafoam buildings of Main Street to green fields and hills as we reach the outskirts of town. Gusts of wind whip at my hair while I climb out, met with the sight of a gray industrial-looking shed of sorts. The dirt path and barren grassy meadows show me just how out of town we are. My eyes widen, and Hunter says, "Relax, Adele. We're just at my dad's auto shop,"

"Oh," I say, sighing with relief.

He grabs my backpack, and I cautiously follow him into the auto shop. An old blue Mustang is suspended by some type of black cord, and plenty of metal tools are set out on a large glass table. Country music blares from an old radio, and the smells of pine, smoke, and oil fill my senses.

"Howdy," a handsome man, a few years older than me, with a scruffy blonde beard and brown eyes looks up from his tool kit.

"Ignore him," Hunter says dismissively, "he thinks he's a Texas man, even though he only spent like two months there for military training."

"Don't mind my cousin," The man extends a hand to me. His voice oozes with charm. It must run in the family. "I'm Colter, but my friends call me Colt."

"It's nice to meet you, Colter," I firmly shake his hand. "I'm Adele."

Hunter laughs smugly behind me.

"We have homework to do," Hunter's tone is stern, but he brings Colt in for some kind of weird handshake where they lock hands and then whistle at the end.

"Come on, man, you bring a pretty girl here for the first time, and I don't even get to interrogate her?" Colter asks.

I take in the resemblance between the two of them. The same sandy blond hair and freckles. Colter has the same coloring and strong, squared, masculine features, but he looks a little rougher around the edges than Hunter. Colter's hair is cropped close to his scalp, contrasting his beard, whereas Hunter has more of a surfer boy haircut. While Hunter is all strong, large muscles, Colter is lean and toned with sharp edges, and a smile that doesn't quite reach his eyes. While Colter's eyes are dark and mysterious, Hunter's eyes are innocent and mesmerizing in another way.

I drop my gaze when I realize I'm blatantly staring at both of them.

"She's a friend," Hunter warns, "and she's off limits, so don't get any ideas."

"All right, all right, that's my cue," Colter smiles and me and points to Hunter. "I'm only here for a few months, but my boy, on the other hand, is here for life."

Hunter doesn't respond. Instead, he heads straight towards a small door behind the equipment, and says, "Holler if you need anything."

I shyly meet Colter's gaze before following Hunter without saying another word.

Hunter smiles sheepishly. "Well, you've met my cousin,"

I look around the small, cramped office for a place to set down my things, but come up short. Files are strewn everywhere: on the crowded desk, on the dark floor, and on the two chairs. Sports memorabilia covers the walls, which feature old black and white newspaper articles and a plaque that reads,

"Watts Family Auto. Since 1924".

"I had no idea you had a family business," I murmur.

Hunter's voice is stern. "Yeah, well, it's not something I like to broadcast,"

Noted.

He clears us some room at the small desk, and pulls up a chair next to me, sitting a little too close for comfort in the tiny room. We fall into a rhythm as I go through the last quiz we took, pausing for any questions he has, and then going through the concepts, sounding like an encyclopedia as I list off the concepts that I've become so familiar with.

"How are you so good at this? It comes so naturally to you." Hunter's pencil creaks as he furiously takes notes.

I shrug. "It's just been my life, I guess. My dad works at a hospital, so it's all we talk about."

Hunter looks up from his notes. "That makes sense."

As he works on some practice questions, my mind begins to wander. I want to ask him why he didn't acknowledge me at school today. Maybe I took my teasing too far.

I don't know how to navigate this with him; talking to him is new territory for me. Hunter and I have attended the same schools since middle school, but never really crossed paths until two months ago. The silence between us now reminds me of that, and I'm desperate to make the feeling go away. Guilt gnaws at my throat, because I've hated him until now, but never bothered to think about how that night could have ended had Hunter not stepped in. He went out of his way for me, and I responded with agitation.

My voice wavers as I prompt him, "What if we review the chapter from last week?"

Luckily, Hunter doesn't seem to notice my shift in mood, because he dives right into studying with me. I'm immediately put at ease by his calm voice as he reads a question aloud.

We're going through the textbook when the door is thrown open, and a man says, "Son?"

His voice is gruff and his expression softens when he sees

me. Hunter looks like a carbon copy of his dad, who shares the same turquoise eyes, only his father's eyes have been hardened by time and struggle. His dark blue overall jumpsuit has faded from years of use and is stained with car grease. His beard is overgrown, and his shaggy light brown hair, which almost covers his eyes, has flecks of gray in it.

"Hey, Dad," Hunter says, "what's up?"

"You have company?" His dad asks, gesturing to me.

"She's tutoring me," Hunter explains.

His dad's tone is dismissive. "Uh-huh, yeah, sure,"

"It's true," I blurt out, surprising myself as my face flushes.

"Well, my mistake then," His father says, extending a hand out to me, "I'm his pops. Don't let him give you too hard of a time."

"I'll try not to," I shake his hand, "I'm Adele."

Hunter gives me a weird glance after his dad leaves the room.

"What?" I ask.

"Nothing, just my dad usually scares people speechless, and you, out of all people, stepped right up," Hunter's lips quirked up. "That was awesome."

"He doesn't scare me," I shrug. "He's just protective."

"That's one word for it," Hunter shakes his head as he laughs. "He doesn't trust me."

I arch a brow as I try, and fail, to contain my laughter. "After our lab, can you blame him?"

Hunter's smile lights up his face. "You are so not what meets the eye, Adele,"

I want to tell him that he's way more than what people see at first glance, but I stop myself, turning back toward what I excel at, studying. Because talking to attractive guys like him, even as a friend, has never been my specialty. The country music from next door seeps through a little louder, and Hunter softly hums along to the tune.

"Do you work here?" I ask quietly.

"Yes and no," Hunter pauses. "During the summer, I'm

here full time, but my dad gives me a break during the school year. Well, this year at least. Colt's back here for a few months, so it's been easier with him around. It's hard to manage with football season, though, and school."

"Wow, that's a lot," I mutter, "how do you manage?"

"I don't," Hunter's smile drops. "That's why I'm failing."

"Well, lucky for you, I'm here to help you," I reply, and our eyes meet.

"Amen to that." He chuckles softly.

An alarm goes off on his phone, and he says, "I have to get home to help with some things since I'm off work tonight. I'll give you a lift home though."

As we walk out, Hunter walks to his dad and shares a moment with him, so I hang back, unable to hear what they're saying, and uncertain of what to do.

Colter dries off his hands on a rag as he finishes working under a suspended car. His brown eyes search my face. "Don't let his dad scare you away; he's just a little guarded. He's been through it; their whole family has. He has a heart of gold, just like his son."

Instead of objecting and telling Colter about how I am just Hunter's tutor, I just nod my head. Hunter's eyes meet mine and he gestures for us to head out, but not before waving to Colter.

As we're walking out, Hunter's dad says, "Nice to meet you, Adele. You come by anytime you need,"

"Thank you," I reply quietly.

As Hunter drives me home, I say, "Thank you for the ride home, especially with everything you have going on. I appreciate it,"

"Anytime," Hunter responds, "and besides, I love driving."

"You do?" I ask, glancing out the window at the beautiful, peaceful scenery around us.

"Yes, when I drive, I can choose to go anywhere. Everything feels limitless like time is frozen still, and everything is up to me," Hunter faces me. "How about you?"

"What about me?" I ask.

"Do you enjoy driving? I don't think I've ever seen you drive before. You always ride with Selena, right?" He asks.

I swallow the lump in my throat, knowing I could easily lie to him. Nobody but Selena knows. But then I think about the way he opened up to me a little, and I think otherwise.

I bite my lip as my voice shakes. "I don't know how to drive,"

It's a half-truth. I don't drive at all. Selena tried to teach me once, and I freaked out, crying and shaking, even though we were only going down her street in broad daylight.

"Your dad never taught you?" He asks.

My dad has tried his best, but driving hasn't come up yet in the "adulting" lessons we have together, probably because my mother passed away in a car accident when I was in the car with her. I was ten years old at the time, and although it was a while ago, the aftermath of it has lingered. I still have a squiggly gash going down my stomach as a reminder, and an immense aversion to driving of any kind. My dad avoids the topic at all costs, as do I.

Now that I think about it, Hunter is one of the only people I've trusted to ride in the car with. I feel safe with him, which says a lot.

I tap my fingers on the window. "Nope,"

"So, when you wrote that on your list, you meant you wanted to learn how to drive down Main Street?" Hunter asks.

"Yes." I turn my head to face him, floored to find kindness in his eyes.

"Please don't tell anyone," I continue, "I have my permit, I just, haven't gotten to the license part yet, even though I'm eighteen."

"I won't tell anyone," Hunter reassures me, "I can teach you."

"Are you sure?" I ask.

"I work at an auto shop," Hunter shrugs. "Cars practically run in my veins."

"That's true," I reply.

He gives me a warm smile. "I mean it, Adele. I'm here for you,"

His words alone give me an extra pep in my step for the rest of the day. Is it possible that I can finally actually learn to drive?

CHAPTER 6

"We survived the first week."

I look up from my desk to see Greg leaning over my desk with a coy smile, his dark hair slicked back. The look he gives me should make me melt, but it doesn't.

"We did," I say, grinning in return.

I freeze, wanting to say more, but not knowing how to. He gives me an expectant smile, and I glance around the room.

To my relief, Greg speaks up. "It's nice to see you looking happier this year, Adele,"

"Thank you, it's been a good year so far. Besides the homework and stress of the future of course," I reply, thankful that he understands how isolating it can be to solely focus on school. He gets it.

"My sentiments exactly," Greg lowers his voice a little. "I've found that going out helps."

He leans in close to me, and it feels like time stills. "I'm thinking about going to Mario's party tonight, it might be fun."

My voice shakes a little as I lamely reply, "Interesting,"

I think he's about to invite me to the party, but the moment between us ends as the bell rings.

As soon as class ends, Greg walks toward me. "Maybe I'll see you tonight?"

I push back the doubt in my mind. "Maybe,"

My face is flushed as I walk away.

At lunch, I tell Selena all about the interaction with Greg, including the way he leaned in toward me when he talked about the party.

Selena's eyes widen. "You have to go, you have to! He practically asked you out,"

I shrug. "He did not, he was just being friendly,"

"Well, it's a start," Selena gushes, "Are you coming tonight? Because, if so, we can get ready at my place."

"I'm still on the fence," I say softly, glancing around at the other groups in the courtyard. Fortunately, everyone else is a ways away.

"Come on," Her eyebrows waggle. "It'll be fun."

Hunter is already seated at our table when I arrive at AP Chem.

He turns toward me. "Are you up for a sunset tomorrow?"

"Tomorrow?" I ask.

Hunter's lips tilt up. "It's supposed to be beautiful tomorrow."

"I'm in, I guess," I meet his gaze. "What time should I meet you?"

His tone is excited like he's already thought this through. "I'll pick you up at 4 am."

He sees the grimace on my face, and says, "I'll bring coffee,"

His smile fades as Mr. Hughes passes back the quizzes from this week.

Hunter whispers, "I failed,"

"That's because it was before I helped you," I reassure him, "yesterday we brought you up to speed."

"You think so?" Hunter lets out a shaky breath. "I need to pass this class."

"I know so," I say, "by the time I'm done tutoring you, you'll have a B,"

"No A?" Hunter asks, lifting a brow.

My tone is light. "Let's not get too ahead of ourselves,"

Hunter's lips quirk up. "I got here early today, and Mr. Hughes offered me a retake, so I won't be in P.E. with you today," His eyes glint with amusement. "You'll have to survive without me, maybe even talk to a few people."

"What a bore," I tease, finding that I genuinely will miss him. Oddly enough, I've dreaded P.E. less when I get to chat with him and see him.

"I'll be back on Monday though," His shoulders slump a little. "That is, assuming I pass the retake."

I smirk at him. "I know you will. You had a pretty great tutor, remember?"

Hunter lowers his voice a little. "I guess it's time to put that to the test,"

My voice is light. "Oh, it's on, Hunter,"

"By the way, Coach Z wants you to run today," Hunter says, "apparently, I'm a distraction. Something about my dazzling smile or something."

I laugh and roll my eyes, but his cheeky smile is quite distracting, and I want to see more of it.

"Good luck on the retake," I say as I begin packing up my backpack.

"Thanks, Adele. I'll see you tomorrow,"

At P.E., I'm completely caught off guard by the amount of running I have to complete. A loud buzzer sounds, and all of my classmates and I have to sprint to the other side of the field before it goes off. The shrill sound startles me every chance that I think I have to finally rest a little.

I stop at one side, catching my breath, until the buzzer goes off again, and I groan. Once the test is finally over, I bask in the feeling of rest, wanting nothing more than to crawl into bed.

As I'm walking toward the locker room on achy legs, Coach Z hollers, "Good job today, Adele,"

"Thank you, coach," I say, still completely out of breath.

Coach Z chuckles. "Maybe Hunter isn't so bad of an influence after all,"

"I guess not," I say, smiling as I walk to my locker.

After school, Selena and I pick up Carlos, who encourages me that I "have" to go to Mario's party, because apparently, word has even spread to the middle school about the "legendary" party that is happening tonight.

I take a quick shower at Selena's house, allowing the cold water and rose body wash to refresh my skin after all the running I did today. I sneak a glance in the mirror, and it hits me that not once has anyone in the locker room made a comment about, or even noticed, the scar running vertically along my stomach. Luckily now it's faded into a light squiggly line that could almost be mistaken for an ab line if my build were slim, which it's not.

But if a room full of people didn't stare, or make comments, then maybe when I'm alone, I can give myself a break, and let it go.

Selena scrunches my waves with leave-in conditioner, letting them air dry curly while she does my makeup. She puts on less makeup than I'm usually comfortable with but I don't say anything, instead trying to go outside of the box a little bit.

Selena gives me a once-over as she hugs me. "You look beautiful,"

"Thank you," I gesture to her, "so do you."

"Now let's go have some fun," Selena turns on a pop song, shimmying her hips as she sings along.

I shake my hair out a little, giggling excitedly about the possibility of seeing a boy at a party tonight. Selena shakes her hair too, laughing, and suddenly we're thirteen again when the biggest concern about our future is what gift we want for Christmas. And I soak in every second of it until the song ends.

The word must have spread fast about Mario's party because it takes us ten minutes to find parking until we settle for a parking spot two streets over.

The bass of the music reverberates through the large house, which sits in the hills, the fanciest part of Harmony Falls. My first party in a while is the full experience, ringing ears and all.

Selena must sense my apprehension because she offers me a small smile as we walk in the unlocked door.

Mario greets us right away. "Selena and Adele, you made it!" I realize that this is one of the first times I've ever been greeted too. Normally when I'm with Selena, people say hello to her and offer me a head nod or a small smile, but this is a nice change.

Suddenly the party doesn't seem so bad. Nothing like the last one I went to.

notice the flush in Selena's cheeks as she chats with Mario, so I head to the kitchen to give them some space, knowing she'll thank me later.

Around ten people are crammed into the kitchen, and I immediately recognize some of them from previous classes.

"I'm glad you came," Greg says, giving me a side hug that takes me a second to return.

"Me too." I put my hands in my pockets.

"Can I get you something to drink?" Greg asks.

"Water, please," I reply, grateful for a diversion.

He comes back seconds later with a water bottle, and I'm met with the realization that we have absolutely nothing to talk about. Every conversation avenue that I try somehow ends up going back to school, or grades, or school again. I want to huff in frustration, irritated that the one guy who may potentially be attracted to me is solely interested because we share the same priority.

I guzzle my water down, instead, nodding my head at the right times, even when I ask him about how his family is doing, and he says, "They're good, they're excited for me to graduate."

After too long of an awkward pause than is socially acceptable, even for me, I excuse myself to go find a drink. After I walk away, I glance back at Greg, only to find him giving a pretty girl his full attention. He leans in close, smiling as he tells some sort of elaborate story, hand motions and all.

I feel my heart pang, realizing that I want to feel that. Not with Greg, since clearly there is no chemistry there, but with someone.

I search the party for people I recognize, but am disappointed when I notice that most of the people here are from student government and art. The lack of a familiar face is just another reminder of the way that I've done a little too good of a job at keeping my head down at school.

The party begins to move in slow motion as panic settles into my chest; I don't even know what to do with myself. Selena is in her natural element, chatting it up with everyone. The music continues to blast more, which helps me to feel like less of an outsider because it's too loud to try to carry a conversation with anyone.

I stand along the wall as I watch Selena join a group of girls who are dancing in the living room to a song I don't even know. The singer's voice captivates me as she passionately expresses a desire to move onto better days, and I can't help but want to sway my hips, wishing I could fit in as effortlessly as her. Instead, I prop my foot against the wall and remain there, alone, for the rest of the night until Selena tells me that she needs to get home for curfew.

As we're walking to the car, Selena faces me. "How did it go with Greg?"

I sigh. "It turns out there's no spark there,"

Selena's eyes tilt down. "Bummer,"

"It's all right," I shrug. "Speaking of sparks, though, how did it go with Mario?"

"We're just friends," she replies, but her eyes are glowing.

"Whatever you say," I tilt my head. "But if you want my two cents, I think that there's a connection there."

"We will see," Selena says, grinning the whole way home.

The air stills as we pull up to my house. I forgot to turn the porch light on, so it's pitch. Selena turns toward me as her engine slows.

"Are you sure you don't want to stay the night?" Selena's voice is laced with concern. "I don't like the idea of you being home alone all night."

"Yes," I assure her, "I'm getting up in like five hours."

"Ahh yikes, that makes sense then," Selena continues, "You know how I am when I don't get my sleep."

I chuckle. "Trust me, I've learned the hard way,"

Selena's eyes meet mine. "Well, call me if you need anything okay? Be safe,"

"I promise I will," I respond.

Selena raises a brow and gives me a questioning glance. "What are you doing up so early anyway?"

"I'm watching the sunrise," I say quietly. I feel guilty, although it's technically not a lie. Instead, I'm just not sharing who I'm watching the sunset with. The last thing I want is for Selena to jump to any conclusions about me and Hunter.

Her tone changes from curiosity to excitement. "That sounds fun!"

I know she wants an invite, but it feels too complicated to try to explain the arrangement I have with Hunter, so I downplay it. "Who even knows if I'll be motivated not to snooze my alarm after staying out so late tonight,"

Selena hugs me goodbye. "True. I had a lot of fun, and I'm so glad you came,"

"Me too,"

Once I'm in bed, my mind races for hours as I play back to the way that I felt no butterflies whatsoever around Greg, despite being so similar and having known each other for some time. Instead, I think about Hunter's goofy smile and his quick wit. I toss and turn as it hits me that in just a few hours, I'll be spending time alone with a boy who does make my heart race. Just a little.

CHAPTER 7

Tap. tap. tap.

A soft thumping sound wakes me up from a deep sleep. I grimace as I open my eyes and adjust to the lighting. I gasp when I see a figure outside my window, but relax when I see that it's Hunter. Remembering our sunrise plans, I slowly crack my window open, shivering when the air comes into my room.

"Hi," I whisper groggily. I rub my eyes, hoping to feel more awake.

"Hi," Hunter says, "I realized I don't have your phone number, so this was the only way I knew how to wake you. If we leave now, we can catch the sunrise, but we could always go another time."

"No, no, I'm coming," I yawn. "Just give me like thirty seconds, and I'll meet you out front."

"Sounds good, I'll be in the car," he says, his hands in his hoodie pocket.

I swiftly turn the light in my room on and assess my appearance: my eyes are still bloodshot from not sleeping, my skin looks pale, and my hair is frizzy as can be, going in all sorts of directions. I shrug and put on some lip balm, brush my teeth, and put my hair up in a clip.

Two minutes later, I'm walking in the cold to Hunter's car. The dark sky does nothing to help me wake up.

As soon as I'm in his car, Hunter hands me a hot thermos, saying, "Here's some chai."

"You are the best," I muse, and he laughs softly.

He drives us up the hills and pulls over at a dirt path.

"This is the perfect viewing spot," he explains.

He takes my hand and leads me to the back of his truck,

where he's set up a couple of blankets along with a spread of fruit and bagels. The bed of the truck offers us the perfect view of the cliffs, the ocean, and the sky that will soon change.

We eat in comfortable silence, cocooned in our respective blankets, watching the dark sky for what feels like hours. My eyes feel weary and I feel myself drifting off to sleep when he murmurs, "Adele, it's time,"

And it's beautiful. The dark sky transforms into a glorious stream of yellow light that hovers over the water, and envelops my view with gold, yellow, and turquoise. The air is crisp and the sky is quiet. Even the waves feel calm. The serenity of the shift to a new day is all-consuming, drawing me in completely to see everything I can while the moment is mine.

And this moment feels like mine because it's just us, for this brief time before the bustle of everything is in full motion. Right now, it's just Hunter and I, staring at the sky, daydreaming about all the possibilities even if we know deep down, that everything is already set for us. But here, at this point, it's just me and the breathtaking peace of a new day.

Looking at Hunter and his baggy hoodie, his small smile, and his entrancing eyes, I can see why he was so excited to share this with me. It's everything that he is, or wants to be. It's the type of scene to make you completely stop what you're doing so you can soak up every second.

"What do you think?" Hunter asks as if my mesmerization and awe aren't written all over my flushed and happy face.

"It's incredible," I muse, "I can't look away, even if I wanted to."

"Right? It's some kind of magic, making someone like me sit still," Hunter says.

"It is something," My eyes meet his. "Thank you for showing me."

"Of course. This," Hunter gestures to the scenery around us, "is what life is about, Adele. This is living."

He has a faraway look in his eyes, and I want to ask more, but I feel the words get stuck in my throat. "I couldn't agree more. This is a nice reminder. Moments like this should be the norm, not the exception,"

The way that the sunlight streams on his golden hair makes him look like a mirage of sorts, and in my sleep-deprived state, being here with him of all people sure feels like one. But somehow, I'm enjoying myself.

"So, Miss AP, do you ever get scared about the future?" His voice is teasing, but his eyes are curious. "I don't mean like school, like classes right now, or next semester, but like next school year? College and all of that?"

"Believe it or not," I tease, "those of us outside of football also have pressure too."

"You do?" He arches a brow and his eyes study my face as if he's seeing me for the first time. And maybe he is. "I figured getting good grades came so easily to you, that your college plans would just be a breeze too."

I let out a shaky breath. "I wish that were the case,"

He lowers his voice. "It's not?"

I glance around at the golden glow of the sun peeking through the clouds as the sky comes to life. The rays illuminate the water. If I listen closely enough, I can hear the humming of birds waking up and the soft rumble of the early morning waves.

"Honestly?" I say softly, "I get scared all the time. It feels like even the choices I'm excited about lead to changes that I don't want. I'm not ready for everything in my life to fall away,"

"That makes sense," Hunter pauses. "I wouldn't say I get scared, just frustrated. I feel stuck here like I keep watching all of my friends make all these plans, but everything is already set out for me."

"So, your cousin wasn't joking then, at the shop?" I ask.

Hunter's eyes meet mine with curiosity and my face flushes. "You have a good memory," He remarks, "but, yes. I'm going to be taking over the shop as soon as I graduate."

My words come out before I can stop myself. "Is that what you want?"

He moves a little closer to me. "I don't mind working at the shop, but I hate the idea of just not being able to even consider anything else,"

"What would you do if you could do anything?" I ask.

"That's the worst part. I don't know," Hunter sighs. "And the idea of leaving my siblings behind feels awful. Maybe all I want is a chance for people to see me differently, instead of looking down on my family."

My heart falls. Outside of his football reputation in the walls of our high school, Hunter is viewed in a negative light. While he's practically worshiped at Harmony Falls High, a lot of the adults in town, my dad included, see his family as outsiders. Even when I wasn't a big fan of Hunter, I never understood why people felt the need to ostracise his family.

My voice becomes tight. "Anyone who judges you based on something so trivial and out of your control doesn't deserve to be close to you anyway,"

"Thanks, Adele. You too. For what it's worth, I respect how hard you work in school. It's nice being around someone who has a vision for their future," Hunter says.

My lips curve into a smile. "Thank you,"

~

The sound of laughter fills my ears as soon as I walk into Selena's house. Selena's dad and Carlos are in the living room, engaged in an intense game of battleship, offering only a nod and a smile as I walk by.

Selena's mom embraces me and gestures toward the living room. "Don't mind them, they've been at it for thirty minutes now. Their game is at a standstill."

She leads me to the kitchen, where Selena is helping to finish dinner. I smile when I see that they've set my chair with a place setting.

Selena's mom waggles her eyebrows. "If you ever want to bring a boy to game night, Mi Amor, you are more than welcome to,"

"Mom!" Selena groans.

"I'm serious, girls. Now that you're Seniors, I think I need to cut you both some slack," her mom says.

I just laugh. "If there are any new developments, you will be the first to know,"

"Well, actually there are some," Selena's voice brightens. "She's tutoring Hunter Watts."

"I remember him. He's a good kid," Selena's mom waggles her brows. "I've been told he's handsome too."

I feel my face flush, especially as I think about how I spent the morning with him and didn't even tell Selena about it, which will now make that time with him seem like an even bigger deal if I were to mention it now.

"I'm just his tutor," I reply.

"Is he paying you?" Selena asks.

"No, he's helping me with some things," I hesitate, "he's helping me to get out of my shell a little more,"

"I like the sound of that," Selena's mom faces me. "That's way better than anything money can buy. Tutor or not, he sounds good for you."

I just smile shyly.

Selena's dad says grace and then we all dig into our food. The stories, inside jokes, and shared memories are a stark contrast to dinners at my house, which feels hollow in comparison to what I have tonight with Selena's family. Selena's Saturday nights are filled with tamales and game nights, an endless stream of community, and happy moments. I guess when I think about the future, that's all I want. The possibility of something more, something where I can experience what it means to feel the joy that comes from loving people. My dad's been gone all weekend, and the house felt the same as it always does when I left earlier today: empty.

Hours pass by as we settle into playing a variety of board games after dinner. After some intense strategy and hilarious bluffing games, we settle for mellow games as it gets later.

"I think I'm going to head in for the night," Selena's mom faces me. "I'm so glad you came tonight, Adele. You're more than welcome to stay the night."

"Thank you for having me,"

"You're always welcome here." As she wraps her arms around me, I breathe in her scent, capturing it, and wondering once again how it'd feel to have a mother to hug every night.

We don't broach the subject, but I know Selena notices sometimes, especially the way I tend to feel about the future.

Fortunately, Selena brightens beside me. "I have an idea," She wears a smug smile on her face.

"What is it?" I fake a yawn, hoping it'll talk her out of whatever wild adventure she wants to drag me on.

Selena doesn't buy it, though. She knows that I'm just as wired as she is right now. Her eyes light up as she murmurs, "Let's go to the corn fields,"

I arch a brow. "*The* corn fields?"

She nods. "It's a rite of passage,"

Rumor has it these abandoned corn fields on the edge of town are haunted. I know they're not, but the idea of wandering around, trespassing on city-owned land, especially after dark, has my hair prickling up on the back of my neck.

One glance at Selena though tells me that it's either this or some kind of hard conversation. I can see the broken aspect in her smile, the way it doesn't reach her eyes. She's already feeling that homesickness creeping in, too. She's going to miss this town as much as me, probably even more.

Sometimes it seems like Selena's family is the only thing that grounds her, with the way she's constantly bouncing around so much. It's almost strange that we've been friends for so long, with the way that she is constantly adding more to her social repertoire, but here we are, and I'm so grateful, I am. But lately, I've been wanting a little more of my own identity, maybe even some friends of my own. I know that discussion, me bringing up the ways I want to branch out socially, would not go well, so instead, I agree to go to the creepy cornfield.

"I'll go," I murmur, "But on one condition."

She tilts her head at me. "What is it?"

I lower my voice a little. "You can't tell anyone about it,"

"Adele, we're not going to get in trouble," Her eyes widen when recognition settles in. "Oh. I won't tell anyone."

After putting myself out there at a party that went horrifically wrong, I've learned that silence is better. People can't bring me down when they don't know anything about me.

I exhale a sigh of relief. "Thank you. I guess we should head out before the whole town starts going there."

The thought of guys from school jumping out from behind the corn already has my heart pounding. The cornfield is notorious for a lot of different things, mainly the odd traditions of doing risky things there and then telling the whole school about it. It's almost taboo at this point, because it has such a muddled reputation, as every Senior wants to experience their last country excursion before they enter the real world.

Although a lot of people stay in Harmony Falls, life after graduation is different. Many choose to fill one of the miscellaneous job openings at one of the local small businesses.

Selena squeals. "This is going to be fun!"

Selena cautiously cracks her front door open, and it hits me that we're sneaking out. I shake the thought and follow her to her car. As the engine rumbles to life, Selena looks around nervously.

She pulls aside to the side of the road near a tall wire fence. The car tires Our view is only illuminated by her brights; there are no streetlights here. We're really in the boondocks out here.

Even Selena lets out a shaky breath as her car lights turn off, emphasizing how dark it is. "Wow,"

As we get out of the car, I'm aware of the stillness out here. I stumble as I find my footing in the gravel.

The only sound I hear is the faint chirping of crickets.

My hands tremble as I clutch my phone for dear life, hoping to illuminate our path a little. The faded "No Trespassing" sign, which is angled to the side, as if somebody knocked it over, adds to the eeriness.

In front of me, Selena slows her pace, choosing to hang back a little. She lacks her usual pin-straight posture. Instead, she is crouched over, almost as if she is anticipating someone is going to pop out and scare us.

I have trouble following a straight line. The leathery texture of the corn leaves brushes against my leg, and I yelp.

As we get deeper into the field, the space between the rows becomes narrower, and I find myself getting scratched by the plants.

I'm certain that I'm covered in dirt now. I want to speak up and tell Selena that I think we've gone far enough, but she is seemingly relaxed now, laughing as she tries to navigate the crops, telling me that there's supposedly a spot in the middle of the field where people have carved their names into the dirt.

I think back to how far the fields sprawled and swallow a lump in my throat. So, we're going to be here awhile. Great.

I'm finally easing into this environment a little, trying to draw from Selena's exhilaration, when I hear something loud rustling in the leaves in front of us. Whatever it is, it's close. I feel fear pulse throughout my entire body as terror takes over, and the reality of something, or someone, else being here, in the middle of nowhere, settles in.

Selena hears it too, and her shrill scream causes my eardrums to ring as she swiftly turns around and yanks my hand. She tries to tug me along, but the way she positions herself makes it so that I'm now behind her, closer to whatever imminent threat lies behind us. As Selena pushes through the crops and races ahead, I feel my legs become as heavy as lead weights. My breath comes out in rattled gasps as I begin to hyperventilate. The instinct for my vision to become cloudy as panic rises in my chest makes the feeling worse because it takes me back to the night when I was powerless.

I'm shaking so much that I'm about to tip over, no doubt jogging at an angle. I try to will my legs to speed up, but I'm unable to, met with great resistance from my joints. It's as if I'm frozen in place, and it's horrifying.

Blood-curdling screams that it takes me a moment to recognize are my own come out at increasing frequency.

I rest my hands on my thighs as I hear a twig snap in front of me. I began spinning around, trying to identify where to go next. Selena must have come back for me, because she rushes toward me, looking just almost as panicked as I am. Her face falls when she takes in my state.

"Adele," Her voice breaks a little. "I'm so sorry."

I exhale a shallow breath, feeling my shoulders slump a little. It takes me a moment for everything to come into focus again. "It's okay,"

She shakes her head, and I notice the tears glistening in her dark eyes. "No, it's not. I should have waited for you,"

I'm still too shaken up to respond. I stand stiffly in place, still overcome with anguish.

Her lips turn down, and I know she's thinking the same thing as me: all of the scars that I thought were healed have just been brewing under the surface, ready to erupt again.

I thought that I could try to experience some of the "normal" things that my classmates do, but apparently, I can't.

Fortunately, Selena drops the subject as soon as we get back to her place.

Still wired from the creepy cornfield, Selena and I sit on the couch and wrap ourselves in fuzzy blankets. We share headphones and listen to emotional songs until our eyelids become droopy.

"I don't tell you this enough," Selena takes her earbuds out and looks at me. "But, you're honestly like a sister to me."

A smile tugs at my lips. "You are too,"

"And you are always welcome here, Adele. We're family," Selena says.

Her words bring tears to my eyes, so I just nod.

She knows I don't like to cry in front of people, so she doesn't push. Instead, she changes the song we're listening to into a happy song and presses play.

We hum along softly, listening to music until we fall asleep. The soft glow of the sun's early rays streaming through the windows wakes me up. Selena is still fast asleep next to me, curled into a ball. I hesitantly take the earbud out of my ear, and press pause on the song we're listening to. The lyrics hit me:

You only call me when it's summer
I will no longer be your lover
Cuz every time I need you
You're nowhere to be found
If all you want is a good time
I guess I'll see you around

Next to me, Selena stirs. "Good morning,"
I yawn. "Good morning,"

I take the long way on my walk home, humming the song softly, looking at the sky with a new appreciation now that I've seen just how beautiful a sunrise here can be. The air feels crisper now that fall is about to transition into full swing. In the next couple of weeks, orange and red leaves will crunch beneath my feet as I brace myself for the chill of winter. And I'm reminded once again that everything will be different before I know it. Next fall, I'll be in a completely different city, and I'll have to start over again. It feels like I'm just going through the motions, but I don't know how to stop, especially since I know how disappointed my dad would be. Medicine feels like the last thing connecting my dad and me, and even then, we still barely talk. The thought has my heart racing, and I immediately rush home.

CHAPTER 8

Today I'm going to Hunter's house for the first time. My stomach is in knots about the idea of how we'll be crossing yet another threshold from acquaintances to friends. After the corn maze disaster, I tried to convince him that I wanted to back out of our deal, but the pleading in his teal eyes broke something in me, and I found myself agreeing to continue tutoring him. When it comes to my list, though, I'm still unsure if I can. A part deep inside of me wants to continue, though, because it's almost as if I have this hope that the list is exactly what I need to finally heal.

Fortunately, P.E. ends late, so I don't have to worry about any questioning glances from my classmates as I walk with Hunter to his truck, which is the last car in the parking lot. He helps me carry my things into his car and softly shuts the door behind me.

We ride in silence past the last inland stretch of town until we arrive at a small, white house with faded, chipping paint. The shades are drawn closed, and a "no soliciting" sign hangs in the window, despite us being a good twenty minutes away from anyone else in Harmony Falls. Two rusty pickup trucks sit in the dirt lot next to the grassy front lawn, which is overgrown with tall, yellow grass and white wildflowers. The small meadows and hills frame the house, which is the only house for miles.

"Wow," I breathe, taking it all in. I have to take wide strides to avoid stepping on the pretty flowers that line his lawn.

Hunter runs his hand through the front of his hair. "It's a little...out of date," He shrugs. "It's probably not what you were expecting. I don't bring people over much."

"I didn't mean anything negative by it," I reassure him, "I

think it's beautiful. I can't believe I've never been out here before. I just love the flowers out here."

I glance around me one more time, letting it sink in. It almost feels bittersweet to find another pretty nook of town, because I should be finding other things to be excited about, like the East Coast colleges that my dad keeps bringing up Instead, I'm discovering even more reasons why I want to stay here.

"So, you're a country girl at heart then? Who knew?" Hunter gives me the cheesy kind of smile that a lot of people would melt over. Only it feels special to me right now, because there's an unspoken agreement between us, that we know that crossing that line is a terrible idea.

Other than him being completely out of my league, it's just impossible, given our lives are going in two completely different directions. Which makes this friendship easy. I like simple and predictable, and surprisingly, this connection between us is just that. So even charming looks like the one he's giving me right now won't phase me.

As we walk into the house, I find myself surprised that there are no pictures on display. The walls are completely barren, with no inspirational quotes, artwork, or decor at all. A cowboy hat hangs over the television, serving as the only piece of decoration within the entire space. A few dusty pairs of leather work boots are lined up by the door. Instead of a rug, a black towel, which is threadbare, has been laid down on the carpet.

"I'd offer you a tour, but this is pretty much it," Hunter murmurs.

He lacks the usual confidence he carries himself with, and it makes me realize that growing up on the outskirts has come with its negative stigma. It surprises me that that has affected him at all because he seems so secure in his identity. But, now that I think about it, a lot of that has been in football.

I stay quiet and busy myself with setting up my school supplies. Explaining thermodynamics to him sounds way easier than asking him about why his house has no pictures or memorabilia.

We are completely immersed in studying when a giddy and soft voice interrupts us.

"I love your hair,"

I look up from my notebook to see a girl with straight blonde hair and light green eyes. She's a few inches shorter than me and stands tall with pride.

Surprised by her kindness, my voice comes out peppier than usual. "Thank you, your hair is pretty too,"

I see Hunter give me a curious look as he watches our interaction, no doubt holding back a grin.

She offers me a shy smile. Soft, light brown freckles line her slim face. "I'm Shelby."

I shake her hand. "I'm Adele,"

"I'm his sister, by the way, not his girlfriend," She leans in. He's single."

Shelby's boldness makes me giggle, and I have to clasp my hand over my mouth to hold back. Hunter just laughs and shakes his head. His eyes tilt up as he continues chuckling. He gives me a knowing smile, and I feel my face flush.

"I think that's my cue to make dinner," Hunter announces.

I start scooting my chair to leave when Hunter faces me. "You're welcome to stay for dinner. I can't make any promises about the food though."

Shelby's eyes gleam with humor. "You've been warned."

Hunter turns toward Shelby. "Gratitude goes a long way, you know. I'll remember this next time you're running late for school and need help packing your lunch."

He begins cooking up a storm in the kitchen, putting Shelby and me to work at setting the table and making a salad for everyone.

Shelby and I talk while we help out, and I learn that Shelby is in eighth grade and wants to learn how to surf, but that Hunter hasn't taught her yet.

I'm rustling around for some oven mitts when I find a small, wrinkled flashcard with cursive writing on it. I pick it up and try to get a closer look, but Hunter furrows his brows and gives me a questioning stare, and I immediately put it back. I feel my face flush from snooping, which is totally unlike me. My unease fades as we are joined by Colter, who is followed in by a young boy who has Hunter's eyes and sandy blonde hair.

His hair hangs in his eyes, and he is drowning in his football jersey.

He gives me the biggest smile and hug when he sees me. I feel myself return his hug, and grin in surprise.

"I'm Austin," he says.

My voice softens. "I'm Adele,"

Colter gives me a side hug as his eyes roam over me. "Hunter told me we have a special guest."

I glance at Hunter, and he shrugs. "It was the only way for this fool to leave you alone. But it still didn't work,"

"How was practice?" Hunter playfully pushes his brother's hair out of his eyes as he hugs him.

Austin beams at him. "Amazing! Coach let me run a few plays,"

"He did, huh?" Hunter says, "I'm so proud of you. Let's get you fed after all that hard work."

After the five of us sit down, we have a meal, unlike everything I've ever had before. Hunter's pasta bake is so chewy that it sticks to my teeth, and Shelby and I exchange a smile from across the table as we try to contain our laughter.

Everyone in his family talks simultaneously, sharing their opinions and stories at different volumes. Somehow everyone manages to understand one another, despite the gradually increasing noise of the chatter in the room. The night is filled with stories of funny memories. As Austin tells us the play-by-play of his first week of fifth grade, I accidentally meet Hunter's gaze, and I find myself wondering what is going through his mind with me being here. Because somehow, in this room where I really shouldn't fit, I don't feel out of place at all. I feel completely at home. His lips quirk up, and I quickly look away, feeling my cheeks warm.

Not once does the conversation of medical school or

degrees come up. Instead, Hunter's siblings are fascinated by how I'm just now only taking P.E. and offer to help me if I ever want to learn any sports. Hunter assures them that I already have him as a running coach, enthusiastically regaling the way he beat me in our race on the track. His younger brother lists off tons of running advice for me to improve my times so that I can "leave Hunter in the dust,"

Hunter and I exchange a smile from across the table as his sister tells me once again that she loves my hair. I've never met a family this loud and I love it. A part of me wants to capture this moment, the smiling faces around me, the incessant chatter and laughter, the smell of Italian spices, the warmth of Hunter's gaze, and save it for a later date as a reminder that memories like this still exist.

After dinner, I help Hunter collect everyone's plates as his siblings start getting ready for bed. As soon as everyone has left the room, Hunter turns to me. "Thank you for coming tonight. I'm sure it's much different than what you're used to,"

"Different is good. Thanks for having me," I respond.

Hunter's brows furrow. "It was nice having someone here as a buffer. I hope it wasn't too crazy for you,"

I pause and face him. "Trust me, I like chaos. It's a nice change,"

"It is?" Hunter asks.

"Family dinners at my house are very quiet," I explain. My voice somehow loses the zeal it had earlier when I was meeting Shelby earlier. I feel hollow just thinking about my house.

He gives me a concerned look, so I quickly recover, "I have Selena's family, though, for when I want to go to a game night and experience a loud family, so I get the best of both,"

"That is very true," Hunter nods. "I think I can picture Selena's family like that."

The way he refers to her so casually should remind me that he and I run in completely separate social circles, but instead, it helps me to see that maybe we're not so different after all.

"It's something," I say.

"Speaking of fun experiences, it's your turn to check off one of the next items on your list. Which one do you want to do next?" Hunter asks. "I have some ideas, but I wanted to hear your thoughts first."

Now that everything is in front of me, I find myself panicking. Where do I even start?

Hunter's voice softens. "I have an idea,"

~

"Do you trust me?" Hunter asks.

I pause. "Surprisingly, yes,"

"Good, then trust that I'll be right here to help you," Hunter reassures me. His proximity has me feeling all kinds of things right now; it makes me wonder if he feels the chemistry too.

Since I couldn't pinpoint anything on my list that I was excited about, Hunter is teaching me how to surf.

We're trying to get a lesson in before school starts in an hour, so we've rushed through the basics, which is why I am currently shivering and dripping wet as I stand beside the surfboard. The frigid water is up to my belly button, and my soaking wet hair has my teeth chattering. My feet brush against slippery seaweed on the ocean floor, and I decide that I'd rather be on the glossy smooth surfboard instead of having my ankles in the water, which honestly looks a little murky today. I reach my arms to wrap around the board, ready to try to climb on to attempt to catch a wave again.

Just as I'm about to bring my knees onto the board, a huge wave crashes into us, and I feel my feet give out beneath me. Still attached to my wrist, the board whips me around as the wave violently rustles my surroundings. I gasp for air as the salt water stings my eyes and overwhelms me. Panic begins to settle in as I'm throttled around, pulled toward the sea. Everything moves in slow motion as the current picks up.

I hear Hunter's voice in my ear as my knees buckle and I'm taken toward the deeper depths of the sea.

"Hey, hey, I've got you,"

I feel Hunter's hands firmly wrap around my waist as he leans down to help me. My body goes limp in his strong touch. He gently lifts me out of the water, bridal style, carrying me as if I'm as light as a paperweight. My throat feels raw as I sputter the acidic water, still struggling for air. He applies light pressure on my lower back, which helps me cough so that I can breathe again. If I wasn't so terrified, I'm certain that I'd be radiating heat at the connection of the way his hand gingerly connected with my back. I glance up, trying to maintain a neutral facial expression at the sight of his swim shirt clinging to the muscles in his chest.

Fortunately for me, before I can get any crazy ideas, like touching his impeccable body, my hair falls in my face and hangs in dripping ringlets around my eyes. His fingers push a strand back behind my ear.

I'm still coughing, but my apprehension fades as I see the relieved smile he gives me, which lights up his entire face. Despite the chaos of the waves, he looks completely at home here in the water.

My voice trembles. "I think you just saved my life,"

He pulls me closer as the waves become calmer as we enter the shallower water. Hunter shakes his head and sighs. "You have no idea how glad I am that you're okay,"

Even though I know he's a little panicked, which I can tell from the intensity in his gaze, I appreciate that he doesn't show it. He stayed strong for me and immediately stepped in and helped me rather than freaking out. The way he responded was exactly what I needed, almost as if he knew how to best handle the situation. If he had panicked, I probably would have had an anxiety attack. Instead of fear, I just feel relief and gratitude.

He continues to carry me to the car, reaching into the backseat for a sweatshirt. As soon as the soft warmth of the hoodie surrounds me, I sigh with happiness. "Thank you for this, and for saving my life."

"Anytime, Anderson," He just chuckles. "I know we only

have ten minutes till the first period, but would you want to warm up first? I'll buy you a hot coffee."

I nod because I don't want this outing to end yet. Time flies by with him, and I'm not ready to go back to reality. I prefer the bubble that forms around us when we're together, even when I'm drowning. "A hot drink sounds great right now. Thank you,"

"It's the least I can do after dragging you into one of the worst riptides I've ever seen," Hunter says.

At the Java Shoppe, we're quiet as we sip our drinks. I put my hair into a bun, and focus on keeping my hands on the steaming mug in my hands, which helps to warm me up.

For the first time in my life, I skipped the first period of school, and I'm enjoying it. So far, the world hasn't crashed down on me yet. It's comforting to know.

The soft hum of the ambiance music at the Java Shoppe is soothing as the realization sinks in.

"Out there, was I going to drown?" I ask, my voice barely above a whisper.

The emotion in Hunter's tone surprises me and shakes me to my core. "Not on my watch, you weren't. I would've drowned first before letting anything happen to you."

His words take me aback, and I just sit in stunned silence for a couple of seconds.

They remind me of the same passion he had when he was warning me not to walk alone in the dark when I ran into him at the beach. Is he protective of me after the events of the party? As much as I want to ask him, I'm not ready to let him in on just how affected I am by what happened last summer.

Hunter's eyes study mine. "What's on your mind?"

I set my drink down. "Just surprised is all, I mean you put your safety at risk for mine,"

Hunter's voice sounds more assured than it ever has. "Well, don't be. I'm going to keep you safe, Adele. You can count on me for that,"

"Well, thank you," I say quietly, "I'll try to stay out of

trouble."

His tone is amused, but his eyes are serious as we connect. "Knowing you, I wouldn't be so sure. Trouble seems to have a way of finding you,"

I think back to the cornfield outing with Selena, and the way I completely fell apart.

"I guess it does," I reply.

"Fortunately, I'm here, so you don't have to go it alone," Hunter says.

I set my drink down. "I'm glad to be of service as your tutor then,"

"I would argue that I'm tutoring you as well," Hunter says, a small smile on the edge of his lips.

"Is that so?" I ask.

"Yes," Hunter challenges me, "look me in the eye and tell me you haven't been having fun living a little more."

His turquoise eyes lock on mine, and I feel my face tingle as blood rushes to my face. Rather than shyly dropping my gaze, I hold his stare and smile back.

"I am," I say.

His smile slips. "I hope today doesn't cause you to doubt your list again,"

I shake my head. "It won't,"

He tilts his head toward me, giving me his full attention. "What made you start having second thoughts?"

Looking at his perfectly boy-next-door handsome face has me in a trance of sorts, and I can't seem to remember. Until the events of the cornfield come back to me. "Let's just say, don't go to the abandoned corn fields at night?"

He waggles a brow, but his lips tilt down when he notices my apprehensive facial expression. His features turn into concern. "Do you want to talk about it?"

"Nothing happened, thankfully," I assure him, "I just freaked out over nothing."

His voice softens a little. "It'll get easier. And, besides, the cornfields are creepy at night anyway."

"You've been there?" I ask, curiosity getting the best of me. His eyes glint with humor. "You sound jealous, Anderson," I chuckle. "I wouldn't dream of it," He smiles smugly at me. "Whatever you say, Adele," The look he directs at me gives me shivers, and I take another sip of my drink to distract myself.

On our way back to school, I gasp when I take in my sopping wet hair and flushed, makeup-free face in the mirror. I try to shake out my hair and fix my appearance a little, reaching into my purse for lip gloss. Even my small touch-up does nothing to fix my disheveled appearance. With my flushed cheeks and frizzy brown-black waves that hang limp just past my shoulders, I look like a surf lesson gone wrong. Hunter, on the other hand, looks effortlessly handsome with his slicked-back hair and the fresh tan from this morning.

Hunter chuckles, and says, "You don't need to fluff up your hair, it looks beautiful. It always does,"

I groan. "My hair kind of has a mind of its own,"

"Kind of like you," Hunter's eyes search mine. "I like it."

His words remain in my head the entire day until I see him in AP Chemistry, where he gives me a big smile, and says, "You left your hair down. Wow,"

"I did," I say, feeling a grin take over my whole face, embarrassed about how a guy telling me my hair is pretty could make me this giddy.

Luckily for me, Mr. Hughes starts passing out the pop quiz. I don't miss, however, the smile and extra pep in Hunter's step as he turns his quiz in. I feel warmth take over my body as I realize that maybe, just maybe, I'm one of the reasons that extra joy is there. Seeing his confidence in turning the quiz in brings back a dream that I've spent a long time shoving down. And now that it's taking over my mind, I want to explore what that could look like. Only it might leave me alone, wandering in the waves, this time with no one to take me out.

CHAPTER 9

"He saved your life?" Selena squeals.

Things have been the same between us since the cornfield incident, but only after I reassured her multiple times that I was fine, I just don't want to talk about it. So, we agreed not to bring it up.

"I guess he did, in a way," I reply, "I mean, I was drowning. Turns out I'm not the strongest swimmer."

Selena takes the key out of the ignition and the car becomes quiet as we talk. These kinds of conversations are unusual for our friendship, but they've been happening more frequently lately. I'm not sure how wise it is, though, given that we'll both be leaving shortly. "That makes sense because I can't remember the last time that I saw you go swimming,"

"Me too," I reply.

"What does this mean?" She takes her out of the braid it's in.

"Nothing, really," I set my backpack down. "Just that Hunter and I are friends now?"

Selena says nothing but wears a knowing smile.

"Speaking of new friends, is there any update on Mario?" I ask.

Selena giggles and lowers her voice. "Maybe,"

Now it's my turn to squeal as I say, "Details! Now!"

Selena turned her head toward her house. "Hush, hush. I don't want my mom to hear,"

"Your mom is very on board with the idea of you dating," I say.

"Well, he and I are going to be going to dinner on Friday night," Selena's eyes gleam with enthusiasm, "As a date."

I gasp with excitement. "Tell me everything!"

And so, she does. Selena gushes about how she and Mario have been texting nonstop and bonding over their love for art.

"We just click," Selena explains, "when I'm around him, I feel brighter, happier, and more confident."

I reach out to hug her. "I love that for you,"

Surprised by my affection, she says, "Adele, I could say the same thing about you lately,"

"You have?" I ask.

"Haven't you noticed it? You're feeling things, things I've never seen you feel before," Selena's voice is kind. "You're even leaving your house more."

"You're right," I hesitate. "What do you think it means?"

Selena's voice becomes more hushed. "I don't know, Adele. I just think you're finally allowing yourself to let your walls down,"

I nod. "I am, and it feels so good. Scary, but good,"

I'm about to open my car door to get out when I blurt, "I'm going to try to learn how to drive again,"

Selena gives me a look of concern mixed with hope, probably thinking about the tears I shed the last time we tried.

I glance down. "Hunter is going to teach me, or try to,"

"Wow, that's sweet," Selena's voice becomes gentler, "Does he know about...?" she pauses mid-sentence, ending the conversation like we usually do when things get heavy.

Her reference to the car accident that killed my mom still causes the smile to fall off my face, the same as it always does. I think that'll be a scar that'll always sting.

Still, I understand her concern. She knows about the ugly aftermath of that accident, especially the way I couldn't even be in a car for the longest time.

As a result, the idea of driving a car is even more terrifying, especially now that I know death is a possibility every time I'm inside of an automobile.

What began as turning down invitations eventually progressed into my world becoming as small as possible.

My one solo attempt to step out and take my life back after anxiety only ended in ragged breaths and tears.

"He doesn't, which is exactly why I think it'll be easier," I explain.

Selena's eyes widen. "You're not going to tell him?"

I shrug. "I might, but not yet," I can see her trying to hold her tongue. Her facial expression twists into one of concern.

She plasters on a convincing smile, but even her reassurance lacks her usual zeal. "When the time is right, you'll know,"

"Thank you," I say, giving her a quick hug as I get out of the car. To my surprise, my dad's car is in the driveway. I'm greeted with the smell of rich tomato sauce and homemade pizza crust as I walk in. I can't even remember the last time my dad cooked, let alone made my favorite dish. When I was younger, we'd love to experiment with all kinds of silly toppings, trying to see who could come up with the most creative pizza.

"This is a nice surprise," I murmur.

My dad looks up at me from where he is rolling out the pizza dough, where the kitchen counter is covered with specks of flour.

"Perfect timing." He gestures for me to wash my hands before we get to work.

Dad wears a bright smile. "How was school today?"

I feel a pit form in my stomach as I think back to skipping my first-period class today. Guilt rolls off my tongue as I plaster on a grin. My voice squeaky as I say, "Great!"

"Mr. Hughes called me to tell me that you earned 100 percent on the most recent pop quiz he administered! He says that you're the first person to ever score that high in such a difficult subject, thermodynamics," My dad hands me a ball of pizza dough to roll out. "Which is why we're celebrating!"

Suddenly I wish I was being scolded. Why is it that we have to have a reason to do something as simple as making pizza together? Am I not even worth his time to make dinner together unless I earn it?

He eyes me. "Adele, this is great news! Don't be so humble, kiddo!"

Dad feels so far away from me lately that even this whole interaction feels forced.

"Thanks, Dad," My voice feels numb, but I try to fake some enthusiasm. "I guess I've been focusing a lot in that class lately."

His tone becomes louder. "Well, keep doing what you're doing, because it sounds like you could be in the running for some incredible scholarships!"

Not once does my dad catch onto the change in my facial expression at that word, the continuous reminder of change. Instead, he drones on and on for what feels like decades about a game plan. I don't even bother making a silly pizza either; I just throw some sauce on and pick at it, trying to feign excitement as he talks about colleges on the East Coast, thousands of miles away from the life I know.

When it hits me that all of this is real and will be happening soon, I excuse myself from the table, saying, "I'm excited, Dad! Thanks for the pizza! I think I just need to get some of this extra energy out with a run so I can focus more on my homework tonight,"

"Good idea," My dad says, giving me a quick hug, "I'm so proud of you."

The words should fill some kind of void, or even spark enthusiasm in me, but they don't. Instead, they make me nauseous, like I have to earn my voice or something. And, even worse, they remind me of myself. The cold, cut-off nature of his mannerisms is something I have lived out in my own life.

As I'm leaving for a run, I peer around my living room at the pictures we have hanging on the walls. One photo of my dad and me stands out to me because it features me holding up an old academic decathlon trophy. I'm beaming, and my dad is radiating pride and happiness beside me. It seems like nothing's changed since none of the photos in our house are recent. They're all centered on outward appearances and accomplishments.

Although the hallways and living room are filled to the brim with an assortment of shallow, scripted photos that mimic my family, this house feels a whole lot emptier than Hunter's house, the small, barren house with no photos at all. I long to be there now, or maybe even just anywhere but here.

My sadness propels me as my feet pound the pavement, each step becoming faster as a loud thud. Tears stream from my eyes as I look up at the night sky, my hands on my knees as I catch my breath, wondering why I'm supposed to navigate all of this alone. Why did we have to lose my mom? And why does it feel like some switch inside my brain, which never let me feel anything at all, was turned on when Hunter came into my life? What does it all mean, and why do I find myself wanting to explore it all more, even though I know I shouldn't?

Even a long, hot shower doesn't calm down the nerves that are still bubbling up inside of me. I do something that I know would get me grounded, solely because of not asking my dad for permission. Or maybe because it would be too hard to ask my dad about it.

The metal keys jingle in my hand as I tiptoe out the front door, which quietly creaks as I sneak out to the driveway. With a blanket wrapped around me, I quietly climbed into my dad's car. I bask in the smell of crisp, clean, scent, and close my eyes while I take in my surroundings. Small pieces of my mom slowly come back to me: the way her warm, soft voice used to read stories to me before bed, her quiet laugh while we'd watch romantic movies together, and the way she'd cover my eyes during any kiss scenes, the smell of gardenia and lily that lingered in every room she'd walk into. She's been slowly slipping away from me, her memories falling out of my grasp, just like everything else in my life. I lost her when I was so young that people tend to shake their heads, softly assuming that I cannot even miss her. And maybe they're right, I can't be weighed down by such a distant memory, but I sure miss my dad. Because losing her caused me to lose him. Because the dad who used to be so silly and full of life, has become a robot of sorts, and I don't know how to get him back without the risk of losing him completely.

I stay in the car for far too long, until my eyelids become heavy and sleep starts to take over.

~

"Are you okay?" Selena asks me, probably for the second time, if I were to guess based on the abruptness of her tone.

"Yes, I'm fine," I say, continuing to pick at my food.

"What's wrong?" She asks.

"Things are just weird with my dad," I sigh. "It just feels like he only cares about me when I'm doing well in school."

"Geeze, that is so frustrating." Selena's eyes meet mine with concern, lingering on the outfit of choice today: a baggy black hoodie that goes down to the knees of my leggings. I hug my legs as I fill her in on the events of last night, leaving out the part where I cried in my dad's car.

"Maybe he just needs some time? I think he'll eventually realize that he's missing out by keeping you at arm's length," Selena says.

I glance down. "Maybe so,"

"You know what I'd do? I'd do the complete opposite," Selena's eyes light up with confidence. "Rather than pushing him away, try to show him what good can come out of actually acknowledging your emotions. Let him in your life, let him see the way you've changed recently."

"Thanks, Selena," I realize she's right. "I appreciate you."

"You too!" Selena says.

"But, anyway, on a more positive note," I say, "I am going to wear the P.E. uniform today instead of sweats. I'm gonna try to be a little more confident."

"Yes, finally!" Selena says, clapping her hands together.

"Key word trying," I respond.

Hunter is already sitting down when I get to AP Chem. His smile is brimming with pride as he shows me that he got a C+ on the last quiz, which means that he's no longer failing the class.

I squeal with so much excitement for him that I almost jump out of my seat. Mr. Hughes catches onto my excitement, giving me a thumbs up as class starts, mistaking my reaction for joy over my own 100%, which I completely forgot about until now.

As soon as class ends, Hunter beams at me. "Thank you so much, Adele,"

"You're so welcome," I shrug. "You're the one who put the hard work in."

"I couldn't have done it without you," Hunter says.

I'm about to roll my eyes, but I feel my face light up in a smile instead, knowing just how much this could change the possibilities of his future, even if only in the short term. Now that I've gotten more of a glimpse of his life, I recognize how much of an outlet football is for him. It's the only thing in his entire life, and I don't want it taken from him. Especially since it means so much to him.

Mr. Hughes calls me to his desk, and Hunter says, "See you in P.E.? Or do you want me to wait for you?"

His gesture doesn't go unnoticed. The thought of him walking me to class makes me blush.

"That's okay, thank you though. I'll see you there," I assure him.

As soon as everyone has filed out of the classroom, Mr. Hughes says, "Adele, I am so proud of you. Tremendous job on the quiz. Your hard work in my class, both on your assignments and assisting other students, is noticed and is commendable,"

"Thank you," I respond.

"I wanted to tell you about an opportunity that I think you might be interested in," Mr. Hughes says, "It's only a one-day commitment, but I think you'd enjoy it, given how skilled you are at science and tutoring,"

He pulls out a flyer that reads, "Science Field Day, Saturday, September 15th from 9 am-2 pm at Harmony Falls Community Center." I glance up from the flyer at him in confusion.

"This is an opportunity for you to have some experience with introducing some science concepts to kids in a fun way," Mr. Hughes explains, "You'll be able to do some fun experiments and meet some other people in the community."

"I don't know, I'm not a leader of any sort," I reply, "I hardly talk to my peers at school, and I've gone to school with most of them since kindergarten."

"What better way to grow than to challenge yourself?" Mr. Hughes says, "Please promise me you'll think about it."

"I will," I reply.

As I'm leaving the classroom, Mr. Hughes lowers his voice. "Adele, I think this is exactly what you've been looking for. It may even lead you into something different than you could've imagined. But the only way to find out is to go,"

The tug in my heart to attend is strong, but doubt is holding me back because this does not align with the plan my dad and I created.

"I'll keep that in mind, thank you," I say before hurrying off to P.E., another part of this day that is going to challenge me.

I skim the flyer once again before throwing it in my locker.

I release a shaky breath as I smooth the silky black athletic shorts over my legs. I can do this. With Selena's encouragement in mind, I quickly leave the locker room and head out to the field before I can change my decision.

I look around for Hunter but see no sign of him on the field, so I join the group and try to blend into the back of the herd of other students walking around the track. I go through the motions, pushing back any doubt in my head, and find that P.E. is a lot less dreadful when I'm not sweating buckets wearing sweatpants during the peak heat of summer.

I still walk when I'm supposed to be running laps though. Baby steps for now.

After Coach Z releases us for the day, I weave through the crowd and nearly topple over Hunter, who has to reach his arms around me to prevent us both from falling to the ground. I don't miss the firmness of his strong biceps as he keeps me steady. Goosebumps form on my arms at his lingering touch.

Embarrassment floods my cheeks. "Are you okay? Sorry, I'm such a klutz," I say.

Hunter steadies me with his hands, finally releasing them after he ensures I'm okay. "I'm fine. No, no, I'm the one who should be sorry. I was standing so close because I wasn't sure if it was you. I almost didn't recognize you,"

It's probably the hot sun and heat from the workout he just had, but is Hunter blushing? I must be mistaken. Even if he is, it's certainly not because of me.

"I thought I'd give the uniform a go today." I awkwardly gesture to the shorts that hit mid-thigh and the stretchy black t-shirt that fits a little too tight for my liking.

"I'm glad you did," Hunter says, "Confidence looks good on you, Adele," before he walks to the locker room, leaving me flustered.

CHAPTER 10

I'm hanging out with Jackie for the first time. We've been talking more in study hall lately, so it was an immediate yes when she asked me. I almost felt guilty as I climbed into her older brother, Braxton's car, after school instead of Selena's. But here I am, trying to evade questions from Jackie's friend, Ava.

After studying for a couple of hours, which mainly consisted of Ava and Jackie deciding between outfits, of which I was no help, we eventually started making our way to the Java Shoppe.

The loud music Baxton is playing does nothing to quiet the countless inquiries of Ava, who is sitting to the right of me. Her dark eyes light up as she leans in and asks, "Is Senior year as exciting as everyone says it is? What's the craziest thing you've done?"

I'm wedged between Ava and Jackie, so I glance at both girls, who are anxiously awaiting my response, no doubt about to be disappointed.

But then I think back to all of the strange things that have already happened this year. Most of them lead back to Hunter, but I shake the thought for now. So far, this year has had a little more jazz than previous years. "Surprisingly, yes," I pause. "I haven't done anything too wild yet though. Except for going to the haunted cornfield, I guess."

Ava gawks at me. "You went there?"

I feel my face heat as I nod. "Yes. With my best friend,"

My eyes meet Braxton's in the rearview mirror. Braxton looks familiar, but I can't quite place him. To my relief, he doesn't look like he runs in the same circles as the people from the party last summer. With his closely cropped dark hair and a faded old band t-shirt, he appears to be a part of a completely different crowd.

He laughs a throaty laugh. "I'm impressed. That takes guts,"

I grin. "Trust me, I don't think I'll be going back, so I don't know how brave that makes me. Once was enough,"

Jackie brightens beside me. "I'm the same way," she glances at Ava. "If it weren't for this one, I don't think I'd do half of the crazy things I do."

Ava's dark, sleek hair flows as she laughs. "You love me for it,"

Jackie sighs. "I do,"

While I try my best to field the invasive questions Ava has about some secret Prom after party, I feel myself freeze a little. Not only have I not heard of it, but Prom is a good six months away, and I'm not even certain if I'll be attending or not.

In the front seat, Braxton whispers under his breath, "Ava, she hasn't heard of half of these things. Neither have I,"

Ava eyes me expectantly. "Well, now she has,"

"What concert are we seeing tonight?" I ask, hoping to change the subject to something that doesn't involve me being in the hot seat.

Jackie brightens next to me. "Braxton's" she says proudly, "his band is playing at the Java Shoppe tonight."

"That's great," I murmur, "I didn't know they have live music."

Ava replies, "Tonight is a concert, but they also have open mic nights occasionally."

"They do?" I ask.

Jackie offers me a kind smile. "Do you sing?"

I feel my face flush as I admit something that not even Selena knows much about. "A little," I shrug. "I'm not at a performance level though."

Braxton quips, "It's art, Adele. There's no such thing as being good enough," His voice lowers a little. "At least, there shouldn't be."

The Java Shoppe is bustling with people, and I have to squeeze into a tiny table with Ava and Jackie on both sides of me. The sweet smell of cinnamon and nutmeg wafts through the air, filling my senses. The scent brings me back to the coffee dates I used to have with my parents. Even the colorful, abstract artwork in the back corner hasn't changed. It's comforting that it's still here.

I glance around at the different groups of people that have come out to support Braxton and his band, recognizing a couple of people from around the school. Some people are crammed into a small table, like me, and others are gathered in the same cliques they talk to at school all day. Once his rich voice begins belting into the microphone, the room becomes silent as we're transported to wherever he's taking us. And it is quite an emotional journey as he starts with a heartwrenching song about shattered promises. His eyes are shut, but a serene smile fills his face as he switches to a piece about midnight kisses. The overwhelming peace he has while he sings, unknowingly capturing the attention of the entire room, captivates me. Because he feels so free, even with all eyes on him. His eyes don't flutter open until after the applause stops.

I glance down, surprised to find myself standing, joining in on the clapping.

Jackie whisper-yells next to me. "Aren't they great?"

I nod, feeling my heart melt about her being so proud of her brother. It reminds me of the way Hunter is with his siblings.

"They're incredible," I breathe.

As the music picks up, and Braxton's band begins playing more mainstream covers, Ava leans in toward me and Jackie. "Let's dance,"

I remain in place in my seat, uncertain if I'm included in the invitation, and unsure if I want to.

Jackie faces me. "It'll be fun!"

My lips quirk up. "Okay,"

Ava loops her arms through mine and Jackie's, leading us to the center of the Java Shoppe, where tables have been cleared to create a little makeshift dance floor. Ava's smooth hair cascades down her back as she dances with ease. Jackie pulls me into their little circle.

People begin filing in behind us, filling the space, and for the first time in a while, my heart doesn't race, because I'm safe here. I glance between my new friends, and I allow the music to whisk me away to another place. It takes a few minutes, and some encouragement from Jackie, who keeps making me laugh by shaking her hips, but I eventually find my own, albeit awkward, rhythm as I sway alongside the crowd around us to the music.

I allow my eyes to close, letting the euphoric sensation of the music take over me. I throw myself into dancing like no one's watching. I'm way offbeat, and I can't help the giggles that escape as I try to keep up with my friends. I feel warmth radiate through me as the song slows, and I glance up to see Hunter across the room, his gaze directly on me. Curiosity fills his eyes as he takes me in. The way his eyes light up as they meet mine sends thrills of euphoria down my spine. His gaze is locked on me, and it gives me a dose of courage to continue dancing. My hair flies in my face as I let the music move me. I offer him a shy smile before returning my focus to Ava and Jackie, who look like they're in a world of their own as they sing along to the music. When I look back in his direction, he's disappeared into the crowd. It should be another reminder of the way we run in different circles, but instead, it fuels the desire I have to be near him. Because I know I wasn't imagining the way his eyes lingered on mine, if only for a moment. There was some kind of connection while I danced, and I know he felt it too.

The feeling stays with me long after the concert ends when everyone is mingling throughout the room. After the band begins taking down some of the set, Braxton walks up to Jackie, Ava, and me.

Braxton tilts his head toward me. "Do you want to try it?"

I glance around at the crowd around us. "Here? Now?"

He shrugs. "You said you sing, right? What better time

than now?"
   I look down. "I don't know,"
   "Another time then," His voice softens. "Do you write?"
   I hesitate, then nod. "Yes, a little,"
   I pause. "How do you know?"
   He chuckles. "Because I know that look,"
   I lower my voice, intrigued. "What look?"
   His eyes gleamed with humor. "That look you get when someone is on your mind, and it's driving you nuts,"
   I feel my face heat up. Am I really that see-through?
   Braxton reassures me, "I only know that because I've been there."
   I tilt my head, doing a double take. "You have?"
   His laughter catches me off guard. "Yes, and you know what?" His eyes meet mine. "It's the best time to write."
   "I guess that's true,"
   He offers me a kind smile. "Promise me you'll think about singing here someday. It could be good for you,"
   After the place clears out, Braxton invites me onto the small stage. "Come on, Adele. It's just us here,"
   I take a shallow breath.
   He's right.
   What better time than now?
   The lights are dimmed, and it's just me, Jackie, Ava, and Braxton. Ava's eyes widen as I step on the stage, and Jackie gives me a reassuring smile.
   Despite the miniscule crowd, I still close my eyes as I lean into the microphone.
   I reflect on the events of the summer, and how affected I still am from the aftermath of everything. And, I let the courage of dancing earlier tonight carry into singing. My voice sounds completely broken, haunted even, but it's the truth, so I continue anyway.

   The lyrics take me back to the hopeless sensation that followed me after I lost my voice, and just how difficult it's been trying to get it back. Mostly, though, they just speak to the way that I'm stumbling around when it comes to navigating all of the feelings I've had lately. I guess after shoving everything down for so long, it's only natural that I'd be overcome with a plethora of feelings.

Wandering in the dark
Can't see where to start
Because this is my first time
It feels like in a long time
That I've tried
And I don't wanna lose sight
Of why I made these changes
One mistake could erase it

One step in front of the other
I can't get too close to another
After what I've been through
It feels like it's no use

Expanding my world
One step at a time
Taking back all the memories
Of what could've been mine
I'm scared to fall again
And Cuz I know that I'd shatter
And I used to be fearless
But this is me after

I can't take a chance
When everything's tainted
So why chase romance
When we might not make it
One step in front of the other
I can't get too close to another
After what I've been through
It feels like it's no use

Expanding my world
One step at a time
Taking back all the memories
That should have been mine
I'm scared to fall again
And Cuz I know that I'd shatter
And I used to be fearless
But this is me after

I lean into you
But never too close
I can't tell you the truth
That's just how it goes

Everyone is silent until Ava is the first to speak up.

She squeals, "Wow, you have some pipes!"

I turn toward Braxton, who gives me a reassuring smile. He understands the process of pouring your heart into the words, in the hope that the final product will somehow reflect a portion of the pain you feel.

Braxton clears his throat. "Wow, Adele,"

Jackie's beaming. "You have to sing that at the open mic in a couple of weeks!"

I shrug. "You think so?"

Jackie nods. "I know so,"

I climb down from the stage, noticing how weightless I feel after singing my soul out up there. Would I still feel the same way after singing in front of a bunch of people?

I'm surprised to find Hunter's truck parked outside of my place when Braxton drops me off.

I give Jackie a quick hug goodbye before walking toward where Hunter is idling.

I gently tap on his window, and he rolls it down, greeting me with a lazy smile.

"Hi," he whispers.

"Hi," My voice is hesitant because this feels like new

territory, and I'm not sure how to navigate it.

Because I certainly don't show up at my friend's houses late at night.

The car whirs as it turns off, leaving me in the dark.

I glance toward my house.

He smiles softly at me.

I'm still standing in place. Do I climb in his truck? Wait for him to get out? Let this strange moment pass between us?

As the options overwhelm me, Hunter murmurs, "I didn't get a chance to properly say hi to you earlier,"

I look down. "That's okay,"

His voice is hesitant. "I understand if you're too tired, but would you want to go for a drive? I can't sleep, I've got too much running through my mind right now."

I nod, settling on climbing in. The air stills between us, and we sit in silence as the sound of me clicking my seatbelt into place is the only thing I hear for a moment.

"Could we just sit here instead of going anywhere?" His eyes meet mine. "It's nice doing nothing."

My lips tilt up into a shy smile. "I'll keep you company,"

His keys jangle as he turns the car on once again.

The engine revs to life, and the lights brighten, giving me a glimpse of just how worn out he looks right now.

He has the same radiating smile he always has, but it looks forced.

I folded my hands in my lap, wishing I was a good conversationalist.

Hunter doesn't seem to mind though. His shoulders settle as he relaxes more. He gently taps his hands on the steering wheel. "It was really sweet watching you have fun with some different friends,"

I want to feel embarrassed, but it feels safe with him because I know he's just being kind. He's happy for me because he realizes how hard it is for me to let people in.

I feel my eyes light up a little. "Thank you,"

He murmurs, "You were quite the dancer,"

I giggle. "I think I'll leave the performing to you football players,"

His tone is playful. "So, you liked my performance, huh?"

It should be a cute little banter, but instead, it reminds me that I shouldn't be next to him right now. A pretty, trim cheerleader should be here instead of me.

I just shrug. "I don't think you're lacking in fans,"

His laughter echoes throughout the car and he shakes his head. "Trust me, it comes with its drawbacks,"

I tilt my head. I give him the space; this is his chance to open up if he wants to. "I'm here to listen if you'd like to talk about it,"

He sighs. "Sometimes, it just feels like the pressure is making me someone I don't want to be,"

My eyes search his. "How so?"

His brows furrow. "I don't want to be the kind of person that doesn't care about other people,"

I shake my head. "That's not you, though,"

He runs a hand through his hair and turns down the heater so that it's no longer on full blast. "Sometimes I feel like I look around me, and wonder how many of the people I surround myself with are only there because of football," He hesitates. "I mean, how many people have I blown off because they didn't fit into my little bubble?"

I want to reach for him, but I don't. Instead, I say, "Hunter, look at me," I lower my voice a little. "You know who you are. Don't let football, or anything else for that matter, take that away from you. And if you forget who you are, just look at your siblings, and at the joy that's found in them when you come home," I gesture around us as I wave my hands around. "Don't get so lost in all of the details of everything that you miss what it's really about."

His eyes look far away. "You're right. Thanks, Adele,"

We sit in silence for what feels like hours, both of us just sitting alone with our thoughts. Even as my eyes become droopy, I stay by his side until he whispers, "This helped a lot. Thank you,"

I nod my head. "Anytime,"

His expression shifts as his lips quirk up. "Tomorrow, I'll be helping you," Somehow, in his truck, we've created some kind of sanctuary, and I don't want to leave. Just his presence has become so familiar, and so comforting to me. Even just sitting with him now feels like it did the night he drove me home. How is it that being around him helps me to feel so at peace?

I can't seem to get enough of whatever emotion it is that he seems to evoke in me.

I hesitate. "What's next on the list?"

He lowers his voice a little as if he's aware of how much this means to me. "I'm going to teach you how to drive,"

I let out a shaky breath. "Oh boy,"

His voice cuts through my fear when he says, "I know you can do it, Adele. I believe in you,"

His words remain in my mind long after he pulls out of the driveway.

CHAPTER 11

"I can't do this. This was a mistake," My voice comes out in shaky breaths as I try to calm down my breathing before it turns into hyperventilation.

It feels like my heart is going to pound out of my chest, and I haven't even driven yet. My hands shake on the steering wheel. I'm certain my knuckles are going to turn blue from my firm grasp on it.

With trembling fingers, I let my hair out of its clip, allowing my waves to cascade over my face in the hope that it would hide the fear written on my features.

Hunter can see right through me though.

He looks at me with patient and kind eyes, gently saying, "Adele, I'm happy to take these driving lessons at your pace. Let's just pause for a second and let you catch your breath,"

His kind words help to slow my ragged breathing, especially when he says, "You're safe,"

We're still on the dirt lot near his dad's auto shop, in the same place we began. Hunter thought it would be easier to practice in the middle of nowhere, but so far I've been too scared to even put my foot on the gas. I keep overthinking things and forgetting the fundamentals of driving. I have adjusted my grip on the steering wheel multiple times. Hunter calmly reassured me each time, even going as far as placing his hands over mine to position them correctly. Just that motion alone helped to calm my nerves a little. Unfortunately, now I'm back to square one.

"Is it gas then brake, or brake then gas?" I ask.

"What?" Hunter asks.

My voice is frantic. "Which one is the one on the left?"

"The brake," He says, "we don't have to start using it today though. Let's just get you comfortable."

That's probably a good call since my foot feels heavy from being so shaky, and I'm not sure I'd be able to take my foot off the gas. The thought alone has my heart racing again.

"It's okay, Adele," Hunter places his hand on my forearm and lightly caresses my arm. His small act of comfort, although a friendly one, changes something in me, replacing my panic with calm. Suddenly the cold sweat and shaky feeling reverberating throughout my body is replaced with an overwhelming peace. "I'm here to listen whenever you're ready to share. Even if that's not today."

"My mom died in a car accident," My voice is hurried and uncertain. "I was in the car with her."

Rather than giving me the usual dreaded look of pity, or a rushed response, Hunter puts his hand over mine and gives me his full attention, allowing me the space to share. The warmth of his touch sends butterflies to my stomach, but I shake off the feeling as if it simply being an effect of a guy touching my hand for the first time.

"It was a long time ago, but I guess I'm still a little shaken up by it. Even just riding in the car with people freaks me out sometimes, which is why I usually only ride with Selena. And, well, with you too, I guess. When I have to ride with people I don't know well, which rarely happens, especially recently, my heart starts to pound out of my chest and my entire body gets so shaky that I feel numb. It almost makes everything feel like too much effort," I say, letting out a sad chuckle.

Only Hunter doesn't laugh. He looks at me with such an intensity that I never believed was possible for him. "Thanks for trusting me, Adele. I can't even imagine what that's like. Please just know that I'm here for you. I'm in your corner,"

"Thank you, I really appreciate it," I say, turning my gaze back toward the steering wheel as I see the light in his eyes as our gazes meet. "I guess you could say it's been a hindrance to me socially since it makes making plans hard. Which I guess brings me to why I was so upset at you over the summer." My eyes betray me as tears escape.

"Upset? What?" Hunter asks.

"My... anxiety has led people to believe that I think I'm better than them or something, especially when I don't go to many events. At first, I was fine being known as the science nerd; I didn't mind it. I liked being able to just keep my head down and go through high school without making any waves," I smile sadly. "But then being known by the entire school as someone who has never been kissed and was outed to everyone as being afraid of it? I was humiliated, I mean, the looks I got from people, the whispers as I walked by, just made me want to disappear even more."

"Adele, I'm so sorry," Hunter's voice cracks slightly. "I was just trying to protect you. The last thing I wanted to do was hurt you. It was wrong of me to publicly make a big deal of it like that. And for that, I'm so sorry. I hope you can forgive me."

"No, no, Hunter, I can see now that you meant well," I assure him, "That guy was being a little aggressive toward me, so looking back, I appreciate you stepping in. I guess I'm just embarrassed is all."

Over the summer, I snuck out alone and walked a few streets down to what was supposed to be one of the wildest, most fun parties of the year. Selena was out of town, so I was on my own, desperate to try to live outside of my head and the four walls of my bedroom for once. So, I put on the only party-worthy outfit I owned, a tight knee-length black spandex dress I'd bought online a couple of summers before. The dress was tighter than anything I'd normally wear, but I wanted to step out a little.

At first, the party was as fun as I'd hoped, as even just being a fly on the wall, listening to the music and people-watching was enjoyable for me. But then, the time for truth or dare came, and the party host, Sean, dared Mitch, a guy who thank goodness went to high school in Meadowbrook, the town next door, to kiss me, in front of everyone. Mitch mistook my blatant surprise and hesitation as an invitation to kiss in private instead and started putting his hands around my waist, trying to force me to go to the other room with him. Naturally, I blurted out that it was my first kiss, which garnered even more attention from everyone at the party. Everything came to a complete standstill as everyone stopped what they were doing to watch the drama that ensued.

To my shock, Hunter, whom I think I'd spoken to a handful of times the entire time I'd known him before this, stepped in and demanded that Mitch take his hands off me. In response, Mitch shoved me at Hunter, which angered him even more. Hunter managed to keep his cool, aside from telling all of the guys to respect me and to "stay away, far, far away," from me, sounding like my dad instead of an acquaintance. While Hunter drove me home, the word about me spread to the whole school. The few events that I tried to attend, like the school year kickoff, were filled with people talking about me right in front of me. Apparently, everyone was surprised that as a Senior, I'd never kissed anyone, and when given the chance to kiss a "catch" like Mitch, I'd pass on the opportunity. It's still a little embarrassing, but it is what it is.

With the way my skin tingles right now with Hunter's hand over mine, I'm starting to question my aversion to kissing.

"It took everything in me not to punch him for putting his hands on you like that without your permission," Hunter's eyes scan me, once again ensuring that I'm okay. "I am sorry for making a scene though. I guess I just wanted your first kiss to be special, not with some tool like that, who couldn't recognize what it means to you."

I just wanted your first kiss to be special.

I want to scream that if it was with him, it would be special, but I don't.

"Well, surprise, it still hasn't happened yet," I laugh but it comes out strangled. "It turns out that guys get kind of hesitant to start something with me."

"Anyone who will get to know you in that way is lucky, Adele," Hunter says.

His face is centimeters from mine, so close that I have a front-row view of the cute freckles that line his nose, the innocence and goodness in his eyes that I never noticed till now, and the joy behind his smile, despite the burdens he carries each day.

"Thank you," I whisper, itching to lean in more and close the space between us. I'm desperate to know if kissing him feels anything like I could've imagined, knowing it'll be better.

"When it happens for you, it will be special," Hunter inches back to increase the distance between us once again, his eyes still on mine, "Now, let's get you familiar with the brake and gas."

And the moment between us fades so instantly that I'm sure I imagined it. So, I focus on moving my foot between the brake and the gas, which is simpler after the lingering comfort of his touch.

As he turns the car off, about to drop me off at my house, I say, "Wait,"

The car is dead silent, with not even the engine to break up the quiet.

I glance at him. "Thank you, for today. Thanks for listening, and for being there,"

"Anytime," Hunter replies, "thanks for trusting me."

As I walk up to my front door, I glance over my shoulder to see him still waiting for me to go inside. The thought makes me flush.

"Did Selena get a new car?" Dad asks as I walk into the house.

"What?" I ask, still in a trance of sorts as I think about the butterflies in my chest right now.

Hunter sees me. He gets me. Maybe we're not so different after all.

"Who dropped you off just now?" Dad asks, any remnant of a smile from yesterday completely vanished from his face. Even his tone sounds entirely different, the same stiff, cordial voice as usual. Yesterday feels like a dream now, and the chance of laughing again and making pizzas feels impossible.

"Hunter Watts," I try to keep my tone nonchalant, despite panicking on the inside. "I'm tutoring him in AP Chem."

I feel guilty, even though it's the truth. I am just tutoring him, in a very temporary agreement, but there's a tiny part of me that wants more.

Dad's exasperation evident in the way his voice rises slightly. "Don't you have enough on your plate?"

I want to tell him that until lately, I've had nothing on my plate. I'm tired of all my Friday nights consisting of reading alone in my room when I could be spending time with other people. That leaving the house doesn't have to be equated with something terrible happening to me. Mostly, though, I want to tell him that I miss the man he used to be, and I'm not sure if I'll ever have that back. "I promise I'm doing fine balancing it all,"

"I trust you," My dad says, emphasizing how this newfound freedom, this independence I've had lately since he's been traveling for work so much, is something that can be taken away in an instant. The thought alone brings on nausea and makes me want to end this conversation as fast as humanly possible.

"Thanks, Dad," I say, "speaking of which, I was invited by Mr. Hughes to volunteer at a science event happening at the Community Center this weekend. It could be good for my college applications."

The last part is a stretch since it's a one-day youth event, but something is telling me to show up that day.

His voice softens. "That's wonderful, Adele. Good for you for stepping up,"

We're in the living room, and it's time for dinner, but neither of us seems to be in the frame of mind to sit down and share a meal.

"Thank you, I'm excited about it. It'll be a good opportunity," I respond.

"Are you hungry, kiddo?" My dad asks, his tone suddenly shifting to friendly now that he's gotten some assurance that I'm not throwing my life away.

"Not really, I want to read ahead for the next AP Chem quiz," My smile is forced. "I'll probably just grab a snack later."

"Okay, well I'll be catching up on some work in my room if you need anything," My dad says, "so holler if you need anything,"

"Thanks, Dad," I say.

I'm about to walk away when I remember Selena's words about not pushing my dad away. So instead, I give him a hug, noticing it takes him a second to reciprocate.

His features are etched with a warning. "Adele, please be careful with that boy,"

A second passes before I remember who he's referring to.

"Dad, I'm just tutoring him," I reassure him. "And besides, we're friends, it's not like that."

"I didn't mean like that," My dad's brows furrow. "I would just hate to see either of you get hurt."

I pull away from the hug and ask him, "What do you mean?"

"Well, I know you haven't dated," Dad clears his throat. "But you're so close to the finish line, you might as well stick it out now and wait until you're in college. There's no use wasting time on high school romance, especially when it means hurting a boy that's already been through enough as it is."

"What?" I ask.

"All I'm trying to say is, wait it out. The right man will come when you're in college, well probably in medical school. You've got a long road of studies ahead of you, Adele. There's no sense in complicating it," Dad's eyes meet mine. "Especially with someone who is staying here in Harmony Falls. It wouldn't be fair to him."

I want to ask him more about Hunter's past, but I realize it's not fair to Hunter. He'll share with me if he wants to.

"Thanks, Dad. I'll keep my eye on the prize," I assure him.

Dad grins. "That's what we Andersons do,"

The thought of my mother crosses my mind once again.

Was she the same as him, or did she completely take his world off his axis, the same way Hunter's done to mine?

CHAPTER 12

"One, two, three, go!" I shout, my voice followed by the echo of the kids' laughter as two first-grade girls, Tali and Rae, release their egg drop off of the side of the gymnasium bleachers to the padded area below. The homemade device crackles as it falls.

Science Day has been incredible so far. Sandra, the director of the Community Center, threw me straight in, immediately giving me a group of ten first graders to supervise. All of the stations so far have been fun, but this one has been the best. The kids I've been with today have been so full of life and energy that it's brought out an enthusiasm in me that I didn't even know existed. Even the pep in my voice feels genuine as I lead them through releasing their eggs, wrapped with tape, tissues, and mini cutouts of egg cartons. The giggles that follow each "drop" have me nearly keeling over in laughter, especially when the kids celebrate that their egg survived the fall.

I'm on my hands and knees, helping the kids clean up remnants of tissues and tape before we move on to the next center. I'm able to usher them to the next center with ease, using the chant I learned not ten minutes before I was given an entire group to supervise: "Macaroni and cheese..." I say a goofy smile on my face that mirrors the smiles of the kids.

"Everybody freeze," the kids say at an ear-splitting volume as they line up to move rooms.

I walk backward, leading my group toward a small, bright blue classroom with the floor and desks completely covered in garbage bags.

"Time to...make slime!" I say, reading the theme of this final center.

Minutes later, the room is filled with laughter as the kids play with the sticky, glittery, colorful goo.

"Best day ever!" Rae says, smiling widely.

And it is great. The curiosity and the endless laughter from the kids in my group make the day go by in a blink. Sandra, the Community Center director, pulls me aside while the kids are finishing up, and gives me a warm hug. "Thank you for your help today,"

"It was a pleasure. I had a lot of fun," I notice the kids in my group laughing together as they compete to see who can pick up the most pieces of trash off the floor.

"Do you have a lot of previous experience with kids?" Sandra asks.

I shake my head. "Me? I have none, I'm an only child,"

"Well, Adele, you are quite the natural at this," Sandra offers me a smile. "It might be something to think about."

Before I can respond, she walks away to check on the next group.

After the "Awards Ceremony", where each kid receives a red ribbon and a miniature science lab kit filled with small beakers and a magnifying glass, I'm about ready to walk home when a familiar voice says my name. Turning, I'm met with a big, enthusiastic hug from Hunter's sister, Shelby.

I hug her back. "Hi!"

"Hi!" She is glowing with happiness as she practically bounces up and down, still on a high from the excitement of the day.

"Did you have fun today? Which group were you in?" I ask her.

Shelby is beaming. "I was volunteering. I was helping in Miss Sandra's group,"

"Wow, that's so nice of you," I'm moved that Shelby, who doesn't seem to have much free time, would spend a Saturday giving back to younger kids in the community.

"It is," I hear Hunter's voice say, laced with an emotion I can't recognize. Pride for his sister, if I were to guess. I was so caught up in enthusiasm over seeing Shelby that I didn't even notice Hunter was here.

"Hi," I say quietly, feeling lame for not having something witty to say.

Hunter glances at me as if he's equally surprised to find me here too. "Hi,"

We begin walking side by side as Shelby races ahead of us, stopping along the way to give hugs to several people she recognizes on her way out.

"I wasn't expecting to see you here," Hunter says, "how was it?"

The hallway around us is still abuzz with excitement, filled with enthusiastic kids showing their families their

I grin. "It was great,"

"You seem very happy," Hunter gestures around us. "Then again, you're kind of in your element here, with science and all."

"I am," My lips tilt up. "It turns out I might be better with kids than people my age."

Shelby, who's just a few feet ahead of us now, exclaims, "I agree! She was amazing, she let everyone make tons of slime!"

And for some reason, the big smile she gives me has my heart swelling with pride.

I'm about to part ways with them, turning to walk toward my house, when Hunter pauses. "Are you hungry? I was going to take this one home for some lunch,"

I glance at the ground. "Oh no, I wouldn't want to impose,"

Hunter faces me. "I'd love for you to join us,"

"Please come, Adele! Please?" Shelby says, making a pouty face.

"I'd love to," I say, following Hunter's lead as he opens the passenger door for me.

He opens the back door for his sister and shuts it behind her, and I melt over him once again. There's something about the little things he does for the people around him that makes me all warm and fuzzy.

"I love this song, turn it up!" Shelby says from the back

seat.

"I can't even hear it. How do you hear it from the back?" Hunter asks in a teasing voice, turning the volume up.

"Probably all those loud noises from the auto shop," Shelby quips, causing me to laugh.

Hunter chuckles and shakes his head as Shelby sings along at the top of her lungs. I love the country song playing too, so I slowly start singing along, feeling less shy since the radio is blaring loud anyway.

Once we get to the house, Hunter puts me to work in the kitchen, offering me an apron as we roll up our sleeves.

"What's on the menu for today?" Shelby asks.

"Paninis," Hunter responds.

Shelby groans. "But I'm starving, they didn't even have snacks at the Science Day,"

I think back to the many meals that I've come up with on a whim when I've been home alone. "I have an idea," I say, "What ingredients do you have?"

"Be my guest," Hunter says, gesturing toward the fridge.

To my luck, it's filled with Roma tomatoes and basil.

"How about you cook the pasta and I will cook the chicken?" I glance at Hunter. "That is, is it okay if we use it? I'll make it go a long way."

"That works for me," Hunter says, turning to Shelby. "How about pasta?"

Shelby's eyes tilt up. "Now we're talking,"

I hold back a laugh at her assertiveness.

Hunter waves his hands toward Shelby. "You go rest, Shelby, you've had a busy week."

Shelby gives him a small salute as she walks out of the kitchen, leaving me alone with Hunter.

I'm grateful to have a task to focus on since conversations are not my strong suit.

I'm cutting the chicken into thin slices when Hunter says, "You have a beautiful voice, by the way,"

I feel my face flush. "Oh, umm, thank you,"

"I mean it, Adele," His eyes search mine. "You're talented."

Singing is an ingrained part of me at this point, but I don't share it with anyone, probably because it's the last tether between us. I remember the way she used to fill the house with her melodic voice as she whipped up delicious-smelling recipes that filled the entire house with the aroma of Italian spices. The meal Hunter and I are making today reminds me of her. She never wrote her recipes down, instead encouraging me to "use my heart" when helping her cook, which usually went dreadfully wrong. After she passed, and my dad began spending more time at work, I tried to recreate those recipes I remembered her by. It felt like I was grasping at straws when it came to keeping my connection to her alive. This was mainly because my dad completely shut down after her death.

As I'm cooking the chicken on the stove with heavy cream and spices, Hunter asks, "When did you learn to cook?"

My response is hurried; I'm not ready to go there right now. His question makes it sink in just how lonely things have been at home. "We don't eat much together at my house anymore but this is one of the only things I know how to cook."

Hunter raises his eyebrows in concern and says, "I'm sorry, Adele,"

"It's okay. It's just the way it is," I say, plastering a smile on my face as I go back to stirring the Italian spiced chicken, adding some fresh tomatoes and cheese until everything melts together.

Hunter's eyes search mine. "It's not how it should be, though. You deserve more than that," The kitchen instantly feels too small, with him right next to me making such a bold statement so casually.

I smile at him, feeling more at home at his place than I have in mine in months.

"Thank you," I say, "I know it will get better."

Before I have a chance to react, a loud buzzing sound echoes throughout the small space, and I cover my hands over my ears while my heart races. Smoke fills the room and Hunter gently takes my hand and guides me to the edge of the kitchen since I'm frozen in place. His words feel distant, and they echo in my head as he asks me to open a window.

He moves with speed and calmness as he carefully drains the pasta noodles and turns off the stove. I'm still too startled to move until he's next to me and opening the window to let some fresh air in. It feels like I can't get enough air as the room around me becomes a blur.

"Hey, Adele, it's okay," Hunter whispers in my ear, "I just cooked the noodles on too high of heat. We're safe, I promise."

I nod softly, wondering if there will ever be a point in my life where even the smallest things don't feel like life or death. Trauma has a way of sticking around my life like an ugly cloud that's not always visible, but it's constantly there. Hunter doesn't press the issue, though. Instead, he gestures for me to join him at the table. "If that fire alarm didn't wake Shelby up, she must be exhausted. I'll let her sleep a little longer,"

Hunter and I eat in comfortable silence while I notice the way I feel different around him. Confident, even. He's the captain of the football team, and I'm completely new to this whole exercise thing, which shows, but he's not once ever made a comment of any kind about it. If anything, his teasing about P.E. has been an encouraging distraction from my insecurities. Hunter has been cheering me on. Even Mitch's last words to me at the party that night, "I wouldn't have wanted to be with you anyway. I was just doing you a favor," don't hold much weight when I'm around Hunter, who doesn't seem to care.

I wonder what Hunter's type is. I think back to the way that I've stayed out of the gossip mill at school and realize that I can't remember him dating anyone. If I were to guess, he probably goes for cheerleaders. Someone more in his league, I suppose. I almost laugh at the thought of me even thinking I'd have a chance with him; that would be nearly impossible.

"What's going through your mind? You're smiling a lot," Hunter says, breaking me out of my spiraling daze.

"Nothing," I say quickly.

"It sure must be something big because it's causing you to push your food around, and this is one of the best meals I've ever had," Hunter's voice is light. "You'll need to teach me. Thanks, Adele. I think once my siblings try this, they'll want to replace me with you."

I chuckle. "Nothing could replace you,"

Hunter's lips quirk up. "I can't tell if you mean that in a good or a bad way,"

"I guess you'll never know," I say smugly.

He's beaming now. "Well, come on silly, and finish your food quickly because I have something to show you,"

~

"This is beautiful out here," I say, looking out at the grassy hills that Hunter has led me to.

"I thought you'd like it," Hunter gestures to the meadows around us. "I saw how happy you were looking at all of the wildflowers near my house."

He grabs my hand and leads me to the top of a large hill while gusts of wind whip through my hair. We're up quite high, and other than his house, there's nothing for miles. The grass and flowers line the surrounding hills, and it feels like we're in a completely different place instead of the edge of town.

"Now for the fun part," he says when we reach the top, gesturing to two large, flat pieces of cardboard.

I arch my brow. "What?" I glance at him.

He gives me a mischievous smile and says, "We're going sledding,"

When I give him a blank stare, his lips tilt up into a half-smile. "You've never done this before?"

I shrug. "No,"

"You'll love it," His eyes search mine. "Trust me on this."

My legs tremble a little as I crouch down to sit on the thin cardboard, surprised that I'm relying on it to carry me down safely.

Hunter's rich voice sends goosebumps up my neck as he bends down right behind me to whisper, "Let me know when you're ready, Anderson,"

"I'm ready," I breathe.

His hand firmly connects with the small of my back as he sends me off.

I squeal since I have nothing to grab onto for dear life as I go gliding down the hill, laughing as my quick, exhilarating ride ends with a thump as the "sled" comes to a stop and the land becomes rockier. Hunter comes riding behind me, nearly colliding with me, causing me to giggle.

"Again!" I say, grabbing his hand now and leading us up the hill.

He just gives me a cheeky smile and squeezes my hand in his. I'm having too much fun to try and dissect the warm feeling that's radiating through my chest right now.

We sled for what feels like hours until my legs are sore and my jeans are covered in dirt. I marvel at the sky around us as it transforms into an assortment of orange and pink tones while the sun takes up the entire sky at once, entrancing me. The beams of the sun spread out diagonally, creating the most beautiful clouds. I can't look away. Before I know it, Hunter is pushing a piece of hair out of my eyes and putting a small pink flower behind my ear. I shiver at his touch.

With his other hand, he hands me a small flower, saying, "Blow on it and make a wish,"

"It's not a dandelion," I say, desperate to say something to fill the moment.

"It's the same concept," His eyes meet mine. "Make a wish anyway. It just might come true."

I grin and gently blow on the flower. I feel my smile take over my entire face as my eyelids flutter shut. I might as well go all out with this wishing thing, just for good luck.

Even though I don't believe in wishes, I wish for him anyway. For some kind of glimmer of hope that he feels the same way around me.

"What did you wish for?" He leans in with a mischievous smile. His eyes are still locked on me, and all I want is to stay here in this moment with him.

I glance down as a flush creeps in. "If I tell you, it might not come true," I say, too shy to meet his eyes.

"As if," Hunter says, "You can do anything you put your mind to."

"What did you wish for?" I ask.

The last rays of the sun fade beneath the hills, leaving the sky as a beautiful, dark canvas of colors.

"For more days like this where I can slow down and appreciate all of the incredible things going on in my life. Sometimes I just lose track of what's important," Hunter replies.

His response throws me completely off guard because Hunter has a lot of things he could wish for, yet he wishes for a different mindset. That alone tells me a lot about him. And better yet, it has me thinking about how maybe that's all I'm missing in my own life.

Hunter's tone shifts to worry. "Let's get you safe inside before the coyotes come out,"

I squeal and nearly jump in his arms.

"I'm kidding, Adele," His deep laugh fills my ear as I try to gracefully exit his embrace, the tangled limbs we have going on. "Your reaction was priceless, though. I'm glad to know you trust me."

I think back to him carrying me out of the ocean.

"I mean, you've saved my life, so I trust you with anything now," I say.

"I'm glad to hear it," Hunter replies.

As the night sky becomes darker, we begin to huddle together as he guides us back to his house in the pitch. And even when I'm back at my house, the happiness I feel doesn't fade away. For the first time in my life, I've stopped hiding. And now that I know what it feels like to live like that, I don't want to go back anytime soon.

When my dad tries to scurry into his room, claiming he's going to call in some takeout for us, I offer to cook for us, saying that I need his help.

We dance around each other in the kitchen, trying to find our groove in this unfamiliar territory: actual conversations. Which leaves me as the one to start to try to make a change.

"Science Day was incredible today, Dad," I begin, "I loved every second of it. I had so much fun, I can't even describe how much I enjoyed it."

Happiness settles into his features, and the smile he gives me is hesitant probably because he doesn't smile much anymore. "Wow, Adele, I'm so glad to hear that,"

I think back to how right it felt to be with the children.

"Working with the kids just came so easily to me," I explain, "It felt like second nature."

"Your mother was the same way," Dad says quietly, clearing his throat as he realizes he's brought up the topic we never touch. Only, now I'm more than ready and practically close to pleading with him to tell me more about her.

"She was?" I ask.

"Yes," Dad's lips tilt up into a sad smile. "She loved being goofy and just having fun with children. She loved being a teacher, but mostly, she just loved being a mom. That was her real dream in life, Adele: being your mom. She loved every second."

Dad has a faraway look in his eyes and I know from experience that this moment will dissipate as quickly as it started, so I fight for it.

"I think I'm more similar to her than I thought," I quip.

His tone immediately shifts, and so does the topic of conversation. "What? Like, maybe you see yourself doing pediatrics?"

I want to groan, but I don't, because this is some progress.

"Maybe something like that? I'm realizing that I might want something different out of life," I say.

His words give me a glimmer of hope. "Well, keep doing well in your classes and you'll be able to walk through any door that opens up,"

"Thanks, Dad," I reply, "and we should eat dinner together

more often."

His voice softens a little as if he remembers why we're here in the kitchen. It's almost like he just needed some time to shift out of task mode. "That sounds good to me,"

CHAPTER 13

"Adele, please come! This is totally up your alley, it's a tradition," Selena pleads as we talk outside of my locker, referring to the annual Senior shut-in, which is happening on Saturday, in two days. I never understood the appeal of being stuck inside the school with all of my classmates. For Selena, though, who's pretty involved in the extracurriculars at school, it makes sense, because she'll have plenty of people to goof off with and talk to.

"Mario is going," Selena says as if it's a selling point. They've already been on two dates, and I couldn't be happier for her. That being said, though, his presence will just mean that I'm more likely to be alone the entire night since Selena will be with him the whole time.

"And? If I don't go, you have more time with him," I say, slowly slamming my locker closed.

Selena's eyes widen, and she glances around us. "But we might have our first kiss there. It'll be the third date, after all,"

"At the shut-in? Is that a thing?" I ask, leaning in closer to talk quietly. I had always assumed that the Senior shut-in was just a movie night.

"Yes, it's one of the main reasons people go," Selena says matter-of-factly.

Oh boy. My mind immediately wanders to think about whether a certain boy is going to be there. The last thing I need is to reveal my growing attraction toward him to Selena. Knowing her, she'd be rooting for it and would be even more disappointed than me when I'd inevitably be rejected.

"Who knows, Adele, you might even have your first kiss," Selena's words pique my interest, but I don't let on.

"What about the third date rule?" I ask, but the idea of there being a possibility of something happening in that area of my life is exciting.

"There's only one way to see," Selena says.

"I'll think about it," I say softly, knowing that my answer is still leaning toward no.

"Good, because I think there's someone else who wants you there," Selena says, gesturing toward Hunter, who's walking our way. She can see right through me. Although, I'm pretty sure that my interest in him is written all over my face. The second I saw him, my face lit up.

Selena nods hello to him then quickly walks away, saying, "Think about it, Adele!"

"Hey," Hunter says, and I realize that this is the first time I've seen him in the morning before school, let alone really talked to him much in front of our classmates outside of tutoring and P.E.

"Hi," I reply. I give him a shy smile, then try to hide my excitement, only to look even more awkward. Fortunately, Hunter is nonchalant as ever and doesn't notice my little internal crisis around him.

"What does Selena want you to think about?" Hunter asks.

"Nothing, she's just trying to convince me to go to the Senior shut-in," I say, gaging his reaction.

"You're not going?" He encourages me, "Come on, Adele, it'll be perfect for your list."

Well, when he puts it like that. Plus, if this shut-in is as eventful as Selena says, I might be able to figure out Hunter's type. And then be able to silence the spark I feel towards him because there's nothing like watching someone you like to be with someone else to destroy those feelings. Or so I'd think. If anything, going would help to remind me that he and I are not a good match. More for my sake than his, because he's already gotten the memo.

"I guess it could be fun," I say quietly.

"Come on, think about it?" Hunter asks, giving me puppy

dog eyes as he smiles at me.

With him looking at me like that, there's no chance that I'll be missing the shut-in, whether I like it or not.

As we part ways to go to our different first-period classes, I nearly trip over the air as I rush to make it to class in time. My head is in the clouds as I go back and forth between feeling dread over seeing Hunter with someone else and excitement about the tiny chance of him seeing me in a different light if I do go to the shut-in.

Fortunately for me, a couple of people filed in after me. In study hall, Jackie saved me a spot beside her in the very back row. It feels nice to have people in class looking out for me. Someone reserving a spot for me is a first.

Jackie turns toward me once our teacher is back at her desk after attendance. "Are you going to the shut-in?"

"Maybe, I haven't decided yet," I reply, "is it as crazy as everyone says it is?"

"Yes, and more so," Jackie wears a mischievous grin that tells me I'd be a fool to miss the shut-in. "Which is exactly why you should go. Live a little."

"I wish you were going," I quip.

Jackie sighs. "Me too. Next year," Her eyes dance with excitement though. "Is there someone you're hoping to meet there though?"

I try to hide the carefree smile that spreads across my face at the thought of Hunter. "Maybe," I pause, "I'm not sure if he feels the same."

Jackie nudges me. "If you go to the shut-in, you might find the answer."

I want to be able to live again, I do.

If only it were that easy. Although, I have had a little more courage lately. Things have been slowly getting easier. Am I ready for this though?

I want to be.

I pause. "I'll think about it,"

Throughout the day, the entire school is buzzing about the

shut-in, and it reminds me of the brief time when I was the topic of some people's conversations.

If I show up to the shut-in and let something happen, will people talk again? And, will I care? I think back to how I let their hurtful words affect me when the people who spoke them didn't even know me. While I might be considered behind in that area of life, I'm doing the best I can, and that starts with showing up.

~

"Wow, look at you, I don't know if I could beat you in a race anymore. You have some crazy endurance now," Hunter says as we power walk around the track during P.E. Something tells me that I will not be receiving an A in P.E. this semester, but I'm having far too much fun with Hunter right now to care. Even the fact that I'm wearing shorts again, after so many years of hiding in sweats, is enough to point to his encouragement in my life.

It feels like I'm finally stepping out after so many years of hiding.

My tone is teasing. "Does this mean I'm ready to take up surfing again? We never got to finish our lesson,"

"I'm not so sure about that, I think I almost had a heart attack. I think we'd have to start with swimming lessons," Hunter says.

The thought of him giving me a private swim lesson has me about to faint on the track of awkwardness, but Hunter is completely oblivious to the effect he has on me, and talks about us swimming together as if it's the most normal thing in the world.

"Maybe so," I giggle. "I realized after we went surfing that I hadn't been swimming in years, like since elementary school,"

"Believe me, Adele, I could tell," Hunter says and we both chuckle.

We still have a steady pace going, but I'm not panting like I would have been a few weeks ago. Maybe Hunter is right about me having more endurance now. That progress makes me grin. I'm proud of myself, and it feels good to be doing well at something other than academics.

"What's got you smiling so much?" Hunter asks.

"I'm just proud of myself, I guess. I never thought I'd feel this way," I muse. I draw my arms around myself a little, feeling vulnerable all of a sudden.

"Feel what way?" Hunter asks, pausing to slow down his pace as he leans in a little closer to me.

"Strong. Confident," I say.

"You're one of the most resilient people I know," Hunter's eyes meet mine. "And I'm glad to see you feeling more confident."

Before I can tell him more about everything, Coach Z calls me over to the field, where the rest of the group is playing the game of capturing the flag.

~

I'm currently doing Shelby's makeup before her formal dance. I originally came over to help Hunter study for the first AP Chem exam next week, but I heard Shelby quietly crying in her room when I was in the restroom. Her muffled sobs nearly broke my heart. She told me it was because she wants to get all dolled up for her dance, but doesn't know how to. I immediately offered to assist her.

I gently unclasp the small clips in her hair and get to work at putting some soft waves in her hair with the curling iron I found deep inside the back of the bathroom drawer.

"You are all set, pretty girl," I say, gently turning her shoulders so that she is facing her reflection in the mirror.

"Wow, thank you, Adele, you're the best!" Shelby says, facing me to hug me.

"You are so welcome," I grin. "Now let's go show your brother. He could use a little study break."

We eagerly walk to the main part of the house, the combined living room and kitchen, to where Hunter is staring at the periodic table.

I tap his shoulder, saying, "She is all ready for her first dance,"

The adoration in Hunter's eyes as he stands to hug her,

111

saying, "Shelby, you look beautiful!" brings a smile to my face.

His words feel like fireflies in my heart, lighting up parts of my brain that I didn't know were working until recently.

"It was all Adele, she worked her magic on me," Shelby says, but she's brimming with confidence.

I turn towards her. "There was no magic, Shelby, you're a natural beauty,"

Shelby beams at me, her face radiating with joy, as she asks, "You think so?"

I offer her a kind smile as I reassure her. "I know so,"

This dynamic is different than my usual role as a follower; I like it. It's a refreshing change.

I take a quick photo of them together before Shelby asks to be in one with me. I grin as Hunter makes silly faces at us from behind the camera. Even when he's drooping his lips into a frown, he's still drop-dead handsome. The kind of attractiveness that is wholesome instead of cocky.

I ride with Hunter to drop Shelby off, and a small group of girls standing outside of the dance surround her with a hug as she joins them. She glances back at us one last time before heading inside, and our eyes meet. I give her a thumbs up, and her smile lifts a little more. She stands a little prouder as she walks into the auditorium.

As we're driving off, Hunter lowers his voice. "That was so kind of you, helping her get ready. I don't think I've ever seen her this happy before. She'll be smiling about this for weeks,"

I shrug. "I enjoy spending time with her,"

It's the truth. She's sweet, and it's nice doing something positive for someone else. Maybe Hunter has rubbed off on me in that way, too.

"It means so much to her, having someone like you to look up to," Hunter's voice softens a little. "She doesn't have a lot of girl time like that, being the only girl living in a house of men."

"I'm glad to have been able to help her in that way," I face him, wanting him to know that I mean exactly what I'm about to share. "I know it's not the same, but I have a sense of what it's like, navigating things like that on my own. She's a tough girl, but still so sweet. And she thinks the world of you. She's lucky to have you."

He shrugs as he smiles. "I'm lucky to have her,"

"What you and your siblings have is very special," I reply.

"It is, I'm so happy we've remained close, despite everything," Hunter says quietly.

The sadness in his eyes tells me not to push the subject, so I don't.

Hunter is like a puzzle that I never expected to be so fascinating. The more I learn about him, the more I want to know. Because every time I uncover something new about him, it points to his character. I'd love to discover what shaped him.

He walks around the car to open my car door and begins walking me to my front door. The air is still tonight, and the moonlight provides us with a dim glow.

"I want to tell you what happened with my family but I'm not ready yet," Hunter's eyes meet mine and they're filled with emotion. "It's what a lot of people see, when they look at me, and I don't want to lose that with you. I like how you don't view me as an outcast, the way that some of the people outside of our high school do."

"Hunter, I'm here when you're willing to share, but I want it to be in your timing. Please wait till you're comfortable to share, even if it's never," I say, softly, reminding us both that this is just a temporary thing between us. I know that his revealing his past would only deepen this and complicate things for both of us. A small part of me wishes that would happen, although I know deep down how badly it'll end for me.

"Thank you, Adele," Hunter lowers his voice a little. "I am very happy to have met you."

"Me too," I reply.

He clears his throat. "I know I've been helping you to branch out more with your list and everything, but you've helped me a lot with myself. Seeing my life through your eyes has helped to remind me of just how much I have to be grateful for. I'm even appreciating this town a lot more, especially when I keep seeing just how much you love it,"

My heart swells at the idea of being able to show him Harmony Falls through my eyes. He's done so much more for me, though. He's modeled to me how to view the world through a new lens, one that isn't clouded by fear and doubt. Instead, he's guided me to see the good things that happen when I step out in faith.

My voice wavers a little as the extent of the impact he's had on me settles in. "I feel the same way, I've been learning so much through seeing you with your family. You've been helping me to let down my walls,"

Hunter steps a little closer toward me. "I'm glad,"

He pauses and I find myself wanting to invite him in, but stop myself. I'm already likely going to see him tomorrow night at the shut-in, so there's no need to push it.

"Have a good night, Hunter," I say as we pause by my front door.

"Don't stay up too late tonight, the shut-in is tomorrow, so you're going to need all the rest you can get beforehand," Hunter responds.

I chuckle softly saying, "I still haven't decided if I'm going yet," knowing full well that I will be there no matter what. Now that I know he's attending, I can't seem to say no. I'm unable to stay away from him, despite knowing what's best for me. It's both frustrating and exhilarating at the same time.

"Well, I hope to see you there," Hunter arches a brow. "Because it wouldn't be the same without you. I mean, I'd have to watch the movie they're playing instead of hearing your laughter."

"You might just have to survive it without me," I say in a teasing tone.

"We'll see," Hunter gives me a look that could make me melt like a puddle into the floor. "Goodnight, Adele, and thank you again," and watches me while I walk inside. I smile as the door clicks behind me, feeling giddy.

I'm surely imagining any attraction he feels toward me. Although I secretly wish he felt that pull too.

CHAPTER 14

"I'm not so sure about this," I say to Selena, motioning at the black dress that cinches in at my waist and hugs my hips a little too tight for my liking.

Selena puts her hand on her hips as she gestures toward me. "Well, I am. You look stunning, and it's time to branch out a little,"

Well, if there was any night to take a big chance, tonight would be it.

I take a deep breath and say, "Let's do this,"

As soon as we arrive at the Shut-in, everyone starts dispersing throughout the school, far away from the chaperones in the gymnasium. Selena is immediately whisked away by Mario, who invites me to join them, but I wave them along, knowing how much it means to her to have a special night with him.

As I wander around, looking for someone I know, I begin to freeze. What was I thinking, coming here?

"Adele,"

Hunter's voice behind me feels like a warm embrace.

"Hi," I say.

His eyes gleam with joy. "I'm so glad you made it,"

My heart flutters inside of my chest.

However, not even his kind words can ward off the nerves that I have here, in a new environment. This will be one of the few times I've spent time with my classmates outside of school.

"Me too," I glance down. "I guess, I'm just not sure what to do with myself when I go to things like this."

Hunter waggles his eyebrows. "Well, I have some ideas,"

My face turns beet red and he says, "Don't worry, nothing

crazy. I just thought that maybe we could sneak up to the roof and look at the stars,"

That sounds way better than being in a crowded room with the rest of the student body.

"Won't we get expelled or something?" I ask nervously.

"Us? No, Adele, trust me, they're looking for people who are doing unconventional things tonight. We'll be fine," Hunter reassures me.

Maybe Hunter is more innocent than I thought he was.

"Okay," I gesture toward him. "Lead the way."

He guides me to some rusty, hidden stairwell located behind the storage closet in the gymnasium. Excitement courses through my body at the idea of sneaking into a secret area of the school. Once I see how steep the steps are, though, I pause. I hesitate at the bottom of the lanky staircase, too afraid of falling.

Hunter whispers, "Hey, I'll go behind you. I've got you,"

His hand remains on the small of my back as I walk up the stairwell. Just the simple touch sends rays of comfort throughout my body. The door at the top is already propped open, revealing the drafty breeze. I draw my arms around myself to ward off the cold.

"This is...wow," I murmur. The small rooftop is decorated with fluffy blankets and plush pillows that have been arranged to create a little blanket fort of sorts.

Before I sit down, Hunter wraps a soft hoodie around me.

"Thank you," I say as I take in the tenderness of his touch. Just that small action means a lot to me.

His voice has a hint of a smile to it. "I figured it'd be cold tonight, and I know you love to be cozy,"

Did he plan this for me?

"You're not wrong about that," I say, holding the blanket tighter around me as he chuckles.

I admire the special ambiance he created, just for me. "This is great, though. Thank you,"

He nods, and his face becomes a little pink, a stark contrast to his usual golden tan. "I wanted to make it memorable for you,"

We sit in comfortable silence as we look at the stars.

"Adele, meeting you has changed everything," he whispers.

It takes courage for me to meet his gaze as I ask, "In a good way or a bad way?"

He interlaces my hand in his, and everything feels different.

He gently squeezes my hand. "In the best way,"

"Thank you," I say, keeping my gaze down.

Only he leans in closer and cups the back of my neck with his other hand. Chills form along my spine as his fingers graze my cheek.

"Is there anything else you'd like to add to your list?" Hunter asks, "I know we've done a couple of things, but is there something more you want to do?"

If I was smooth, I'd probably know what to say, but instead, I come up short. I'm not sure where this conversation is going, but it seems like all my resolve disappears when it comes to him.

I find my eyes lingering on his lips as I soak up the way he delicately holds my face in his palm as if he's the lucky one. The light in his eyes tells me that he's pleasantly surprised that I returned the gesture by holding his hand back.

"Did you have something in mind?" I ask, my voice coming out squeaky as a couple of different possibilities pop into my head.

"Well, I was thinking, maybe we could…"

His words get interrupted by a loud clang behind us. I wince at the noise and yelp, immediately standing up.

The intruder yells, "Look who it is!"

My heart stills in my chest as I recognize Sean's voice, hyper-aware of the way my body still stays tense. I stand and turn to face him. It feels like the blood drains from my legs as I see Mitch. My face goes ashen white as the color and life fade from my body, his presence a reminder of his aggression from the last time I saw him.

"What's going on out here? Are you hiding out here?" Mitch asks, his tone cold as ice. His gaze roams over me as if he's judging me, and I find myself shivering. Just his voice alone takes me back to him putting his hands around me, demanding that I "follow through" on a dare. But, most of all, the sharp glare he gives me takes me back to the hurtful words he said about the way I look.

"We were just leaving, it's all yours," Hunter's friendly voice contrasts his stature as he stands tall, almost telling Mitch to turn around with just his body language. I, on the other hand, am cowering behind Hunter, our hands no longer interlaced.

"Now I see why you were so protective of her at the party," Mitch scoffs. "I have to say, though, I'm surprised, Watts. She's not your type, man."

"Why do you care? It's none of your business," Hunter spits out.

Mitch speaks the harsh truth. "But, that's the thing. You're supposed to be the leader of the team, and no one is going to take you seriously if you're with her,"

"Leave them alone, man. Let it go. This is ridiculous, you're being a jerk for no reason," Sean says to Mitch, putting his hands up as if to say, "Sorry".

"I'm just telling the truth, they might as well see it now," Mitch's lips tilt up into a scowl as his eyes land on me just one more time. I shudder under his gaze. "They don't fit together. Better they hear it from me than from the entire school."

I swallow the lump in my throat. My chest burns as I wonder if Hunter sees me the same way that Mitch does. Is this really what everyone sees when they look at me? Maybe I'm even more of an outcast than I thought. Mitch's words are salt on a wound that hasn't healed yet.

Frankly, though, I'm fed up with Mitch's behavior. What he got away with at the party was bad enough. The sight of him makes me nauseous, and I feel a panic attack coming on. He has some nerve, interrupting my one chance to have a special moment with Hunter. It's just not right. Who is he to come in here and destroy something that's going good for me? Who does he think he is?

"Why do you care?" I ask, my words surprising me. Even Hunter looks back at me, a small smile on his face.

"Jealousy isn't a good look on you, Mitch," Hunter quips. Anger flashes in his eyes, but I give him a warning look. I will not allow Hunter to throw away his future for some tool like Mitch. He's not worth the punch.

"I'm not jealous, I'm just trying to prevent you from wasting your time," Mitch says.

"We're heading out now, thanks for the advice though," Hunter says, lacing his arm through mine as we hurriedly walk toward the stairwell. I look over my shoulder and see Mitch's blatant rage still visible on his face, which is twisted into a frown.

Once we're down the stairwell, Hunter leads us to a quiet, dark hallway where it's just the two of us. It took me a couple of seconds to catch my breath after the tense conversation with Mitch, who outright stated my inner fears out loud. Hunter gently reaches for me as he faces me.

My initial panic over seeing Mitch again has been replaced by insecurity, but I don't know how to voice it. My doubt must be written all over my face because Hunter eyes me with concern.

He wraps his arms around my waist and pulls me into him, He leans his head down toward me. "Can we talk about what just happened?"

I feel exposed under his gaze.

"Sure," I say nervously.

Hunter's breath tickles my neck as he whispers, "I don't know what he even meant by that, but it wasn't right of him to say that. The only reason I didn't retaliate was because I didn't want to stoop to his level, and I didn't feel like getting suspended. Especially when I sit next to such a cute tutor every day,"

His fingers palm the crevice at the back of my neck and it

takes me a second to remember that it's all just temporary. But the way we are together feels as natural as waves in the ocean, as if it's another regular rhythm of life. Only this will be ending soon and the tide will turn around and we'll go our separate ways again. This time though he'll leave with a piece of me. Now that I know what it feels like to be caressed by him like this, I find myself wanting more.

A part of me aches to take it a little further but now is not the time.

"It's okay. I'm fine, and we definitely can't have you getting suspended," I whisper.

His other arm, wrapped around my waist, draws me in ever closer, till I'm nearly on my tippy toes from the motion. "Well, I think we fit together,"

"You think so?" I ask breathily, still conscious of the goosebumps all over my arms in response to his touch.

"I know so," He murmurs, "but, I still want to make sure you know so, because if you don't, I might have to clear some things up for you."

I smile shyly, still shocked by Mitch's words, desperately wanting to lean in and tilt my lips upward to mesh our lips together. All I want at this moment is to close the space between us but first I need the assurance and confidence to do it.

My face is still flushed as I ask, "So, you don't see me the way that Mitch does? Do you think that's what everyone else sees when they see us together?"

He tilts my chin up so that my face is angled toward his even more.

His eyes meet mine. "Like what, Adele? Tell me what it is you're afraid of so that I can tell you just how I see you,"

"I'm afraid that everyone judges me the way Mitch did, about this," I say, gesturing to my body in my dress. I look down at the ground, too afraid to hear his response, uncertain if I'm ready for the confirmation that I'm nothing like what he wants.

Hunter's brows knit together. "What, your dress?"

I chuckle softly at his innocence, and whisper, "No, my

umm, my body,"

Something shifts in his gaze.

"Adele, look at me," He whispers.

I slowly look right into his hypnotizing eyes, my body on fire as he stares at me with adoration.

"You're beyond beautiful, inside and out," Hunter whispers.

"You're not wishing I was different?" I ask.

"That would never even cross my mind," Hunter assures me. "I think you're incredible."

He leans down and kisses my forehead, saying, "Adele, we're in this together, I hope you know that. I want this with you,"

I nod slowly and am about to respond when a random chaperone frantically scolds us to "scatter", startling me so much that I fumble my way in the dim hallway to find my way back to the gymnasium before I can get in trouble. It takes me a while to find my sleeping bag since the teachers separated the guys and girls for the night. Despite the craziness of everything that happened, I fall asleep for the last few hours of the shut-in with the biggest smile on my face.

The first rays of sunlight beam through the gymnasium windows, and I slip out the unlocked door, ready to sneak out unnoticed. As much as I enjoyed seeing Hunter last night, I want to spend some time alone to process everything.

I like Hunter, and he feels the same way. It should be simple, but it's not. I want to live, however, like it is. Because the way I light up inside around Hunter isn't something that can be disregarded as just friendship. It's more than that.

His words continue to repeat in my head and bring a smile to my face. I've spent the last few years wanting to be known, and Hunter's seen more of me than anyone else has. He doesn't categorize me like other people have. He's patient, kind, and encouraging. It feels different with him.

I almost sigh with bliss as the door clicks behind me when I get home, too caught up in thinking about Hunter's words to notice anything else.

"Oh good. You're home," Dad says.

I'm immediately blindsided by him, dressed to impress in the business shirt he only wears on special occasions. He stands beside a tall, lanky man with wire-rimmed glasses, looking equally sophisticated in a white business shirt that looks like it's been ironed and pressed multiple times.

I plaster on a smile, trying my best to not look like someone who slept for three hours last night. "Hello,"

"Richard, this is my daughter, Adele. Adele, meet Richard. He is one of the coordinators for the lab research program at Meadowbrook University," my dad says matter-of-factly like he didn't just spring an impromptu interview of sorts on me when he's supposed to be out of town.

When I'm silent for longer than I'm sure is socially acceptable, Richard says, "It's a pleasure to meet you, Adele. Our conference ended early and we both thought it'd be nice to catch up since we're old acquaintances from college. Your father tells me you're quite passionate about medicine,"

"The pleasure is all mine," I say, extending my hand to him, earning a smile from my dad. "Yes, I am interested in every area of the field."

Richard motions for us to sit down on the couch, and makes a small joke about my dad, finally putting me at ease. Richard and I spend the next hour or so talking about science, connecting about different concepts, and swapping stories of labs gone wrong.

"What is your favorite part of science?" Richard asks.

"I love the ability to learn more about the world and to share that with others," I reply, going on to tell him all about Science Day, and how the activities helped the children to have a new love for the way that science could broaden their awareness of why some things are the way they are. My enthusiasm increased as I reflected on how fun it was to volunteer with the children.

"That's something I appreciate about science as well.

That's one of the reasons I became involved at the lab at Meadowbrook University," Richard says.

My jaw nearly drops. My dad is friends with someone who is affiliated with one of the best laboratories nearby, and didn't even think to call me to tell me to dress up nice before having him over? Senior shut-in or not, I live in my faded sweats, and would not have been presentable either way.

Fortunately, Richard seems unfazed by my disheveled appearance. Instead, he is talking a mile a minute about all of the incredible resources at the lab.

"I'm really glad that you can be involved in work that is so aligned with your interests," I tell him, realizing that one benefit of my personality, which I believe is a little dry sometimes, is my ability to speak professionally under pressure. Only this time it doesn't feel robotic like it usually does. Instead, Richard is helping to bridge the gap between my dad and me.

"Adele, I know you have an entire world of opportunity out there, but I want you to know I think you'd be a great candidate for one of our programs. We have programs that you could complete now while you finish out high school, or one over the summer before you go to college," Richard gestures toward Dad. "Your dad tells me you want to attend university out of state, and I think it's wonderful you're considering your options. There is a place for you to gain some valuable experience in a lab setting, if you're interested in that, in the meantime so that you can enter college with confidence."

This could be the compromise I've been waiting for when it comes to college because it involves a program my dad would approve of that is close to home instead of across the country.

"Thank you," I say, "I don't even know what to say. I am very grateful though."

Richard shakes my hand one last time. "I will send your dad the information. Please consider it because it could be beneficial for your future, regardless of what avenue you try to pursue,"

I still feel like I'm floating on a cloud after my dad and I walk Richard out to his car.

"Wow, that was amazing," I muse. It's almost as if a weight has been lifted off my chest.

Dad looks lighter as if a visit with an old classmate reminded him of how he used to be. It gives me a small glimmer of hope.

"That was one of those times where I was in the right place at the right time," He clears his throat. "I'm glad you arrived when you did."

Guilt settles in my stomach. "About that…"

I blush furiously when I think back to the moment Hunter and I were about to have before we were so rudely interrupted. Was he going to kiss me? It sure looked like it.

What would my dad have to say about it?

My dad's words have me fearing the worst. "Let's talk inside,"

My heart begins to race a little. Am I going to be grounded?

I take a shaky breath as I sink into the couch, hugging my arms around myself. I can't seem to relax, no matter how much I'd like to."

My dad's shoulders slouch a little, and he looks just as weary as I am. He settles on the cushion next to me.

If I weren't in trouble right now, I'd almost be relieved about some hint of emotion in his facial expression. It's a nice change. It feels like he's finally coming back.

He purses his lips. "Adele, I'm not quite sure where to start,"

I look down at my knees, wanting to curl into a ball. Yep, I'm screwed.

My dad lets out a defeated sigh. "I'm sorry, kiddo,"

I perk up. "What?"

He shakes his head. "I made a mistake,"

I arch a brow. "Aren't I in trouble?"

Dad's tone softens. "Adele, it's okay. I'm glad you were having fun. I had a long conversation with Richard about it since he's a father too, and I realized I've been too harsh on you. The only reason I've pushed so hard is because I want you to live a good life," Dad glances at me. "But friendships, and fun, and even love, are a part of that too."

"What exactly are you saying?" I ask, my voice shaky and uncertain.

"Well, I don't want to force you into a corner with this medical school thing. I know it's a big decision, and I don't want you to feel pressured to choose a certain school," he says.

Self-assurance rises in me, still there from my conversation with Hunter. I might as well rip off the bandaid now.

"That's the thing, Dad," I pause to let go of any nerves. "I'm not sure about medical school."

He tilts his head. "As in, you aren't certain about which one you want to go to?"

"I don't know if I want to go at all," I reply.

"What?" my dad asks, his voice faltering.

I notice the way his shoulders sag at the news. "I, umm, I'm sorry I didn't tell you sooner, it just didn't seem like the time, and now seemed like a good time,"

Dad faces me. "How long have you felt this way?"

Even at the start of the plan, I felt this uneasiness about it because I knew that medicine wasn't something I wanted to do. I had seen over the years though that it was the sole thing that seemed to bring my dad any kind of excitement about the future ever since Mom passed away. It felt as if I gave him a new task to focus on, that maybe he'd begin acting like himself again. All it did was create even more distance between us because the only connection we had was built on a lie.

I exhale a shaky breath, clutching a pillow to my chest. "A while,"

"Adele, why didn't you tell me?" My dad's eyes meet mine, and I notice kindness in them. So, I tell him the truth.

"I love science, though. I was never lying about that. I just didn't want to let you down. And it seems like medicine is the only thing tying us together these days and I didn't want to lose that," I explain.

I feel like such a fraud, but I'm more concerned about what this means for Dad and me. Will we have something to talk about anymore?

Dad's eyes tilt down as my words sink in. "I'm so sorry, Adele. I'd never want you to feel that way. I promise you that isn't the case, not even close." He gently squeezes my hand. The gesture alone gives me hope that things are changing for the better between us.

"So, you really wouldn't be disappointed in me if I told you I want to do something else? Even after we worked so hard?" I ask.

Dad shakes his head. "Not at all. I'm proud of you for how hard you've worked, and that hard work will take you far into any field,"

"Thanks, Dad. It means a lot to hear that from you," I respond.

Dad smiles awkwardly. "I'll try to tell you more often," My dad smiles awkwardly.

"Thank you," I say, "And I appreciate you."

For the first time in a long time, Dad and I spend the day together, watching old movies from my childhood and embracing the shift that happened tonight. And it feels like things are looking up.

CHAPTER 15

"De-Fense!" Selena yells. Her arm is looped through mine and her other hand is interlaced with Mario, whom she had her first kiss with at the Shut-in. It was everything she had dreamed of and then some.

She's been glowing ever since, and the two have been inseparable all week. At first, she was nervous about changing the dynamic of our friendship, but I assured her that I was happy for her. It's been quite refreshing having a little more space outside of Selena. If anything, it's helped me to have more of an identity of my own. Things with her have been smooth sailing since, aside from the fact that I still haven't told her about the conversation I had with Hunter.

Despite our connection at the Shut-in, Hunter and I haven't had a chance to follow up since, so I'm not sure where we stand. Hunter's been pretty busy this week with football, and we haven't seen each other outside of AP Chem, which has been all pop quizzes lately, giving us only the chance to say hello to each other. He told me today though that he'd see me after the game tonight, which he invited me to, so that's something.

This is my first time at a football game and it's quite the experience so far. It feels like the entire school is here, maybe even the whole town. Selena and I got here early so we were able to snag a spot at the back of the bleachers, giving us a little space away from our school's "Chaos Corner", which is a big mosh pit of students yelling and jumping so much that they shake that entire section of the bleachers.

Selena, who normally sits in the middle of the Chaos Corner, offered me and Mario a choice. Luckily for me, Mario also prefers to have a little more personal space during the games, earning him major brownie points with me. Selena and I came armed and ready with a couple of thermoses of hot chocolate, blankets, and our warm hoodies. October is just around the corner, and the chilly evenings are here to stay, and will only get colder as fall comes into full swing.

On the field, Hunter is completely in his element, acting as if he almost has blinders on as he hurls the ball across the grass with precision to his teammates. Even as a player from the opposite team comes charging at him as he releases the ball, Hunter looks completely in control as he runs from side to side, barely evading the guy. Hunter makes the motion look easy.

Before one of the guys on our team can successfully make it to the other end of the field, he gets completely pummeled by a guy from Meadowbrook, the opposing team. My heart almost falls out of my chest as I take in the sight of him lying on his back on the ground.

Selena squeezes my arm and tells me it's just a part of the game, and that this happens a lot. I audibly exhale when he gets up, completely unscathed, and realize she's right. I've seen the guys run drills before, but this is completely different. All of the team looks in sync as they move across the field with speed.

During the little breaks in the game, Hunter holds up a little whiteboard and makes big gestures as he talks to the guys. I can't help but smile when I see him lead them through a countdown as they put their hands in a circle and lift their palms in the air with a shout. The marching band adds to the enthusiasm of the crowd.

I can't seem to look away from Hunter. He looks like such a natural as he leads the team through different plays. As I squint my eyes at him on the field, I wish I had a better view, one that wasn't blocked by his helmet. Given the small lead that the other team has on us, I can't help but wonder what facial expression he's wearing right now. Is he wearing that cheeky smile he wears when he knows things are going to turn out? Or, are his lips twisted into a frown as the clock continues to tick?

Once the game is tied, and it's down to the last few plays, I am screaming alongside Selena as Hunter chucks the ball across the field. It feels like the game moves in slow motion as the clock begins losing time, and the game comes closer to the end. The guy on our team at the end of the field catches the ball at the last millisecond and runs to cross the line.

A voice over the loudspeaker exclaims, "Touchdown! A win for Harmony Falls!"

The entire crowd erupts into loud cheering, and I find myself jumping up and down with Selena, nearly falling off the bleachers. I nearly fall into the gap in the bleachers as I squeal. Mario and I high-five, and it feels good to be a part of something, even if only as a viewer.

The players and the crowd start sprinting onto the field, creating a sea of people. The players all start taking their bulky helmets off, and I stand on the bleachers, uncertain of what to do since it's my first time. I'm still on the top of the bleachers when I see Hunter looking directly at me from across the field. He smiles widely at me, and at this moment, he looks so overjoyed that I want to kiss him right then and there. Butterflies form in my chest at the thought of him feeling the same way.

Selena turns toward me. "It looks like someone is very happy to see you. Let's go say hi,"

I numbly follow her down the bleachers, nearly tripping again, this time from a mixture of nerves and excitement.

How do I greet him? Should I let on just how overjoyed I am to be around him? I'm pretty sure that I'm beaming right now.

"Hi," I say breathily to Hunter, who still has the cheesiest smile on his face, "You did amazing."

Hunter's eyes gleam with happiness. "Thank you," He holds his helmet under his arm. "We just worked well together as a team tonight."

And once again, I find myself touched by his humility. He called the shots in the game today and was one of the main reasons we won, but he also acknowledges the hard work and team aspect of the game. He could have easily taken all of the credit, especially given how hard he works, but he doesn't.

"You were incredible. You're a natural leader," I say.

It's nothing but the truth. Hunter had a way of being able to strengthen the connection between the team. By encouraging everyone, he helped to shift the entire dynamic during the final portion of the game, when everyone was exhausted. I saw the new energy and zeal that resulted from the meeting that Hunter called as he hyped everyone up.

"I'm just so glad you came," His eyes meet mine. "I'm starting to think you might be my good luck charm."

I flush under his gaze and instead reach out to hug him. He sets his helmet down and envelops me in a close embrace. I inhale the subtle scent of his cologne and allow his body heat to warm me up. His touch is both familiar and new at the same time; an exciting combination that I'm excited to explore more. It's as if I'm comfortable with him and am ready to continue building the connection. Based on the way his body relaxes against mine, I know that it's not just one-sided. He feels it too, this oneness.

"Now this, this is the best reward I've ever gotten," He whispers in my ear. He crouches down and pulls me nearer to him.

A grin takes over my entire face. I'm about to turn my head and attempt to kiss him on the cheek, which would be my first time doing such a thing when I hear Hunter's dad's voice behind us.

"You played great, son," His dad says.

Hunter keeps a firm grasp on me and wraps his arm around my shoulder, turning us both to face his dad, but I long to break us apart, scared that maybe I made a bad first impression on his dad. Dread fills my stomach at the way I was so outspoken when I first met him. Hunter, however, seems completely nonchalant as he holds me.

"Thanks, Dad," Hunter says, almost standing a little taller. A little prouder.

"And, Adele, it's good to see you again," His dad nods at

me. "I want to thank you again for helping my son. Your tutoring is the reason he's in this game tonight."

His emphasis on the word "tutoring" feels strange, as if he thinks this is some kind of weird way for me to motivate his son to do better in school. I want to tell his dad that Hunter did all the hard work himself, but I hold my tongue. The last thing I need is to jump to conclusions. No more second-guessing. If his dad doesn't approve of us, he's going to have to straight up tell me and be ready for a list of reasons in my response, proving him wrong.

My reaction to him stems more from the desire to protect Hunter than my reputation. I'm in too deep when it comes to him.

To my relief, Mario and Selena join us as a group, and we begin making introductions among everyone. Selena's bubbly personality helps to seamlessly transition to conversation, taking Hunter and me out of the hot seat with his dad. In the corner of my eye, Hunter is still radiating joy, which helps me to feel a little more at ease. Based on my past interactions with him, I've learned that he's a little rougher around the edges, so it would make sense that maybe he's more of the tough love type.

After Selena makes a couple of comments about the logistics of the game, I see Hunter's dad visibly relax.

"I was just about to throw some barbecue on the grill," Hunter's dad says, "How about you all join us?"

Selena and I exchange a look, and she replies, "We'd love to," fortunately answering for me since I'm too surprised to answer. I've been to Hunter's house before, but a family dinner with his dad sounds different, so I'm very glad Selena and Mario will be joining us as well.

On the car ride, I catch Selena up on the details of the Shut-in and she squeals the entire time, making Mario and I laugh nonstop. She asks me to repeat the description of the blanket fort twice, interrupting me both times to tell me just how adorable the idea to go to the rooftop was. Her enthusiasm only adds to my excitement as I recall just how sweet it was for

Hunter to plan something special for me.

I left out the part about seeing Mitch there because I didn't want to ruin the moment. I don't want that interaction with him to color the way I felt with Hunter that night.

Once we arrive at Hunter's house, we all meet in the backyard, where Shelby and Austin are playing a game of cornhole. It feels like a classic, old-school Friday night and there's nowhere I'd rather be.

Selena, Mario, Hunter, and I gather around the grill as we make small talk. Hunter offers to give them a tour, and I hang back to watch his siblings play. As I cheer them on, I notice how at home I feel around his siblings.

While Hunter, Mario, and Selena are inside, Hunter's dad approaches me. "I'm glad to see him spending time with a good girl like you, someone with a future. I admit, I had my reservations because my son is known to jump into things, but you've been good for him," He clears his throat. "You've helped him. I've never seen him this happy."

I've never seen him this happy.

Knowing that I'm a small part of the reason behind that makes my soul sing.

"Wow, thank you. I don't know what to say," I reply, "He's a good man, though, and I'm lucky to know him."

"He keeps a lot of responsibilities moving all the time, and he's always been good at that, but things like this?" His dad says, motioning around the yard. "Letting people in hasn't come easy to him. So, it's good seeing him finally pursue something real."

Something real.

His dad's words have me at a loss for what to say back. Is that really what this is? Because it sure feels real to me.

"I've never really done this before," I say quietly, "I've never even had a boyfriend, so I'm new to this."

"It's just a friendship. Don't get too in your head about it, I know how you teenagers can be," His dad says and we both chuckle.

"Sounds good," I respond.

As my friends come back outside, I see Hunter's eyes immediately searching for mine and realize that this might be real after all.

Over dinner, Hunter and I share smiles from across the table as we try not to laugh at Austin asking Mario a million questions about Harmony Falls High School.

Selena even subtly kicks me under the table as Hunter invites me inside to wash the dishes with him and serve desserts, just the two of us. I nearly choke when he says the "just the two of us" part, but quickly recover. I feel giddy as I follow him into the house.

Once we're inside, Hunter lowers his voice a little. "Thanks for coming over. My family loves you by the way. My dad, too. I can just tell,"

I'm washing off a plate and nearly drop it when he says that, still thinking about his dad telling me that what we have is real.

"Thanks for having me," I glance down. "I'm so glad to know them, to know you."

I feel lame for saying that, because we're together, or maybe we aren't, but something is brewing between us, so obviously he already knows I like him.

As soon as I set the dish down, he slowly walks toward me and pushes a strand of my wavy hair behind my ear, but keeps his hand behind the back of my neck. The gesture sends off a whole chain of sparks throughout my body.

"I want to be with you," He delicately draws a circle with his fingers, sending off more chills. The look he gives me makes me nearly melt into the floor. He speaks in a hushed tone. "I guess what I'm trying to say is, will you be my girlfriend, Adele? I know you have experienced people saying rude things in the past, so we can keep it as private as you like, but I want to be with you, whatever that looks like. And even if we don't tell anyone, it's just you and me, Adele. Nobody else,"

Goosebumps run down my spine as his other hand gently cups my cheek.

I tilt my chin up, basking in his gaze. I'm beaming at the notion of him wanting there to be an "Us". My voice raises an octave in pitch as I reply, "I'd like that,"

I'd love that more than anything, I just didn't know it was a possibility until now.

"You would?" He asks, a smile lighting up his face.

"Yes, more than anything," I glance down. "Maybe we could start slow, though when it comes to telling people. Like, just keep it between us for now?"

I don't want anything to come between this connection we share. And I know better than anyone the way that rumors and gossip have a way of poisoning anything good. What I have with Hunter is better than good, it's incredible, and I will not let anyone at school sabotage it.

"Whatever you're most comfortable with," Hunter assures me.

I can't stop looking at his lips, but I find myself planting a kiss on his cheek. I decide after a second that he has a very kissable face and that it feels nice to have that first with him, so I kiss his cheek a couple more times. After I stop, we both laugh softly.

I flush. "Sorry, that was umm, my first time doing that,"

He grins. "Adele, that was the sweetest thing anyone's done for me. You came to my game, cheered me on, had dinner with my family endured my family's weird jokes, and have been kissing my face off,"

"Well, I know, but I'm not really...experienced. I'm new to this," I explain.

He gestures between us. "We're in this together. We'll take this as slow and steady as you'd like and are comfortable with,"

I nod and smile, but just his response makes me want to hurry things up a bit, even though I wouldn't know the first thing about how to do that. Do people open or close their lips when they kiss? I find myself panicking about the details, deciding that I am in desperate need of a future lesson from him on how to kiss.

"Sometimes, I wish I could read your mind," Hunter whispers, "but then I remember just how lucky I am to be one of the people you trust."

"Don't tell Selena this, but I'm pretty sure I share more with you than with her," I respond.

"Your secret's safe with me," Hunter glances toward the door. "Now let's get back to the others before my dad sends someone to come find us."

I chuckle. "Good idea,"

Only before I start walking, he plants a quick kiss on my cheek. Taken by surprise by his gesture, I giggle in response.

He interlaces his fingers through mine. "Thank you for tonight,"

I smile nonstop for the rest of the night: Hunter is my boyfriend now.

CHAPTER 16

I exhale a shaky breath to try to center myself. My fingers grip the steering wheel so hard that they're pale to the point of being almost blue. My dad is teaching me how to drive, his very first time doing so. It took a lot of convincing him, so there's no going back. I have to show him I'm ready for this, especially if I want to explore the option of an internship at Meadowbrook.

"Okay, I think I'm ready," I say, more to myself than to him. I don't think I'll ever be quite prepared to do this, which is exactly why I need to try. My pulse pounds inside of my chest so loudly that I have trouble concentrating. I take another shaky breath. "Let's do this."

"You can do it. We've gone over all the basics. Just take a deep breath," Dad instructs me.

Things have been a little less robotic between us since the conversation we had after Richard left the other day. Knowing that my dad supports my decision to not go to medical school feels like a weight has been lifted. Now that that stressor has been navigated, I'd like to conquer my biggest fear: driving.

So far, this has been a much more difficult feat than fixing things with Dad. If anything, all it has drawn attention to so far is just how far behind I am from my peers. I immediately shake the thought. I'm trying. That has to count for something.

After what feels like hours, I finally muster up the courage to start. My hands tremble as I move the lever from "Park" to "Drive". It takes even more time for me to release my foot off the brake. I yelp at the motion as I make contact with the gas, surprised by how quickly the car accelerates.

And, for the first time in my eighteen years of living, I drive. It feels terrifying to be in control of something so big and fast, but I manage to drive to the end of our cul-de-sac and back a couple of times, remembering where the brake and the gas are this time.

It's no easy, feat though. I have to pull over several times, taking ragged breaths as I try to calm myself down. My dad talks me through it, gently encouraging me to rest and exhale until the panic subsides. The more I push through the terror, the less it seems to affect me.

This is our second official lesson, as we spent an hour helping me get comfortable in a car again, and I feel so grateful that my dad has been showing up for me this way, especially since he hardly ever gets time off.

I spend the next couple of hours driving around my neighborhood until I'm more familiar with things like using my blinkers and braking without causing my dad to lurch forward in the passenger seat. Steering is still something new for me to navigate, as I twist the wheel too far each time, driving as if I'm in a video game with each sharp turn I make.

In a way, it feels like I'm in some sort of simulation as the road becomes a mirage of sorts as the panic settles in. I try to push past it, but can't seem to shake the jittery feeling.

I quickly jump to apologizing as my dad nearly gets whiplash from the way I step on the brakes with a little too much excitement at a stop sign. I glance over at my dad, shocked to find that he's no longer hanging onto the small lever by his door anymore. Instead, he looks completely relaxed. It helps me to settle into driving more.

If he doesn't think we're going to die, then maybe we're not going to. Even just driving down the street feels like life or death, but when I watched my mother die this way, how am I supposed to separate the two? How am I supposed to know the difference?

My thoughts must be written all over my face because Dad clears his throat, interrupting my trance.

"I think we worked up quite an appetite," My dad brightens beside me. "How about we switch, and I can take us out to lunch?"

"You don't have work today?" I ask, not wanting to take him away from a meeting.

He explains, "I told them I'd be unavailable today, no more working on my days off,"

I wrap my arms around him in an awkward car hug. This is the dad I grew up with; it feels like he's gradually coming back. If this was possible, then driving must be too.

He sighs after we break apart. "I'm sorry, I know I should've done that sooner,"

I offer him a kind smile. "Better late than never,"

His new change puts a little wind in my sails, and it shifts the tone for the rest of the day.

As we switch places in the car, my blood pressure immediately drops. I sigh as I settle into the other side of the car, relieved of the duty of keeping us alive, at least for now.

After I hop into the passenger seat, I watch with excitement as the scenery goes from green trees to hints of orange and red in the foliage associated with the beautiful drive to Meadowbrook. Since Meadowbrook is located north of Harmony Falls, the weather is a little cooler, and fall begins to show itself in the leaves and the temperature a couple of weeks sooner. The sight adds to my anticipation of the seasons.

Growing up, my mom loved to do something special to honor each season, but she especially loved fall. She told me there was something about the way that the world began to shift into such earthy colors before emerging into completely different forms later in the spring was a reminder to focus on what was important. She used to encourage me that autumn was a chance to rest and enjoy the fresh air; to spend time enjoying a new opportunity for change. By watching the seasons through her perspective, I was able to get a glimpse of the beautiful scenery here. It wasn't until now though that I truly grasped what she meant.

Mom was someone who fully lived, in the sense that she created a life that she loved. She poured herself into Dad and me and found every possibility to appreciate the simple things in life.

For so long, I felt like if I just continued to shrink the size of my universe, I could avoid all of the pain I'd experienced. The fewer people in my life, the less chance of grief. The fewer places I went, the less chance of death. The less I went out at night, the less chance of something bad happening to me again. It wasn't until Hunter came into my life that I could see all of the joy I was missing too.

I think Mom would be proud of the way I'm living now, especially with driving. She loved to drive; long car rides together were one of our favorite pastimes. Dad used to joke that if he came home to an empty house, he knew Mom and I were just up the highway, coastal wind whipping through our hair as we sang along to her Oldies music.

The day that she passed, we were actually on one of our special drives. When I glance over at Dad, wearing a genuine smile for the first time in a long time, I can sense that Mom is almost here with us in spirit.

If I squint my eyes and think hard enough, I can see her dark waves floating in all directions as she sings along to her favorite song with the windows down.

Dad pulls up to a huge wooden, cabin-style restaurant with an entire rack of motorcycles all lined up and parked in front.

Dad grins. "This place has the best barbecue in town,"

"Sounds perfect," I reply.

And it is. Nestled in the woods just outside of the busy highway, the Barbecue Shack immediately hits my senses with the smell of tangy, savory, and sweet barbecue sauce. I almost gasp when I take my first bite because it's that good. It's easily the best food I've ever eaten. Not only that, but it's a nice gesture on my dad's part and is sure a nice contrast to all of the nights we settled on eating takeout together without any real conversations.

I give him an appreciative look as I set my sandwich down.

"Thank you for taking me here,"

My dad glances down. "I might have had an ulterior motive, driving us up here,"

"What is it?" I ask, noticing his nervous smile.

"Well, I thought, if you wanted to, maybe we could check out the Meadowbrook University campus. The lab is closed today," He explains, "but you could walk around and get a feel for the environment. It might give you an idea of what an internship here is like."

He planned this so I could see the campus, even if it wasn't his original plan for me.

The thought brings a huge grin to my face.

"I'd love that!" I say, immediately gathering our things.

I feel the most peaceful feeling as we pull into the tree-lined road leading to Meadowbrook University. A huge, grassy lawn features plenty of stone benches and tables. Despite it being a Saturday, I see many college students enjoying the autumn weather.

One group of a few girls catches my eye because they're all reading different books on a blanket in the grass, laughing together. I can picture myself being here and reading on the lawn too. Feeling at home here, even. It sinks in that maybe I am excited about college, after all. I was just apprehensive about moving far away. Fortunately, Meadowbrook is close.

While Meadowbrook is a larger city than Harmony Falls, I'm pleasantly surprised to find that Meadowbrook University has all the old-school charm of the schools on the East Coast that I love. The brick-style buildings look like something out of a movie next to the orange leaves of the giant trees. The leaves crunch under my feet, and the crisp air coupled with the rays of sunshine feel like a nap after a long day. Even just being here for all of five minutes, it feels like my blood pressure has gone down.

As my dad and I walk further into campus, which features even more seating areas and a four-story library, I imagine myself walking down these very same walking paths, not as an intern, but as a student.

One building, a tall, rust-colored brick building catches my eye because its roof is angular, as it sits on the hillier part of the upper portion of the campus. I find myself rushing toward it, and my dad chuckles next to me, trying to keep up. I'm almost out of breath from walking so fast, especially in the higher elevation here.

The copper lettering next to the big glass window reads, "College of Education," and I peer inside, finding that the door catches when I try to open it. I squint my eyes, trying to get a closer look but the blaring rays of the sun make it impossible to see inside. I shield my eyes, still unable to view anything.

I'm beginning to walk away when a girl with red hair falling in tousled waves that barely hit above her shoulders opens the door gently.

She says, "I'm not supposed to let anyone in since I'm doing some behind-the-scenes stuff, but you can come inside and check it out if you want,"

I feel something tugging me to go inside.

"Thank you," I reply, "I promise we won't be long."

A large white staircase with jagged edges caused by the steps being paired together in groups of three is a contrast to the colorful murals, children's art, and bright quotes that line the walls, on which there is no blank space. I can't seem to look away as I take it all in. It's so vibrant here.

"Wow, this place is incredible," I breathe.

"Do you want a tour?" The girl asks.

I tilt my head. "Are you sure? I don't want to make you fall behind in your work,"

"It would be a nice break from filing work. Plus, I love it here," she says, extending her hand to me to shake it. "I'm Karissa."

"Adele," I reply.

She gestures toward the hallway. "Follow me,"

I look at my dad, who motions for me to go ahead without him.

"Are you a transfer student or an incoming freshman?"

Karissa asks.

I fall into step behind her, glancing around me at all of the paintings and drawings. I pause at one cute squiggly drawing of a little girl on a slide. "Incoming freshman,"

Karissa tells me all about how she wasn't certain of what she wanted to study, but after the recommendation of her academic advisor, she enrolled in an Intro to Elementary Education course and immediately fell in love. I also learn that she's a junior and works part-time at the dining hall.

As we chat, she points out different classrooms and offers random tidbits of college advice, and all I want is to soak everything in. Our final stop is a smaller classroom, covered with photos of past students pictured with elementary-age students.

"This will be your favorite class, by far," Karissa says, "it'll be the point where you get your first real classroom experience and can dig deep into why you want to be an educator."

She points to an entire wall dedicated to student photos and testimonials, which say their reasons for becoming teachers. One that piques my interest reads, "I want to become an educator because I want to touch the lives of the next generation,"

This is it. I've found it: that fluttery feeling I've been wanting all along when thinking about my future and what I want out of life, specifically what I want to do.

I want to be a teacher. I want to be silly, kind, and impactful while making learning fun for the kids in my care. I want to empower kids to find their voice.

"Wow," I say, "It just feels...right being here. I can't describe it."

Karissa gives me a knowing smile. "That's how I felt, too,"

"Thank you for giving me a tour," I say as our tour comes to a close, "I appreciate it."

"You are so welcome, Adele. I think you'd be right at home here," Karissa says.

She gives me a quick hug before my dad and I leave, and

gives me her phone number saying, "I know you're still deciding and you've got a lot of choices, but here's my number just in case you come here. That way, you'll already have a friend on the first day,"

As my dad and I walked back to the car, I kept gushing about how pretty the campus was, how cool the tour was, and how right being in that classroom felt. I just focus on the cool breeze and the orange trees in my neighborhood, smiling with each crunch with every step I take as my feet come into contact with crisp red and orange leaves that crunch beneath me.

Once we're inside the car, Dad says, "Your mother went to that exact college,"

My eyes widen. "She did? I always thought she went to school out of state or something,"

"No, it's actually where we met," Dad's lips turn upward as he recalls. "We just didn't end up getting together officially until after a few years."

"Why not?" I ask.

"I was chasing her from day one, but it took her some time to see that I was genuine in wanting to build a life with her," He chuckles and has the same far-away look he usually has when he talks about my mom. Only now, his eyes shine a little brighter. They glimmer with hope. "Oddly enough, I've always seen Harmony Falls as some sort of town where people end up without a real choice in the matter. But coming back here, and remembering your mother, reminds me that it truly is a special place. This whole area is. I think that maybe it was just too painful for me to be in Harmony Falls. I think that's part of the reason I was so pushy for you to consider going out of state."

"Did it feel painful, going back to Meadowbrook University today?" I ask.

"It hurt in the dull way it does whenever I think about her, but the joy I felt seeing you there was by far greater," Dad reassures me. "I loved your mother with every fiber of my being, and she's always going to be a part of me and have a place in my heart. But I know that she wouldn't want me to avoid the places she loved. Instead, she'd want me to celebrate her life."

"I love that, and I couldn't agree more," I reply.

As we're approaching the cozy seafoam buildings of Harmony Falls, I'm filled once again with a sense that this is exactly where I'm supposed to be. Silence falls between us, and I'm struck with the courage to say what's been stirring in my heart for a while now. It's now or never.

"I want to be a teacher," I say shakily.

My dad lowers his voice a little. "Are you sure, Adele? I mean, I know you want to feel connected to your mom, and I understand and support that, but she would want you to do what you want,"

"I know, and I appreciate that, Dad," I assure him, "but I can't describe how right it felt being in that building, and that was before I even knew it was where she learned."

"What are you saying, Adele?" Dad asks, the air between us completely shifting.

I'm suddenly afraid that my dad is going to shut down on me, and things will go back to how they used to be between us.

My dad notices my nerves and reassures me, saying, "I'm listening,"

"I love it here in Harmony Falls, Dad. I don't want to go across the country, and I don't want to go to medical school. I love science, but the medical side of it makes me queasy and it always has. But working with those kids at Science Day was different. I loved every second of it, and it felt right. I just can't explain it, and I know you might need some time to start talking to me again, and…"

My dad immediately responds, "Adele, I'm so sorry that I let my wishes for you overpower your own. All I wanted was to give you options for your future. But, Adele, I want to be a more supportive dad for you. I'll support you in this,"

"Thank you," I whisper, scared that happy tears are going to escape my eyes since they're currently misty.

The hug my dad gives me is the final straw for the tears to spill out.

Dad's face falls once he sees my glossy eyes. "Those are good tears, right kiddo?"

I chuckle and I nod my head. "Yes,"

CHAPTER 17

"Adele, there's someone here for you!"

My dad's voice carries throughout the entire house as I finish getting dressed after showering, still on a high from touring Meadowbrook University this afternoon.

"Be right there!" I shout, uncertain if it's Hunter or Selena.

I almost stop in my tracks when I see Hunter in a black cowboy hat, a black, worn flannel-style long-sleeve shirt, faded blue jeans with a brass belt, and black cowboy boots.

"Hi," I say, looking back and forth between my dad and Hunter.

"Hunter tells me you're going country line dancing tonight," Dad says, a small smile on his face. His hands are in his pockets and he shuffles back and forth slightly.

I realize this is the only time my dad has ever met a guy, and we've never really talked about relationships, other than the conversation we recently had about me waiting until medical school to date. I'm not even sure if I'm allowed to date. I was so wrapped up in my excitement that I completely forgot to clear it with my dad.

Hunter looks equally nervous as he fidgets with his cowboy hat. "If that's okay with you, sir, and with you, Adele,"

It becomes completely silent as the three of us look around at each other. I'm the first one to speak up, desperate to smooth things over in a way that will keep Hunter from starting on the wrong foot with my dad.

"Dad, can I talk to you in the kitchen real fast?" I ask, nodding to my dad to follow me.

Once we're alone, I sense my dad's hesitation. His lips twist into a shy half-smile.

"I'm sorry I didn't tell you," I murmur, "I was going to, I promise. I was just so caught up in the tour today. Hunter asked me to be his girlfriend, and I said yes."

I brace myself for a lecture. All I can hope for now is that this doesn't set my dad and me back.

Dad's voice is kind. "Adele, I already know. He asked me for permission a couple of days ago,"

"He what?" I gasp.

"Yes, and I gave him my permission. I thought it was very respectful and considerate. It showed me that he cares about you, and I'm not going to stand in the way of that, especially when he's a good man," My dad says.

"Thanks, Dad. If it helps, I really like him," I say.

"I can already tell that he likes you too," Dad gestures to me. "Now, go enjoy country dancing."

I give him a quick hug. "Thanks,"

Hunter smiles widely at me as soon as I say, "I'd love to go country dancing with you,"

After he shakes hands with my dad, we're off.

He interlaces his hand through mine and escorts us to his truck.

"I like your cowboy hat," I reach on my tippy toes to try to tap it. "It suits you."

"Thank you," His eyebrows waggle. "I'm excited for an excuse to wear it."

His truck creaks as we pull into a gravel parking lot just outside of town where a large wooden barn-style dance hall is already booming with the sounds of stomping boots and old-school, deep country twang music. Twinkly fairy lights are strung above the deck outside and over the inside wooden dance floor.

It's exhilarating how the crowd around us moves completely in sync, thumping their boots and turning every fifteen seconds or so. Hunter and I are in the back cusp of the group, and every few seconds or so, I see him glancing at me with a smile. I know I have the biggest grin on my face, despite having no idea how to keep up with the fast dances, but I'm having the time of my life here with him. The excitement of the people around us revs me up even more, so much so that the loud music feels like it's running through my veins. I find myself clapping along to the rhythm and jumping up and down when the dancing switches to more individual dancing than line dancing.

"Would you like to dance with me?" Hunter asks, holding his hand out to me.

"I'd love to," I say, putting my hand in his, noticing the warmth radiating throughout my body from the simple touch, and I follow him to the deck outside.

"We have the perfect view of the stars out here," Hunter murmurs.

I tilt my head up to the sky, shocked to see so many glittering stars. I want to close my eyes take a mental picture of it and keep it stowed away in my heart forever. I want to capture all of it: the thumping of the country music, the clanging of the boots, the crisp breeze, the dark sky contrasted with flickering stars, and the touch of the man who brought me here tonight.

"Wow, this is beautiful," I whisper.

The music switches to a slower rhythm and Hunter pulls me in closer until my head rests on his shoulder while we dance.

I breathe in his woodsy scent. "I heard you talked to my dad,"

"Yes, I hope that's okay. I just wanted to make my intentions known. I'm old-fashioned, I guess," Hunter says.

Now it's my turn to cup his face with my hand as I look directly into his soul, wanting him to know exactly how much that means to me. "I like that about you,"

We sway for hours, completely in sync as we move into a world of our own. We're so in our element that it takes the flickering light out front to remind us that the dance hall is closing.

"We closed the place down," Hunter whispers, a sheepish smile on his face.

The fluttery sensation in my chest almost prevents me from responding.

"I guess so," I say, my voice coming out breathily.

He checks his watch and says, "It's 9 pm. Do you think we have time for a quick pit stop?"

I surprise myself with my boldness. "Yes,"

He brightens. "I was hoping you'd say that,"

He wraps a jacket around my shoulders and puts his arm around my shoulders as he leads the way. At this point, we're fumbling in the dark as we walk through the tall itchy wild grass. The sound of chirping crickets reinforces that it's just us out there. As the grass becomes thicker, Hunter laces his hand through mine, paving the way for us until we come across a small clearing, a gap in a splintered wooden fence.

"You don't think we'll get arrested out here?" I ask, my voice wary.

"I promise we're safe. I come out here all the time," Hunter assures me.

The certainty in his voice alone brings me the same sense of security I feel whenever I'm with him. I'm about to ask him what we're doing in a random field in the dark when he says, "Here we are,"

I squint in the dark, still uncertain, as I try to register what it is I'm looking at.

"Here, let me show you," he murmurs. Peace fills my entire body as his hand connects with my lower back.

As soon as the light from his phone illuminates our surroundings, I let out a gasp. An entire field of tall pink and lavender wildflowers, a foot or so taller than my head, lies in front of us. I reach out a hand to touch the tall petals, taking in their beauty. I giggle as I race ahead of him, wanting to see how far the fields extend. After taking in how it feels to be surrounded by such pretty flowers, I sneak a glance back at the man behind me, the one who brings an even bigger smile to my face.

"I thought you'd like this place," Hunter says softly.

"How did you find it?" I ask.

There's a temporary flash of sadness in the way his smile slips and his eyes turn downward as he says, "My mother took me here,"

I don't know what to say but I know that he needs me.

So, I reach one hand and place it on his heart, the other around his back, as I hold him. He's held me before but I've never held him. It feels different, but it feels right. He gives me a small smile, then says, "I come here when I miss her,"

I pull him in closer to me as he speaks so softly that I have to concentrate to hear.

"Things were kind of rocky in my house growing up. Dad was so tired all the time from keeping the auto shop afloat, and Mom was working nights in Meadowbrook. My parents had met when they were young, and my mom was visiting Harmony Falls as a tourist. She had longed to travel the world and to experience life to the fullest I guess," His voice cracks. "My dad says that 'small town life wasn't for her', but you'd think having a family to come home to would make that sacrifice worth it, that it'd be enough." He rests his head on my shoulder as he lets me in and allows me to see him.

What I lack in words, I show in the way I embrace him and draw him nearer to me.

Hunter sighs. "I just wish we had been enough for her to stay, especially for my siblings' sake. I don't feel like I have what it takes to help them,"

"You are enough," I whisper, "And your siblings know that they can rely on you. They know that you care and that you keep showing up, even when it's difficult,"

His voice softens a little. "Thank you, Adele. That means a lot coming from you,"

"It's not just how I feel, it's the truth," I say.

"Anderson, you're the only person I've told about this," He says.

"Thanks for trusting me," I say softly.

He pulls back and lifts his head off my shoulder.

Goosebumps form on the back of my neck as he draws me toward him. I gasp as he reaches his hands around my waist and uses the jacket he wraps around me to pulls me close. My forehead is flush against his neck. I know I could kiss his neck if I want to, but he has other ideas. He quietly clears his throat, drawing my gaze upward. I'm appalled to see the trust evident in his face, the way that his entire body has relaxed into mine as if he's completely at ease now that he's told someone that he's not as unaffected by his mother leaving as he displays to the world.

I wonder what expression is displayed on my face, then realize that it's likely the complete serenity I feel around him. It's from the way I know I can always count on him to not only be kind to me but the people around us. Even the way he introduced himself to my dad speaks volumes about the way he consistently approaches things from a place of goodness.

I want to experience whatever this is between us differently, to show him that I care. I long to bring his lips to mine, to express my gratitude to him for showing me that things could be different for me.

Sometimes I'm so wrapped up in my head that it feels like life is moving by me in slow motion, but with Hunter, I can let my guard down and be completely present in each moment.

"Hours feel like seconds with you," Hunter muses. "You know that?"

He puts his cowboy hat on my head and I laugh as it nearly blocks my eyes and weighs my head down.

"That's my favorite part about you," I say.

"Country girl looks good on you," he says gruffly, gently tipping the cowboy hat on my head back so that it doesn't cover my eyes anymore.

I just smile in response, still flushed under his gaze.

Rays of warmth cascade from my head to my toes as he leans in closer, tilting my hat again. I pause, my heart racing as he presses his lips to my forehead. The tender way he touches me makes me feel like I'm a piece of artwork and he's the lucky one when I feel so lucky to be with him.

Somehow, this gesture, something so innocent, feels so special. His touch, the way I nearly melted in his hands while we danced tonight, the way he confided in me, and the intent nature of this night all have me smiling endlessly.

CHAPTER 18

"You're doing it, look at you! I just can't believe it!" Selena says, laughing as we lurch forward and I come to an attempted slow stop at the stop sign near her street.

I was so excited about my recent milestone of driving for the first time, that I borrowed my dad's car to drive her down the road.

"It feels so good, it still doesn't feel real," I say.

"What did Hunter say?" Selena asks.

Just hearing his name makes me flush after last night.

"I am going to surprise him," I explain, "I'm not sure when, but soon."

Selena squeals. "He'll be so excited for you!"

I smile because I know he will. Hunter has a way of lifting me through so much encouragement that I become a brighter, happier version of myself. It's like I found a piece of me that I didn't know existed until I met him.

"I'm really happy with him, Selena," I say, a smile taking over my entire face.

"I know," Selena claps her hands together. "And I love this for you."

After soaking in the joyful feeling of finally taking back some control of my life, I follow Selena inside her house, where we'll be coloring my hair today. After weeks of trying to convince me, she is finally doing it, and I couldn't be more eager.

Mostly though, I'm excited for Hunter's reaction.

As she puts foils in my hair, I tell her all about last night's country dancing and the way that Hunter went to my dad to tell him his intentions.

"He's really into you," Selena sing-songs.

"I'm into him too," I say, "Things just fell into place so smoothly with him, it feels effortless."

"Exactly as it should be," Selena says.

I close my eyes as Selena washes my hair in her kitchen sink, wincing as the cold water sprays on my face.

"I don't know why, but I'm nervous to see it," I say, feeling that same instinct I have to hide like I usually do.

I've never felt pretty. Sure, I've felt smart, and confident, but I've never felt beautiful in the natural beauty way or the glammed-up way. But one glance at myself in the mirror and I feel a shift as I see myself differently. Because the girl staring back at me is glowing. She looks strong and resilient but has a gentle feminine way about her.

"Hunter is going to lose his mind when he sees you," Selena says softly.

"You really think so?" I ask, twirling a strand of hair around my finger while I admire my new highlights.

Selena grins. "I know so,"

"Thank you for doing this for me," I gesture to my hair. "It means a lot to me to feel like this. To feel beautiful."

"You've always been beautiful," Selena's voice softens. "I'm glad you recognize it now."

"I know I didn't need Hunter to tell me anything, but somehow, him being in my life has helped me to see everything in a different light, including myself," I say.

"That's because when a man loves a woman, she blooms," Selena coos.

"I don't know about love," I wave my hand dismissively toward myself. "I haven't even kissed him yet."

Selena gets a dreamy look in her eyes. "Slow and steady is the best way sometimes when you're in it for the long haul, which I know he is,"

The long haul. The phrase alone makes my heart sing because it plants a seed of hope within me that this could go somewhere.

"I told my dad I don't want to go to medical school," I blurt.

"You what?" She asks, her dark eyes widening as she finishes curling my hair.

The light chocolate brown highlights subtly frame my face, giving me the boost of confidence I needed.

"I told him I want to be a teacher," I say, my smile beaming.

"I could see it!" Selena says, hugging me.

I go on to tell her all about the tour of Meadowbrook and how right it felt to be there, especially in the same classroom my mother was in.

"Speaking of exciting things," Selena says, "I was thinking that tonight, we could go shopping for Homecoming dresses."

"That sounds fun," I reply.

As we're about to leave for the store, Selena's mom oohs and ahhs as she admires my new hair color.

"Wow, Adele, you look so grown up," Her mom says, lightly feathering my wavy hair.

"Thank you," I reply, "Selena could be a hairstylist, she's got a gift."

Her mom chuckles. "She's going to be a wonderful hair artist,"

I glance at Selena, giving her a blank look.

Selena gives me a goofy look, her eyebrows raised as she smiles widely.

Selena is beaming. "Guilty as charged,"

"Wait!" I say, "We just had this whole conversation about me not wanting to go to medical school, and you didn't mention anything about wanting to go to hair school?"

Selena shrugs, but she's grinning ear to ear. She's trying to be humble, despite this being an exciting update for her. "I was going to, I was just waiting for the right time,"

It's then that I'm aware of another possible reason for her hesitation: there are no hair schools that I know of in Harmony Falls or Meadowbrook. The nearest cosmetology school is likely in Santa Maria.

I face her. "Well, you are going to be the best hairstylist. I haven't felt this beautiful in a long time,"

Selena's mom says, "I couldn't agree more, Selena. You were born for this, sweetheart. Anyone who colors their hair in the middle of the night is passionate about it,"

As Selena leaves to grab her purse before we leave for the mall, Selena's mom gives me a sheepish smile as she leans in and lowers her voice. "Selena told me that you are dating Hunter Watts,"

"I am," I say, feeling my face redden as I meet her eyes.

"He's a good man," she says.

"He is," I nod. "I'm happy I know him."

"Adele, I've been meaning to talk to you," Selena's mom says, looking toward Selena's room warily.

I lean in slightly, feeling my pulse quicken. Is Selena okay?

"What about? Is it Selena? Is she alright?" I ask, my voice already shaky.

"No, she is fine. Sorry for worrying you, sweetheart," Her mom says, "I just wanted to let you know that I am here for you. I know that all of the milestones of Senior year can be lonely, especially without your mother."

The energy in the room immediately shifts and the all-encompassing peace I feel at Selena's house overwhelms me because I'm moved by just how much her family has taken me in, in such a way that it's changed things completely for me, and my dad.

"Thank you," I feel my voice crack. "That means the world to me."

"Adele, I am glad to see you out of your shell more," She pauses, and her smile looks forced as her plump lips curve into a straight line. "I just, I don't want to see that disappear if he's not in your life anymore."

"Do you think it will?"

Her brows knit together. "No, not at all. But, I just want you to know, Adele, that yes, he's been good for you, but you could have done it on your own,"

"What are you trying to say?" I ask warily.

Is she saying what I think she's saying? That I should just end things with him?

Her eyes meet mine as she gives me a knowing look. "All I'm saying is, don't be so wrapped up in him that you lose sight of who you are,"

I take a look at the fridge across the kitchen, with its family photos, upcoming calendar events, and artwork, and realize that I have no idea who I am, or where I belong in anything anymore. It constantly feels like things are changing right before my eyes, and I'm not quite sure where I fit into the picture. Even in this family, I have no idea where I am supposed to be, especially as graduation gets closer.

"I don't even know who I am," My voice comes out hoarse. "I feel like everyone else has this security that I just don't have. Maybe you're right, though. Maybe I have been making him my security."

I feel the joy deflate out of my chest like a balloon because I realize that I'm just grasping for straws all the time, trying to do all these things that are baby steps for the people around me but feel like milestones for me. Here I am making all this headway in my own life when in reality, I'm just doing the bare minimum. Like driving. Holding hands with a boy. Deciding what I want to do with my life.

"Adele, life is not about what you've been through, or what job you go into. It's about who you become. And you, my dear, are kind, strong, and a fighter. All I was saying is, don't lose sight of that, because you have been so resilient, and I don't want to see things not working out with him to take you back to a bad place again. That's all. I couldn't be prouder of you," Selena's mom says.

Her words are meant to help, but they remind me of an untouchable topic: a period of my life that even Selena won't talk about: the Dark Ages. Two years ago, during Sophomore year, I was struggling with a lot of things at once: driving, my identity, guys, and my relationship with my dad.

Driving was this heavy subject that my dad and I refused to mention, so we were just dancing around one another, too hesitant to broach the topic of me trying to get my permit or my license. As I watched everyone around me get their permits and then eventually go on to get their license, I just continued to get even more isolated at school. Classes had started to become harder, as I was taking AP and honors classes, so I found myself studying more and more. I didn't see Selena very much, until one day we completely hashed it out in her car and I confided in her about what was going on. I just felt so lost, because I had no way of articulating everything that was swimming around in my head all the time.

All I know is that I don't want to go back to being lifeless, timid, and insecure all the time. Now that I do have my confidence back, especially after years of only living in sweatpants every day, I don't want to lose it.

"Thank you for the encouragement," I assure her. "I'm in a good place, and I don't plan on going back."

"You're welcome," Her mom faces me. "And if anything changes, you call us. We're your family too, and family doesn't go through it alone. We'll help you."

"Thanks," I say, hugging her, silently wondering what my mother would have said if she were here.

At the mall, I end up choosing a beautiful black satin dress, silently telling myself that even if I go solo to Homecoming, I will be wearing that dress, and I will feel good. There's no more going back, especially since I now know what it feels like to live.

CHAPTER 19

"Can we take a break yet?" Hunter asks, tilting his head sideways and glancing at me with his captivating eyes.

He's fresh out of football practice and still wearing his jersey, completely unaware of the effect that seeing him has on me. Or maybe he's fully aware and using it to his advantage. Either way, I'm loving it, loving how comfortable we both are now. The transition from friends to more than friends has been seamless so far, which is a relief because it's the part I'm most nervous about. Hunter now has a B in AP Chem, but I'm still tutoring him because A, I love his company, and B, it's kind of fun. I get to practice my future teaching skills.

"We just started," I say.

He reaches his hand out on top of mine, gently claiming me as his, causing me to drop the pencil I'm holding.

"I guess we could take a little break, we have been working pretty hard." I smile slyly.

"That's my girl," Hunter replies, giving me the cheesiest grin.

"What do you want to do?" I ask.

He pauses. "Honestly, I just want to leave this house, it feels like we've been here for hours,"

"I have an idea," I say, "It's going to require you to trust me though,"

His eyes meet mine. "I trust you with my life, Adele,"

"Good, because that's essentially what it is," I reply.

"What?" He asks.

"You'll see, silly," I say, reaching for his hand as he grabs his car keys.

My dad is at a short work conference again, but he

carpooled with a friend and left me his car. Since Hunter doesn't know that I've driven yet, now is the perfect time.

I grin. "You won't be needing those,"

"Oh," he says, giving me a small smile of encouragement.

I take a shaky but excited breath as he holds the door for me and I climb into the car.

I calmly start the car, replaying all of my dad's tips for driving. I can do this. Hunter is patient with me, even as I take a few minutes to fumble with the mirrors and settings in the car. I pull myself together though and we're off.

I'm grateful for the silence as I settle into driving. My nerves eventually cool down, and I take in the beauty of the quaint buildings that line Main Street.

I end up pulling into one of the parking spots on the main drag.

"This is probably only as far as I can drive," I say sheepishly, smiling and looking down as my hands still grab the steering wheel for dear life.

"Adele, I can't believe this! You're doing it! I'm so proud of you," Hunter says, his voice laced with kindness. I never thought I could do this, especially after being so scared for so long.

It feels like the air between us shifts, and I say, "Would you want to go somewhere and watch the sunset?"

He nods. "I'd love to, I know the perfect spot,"

We end up switching spots as he takes over the driving, one hand on the steering wheel and the other on my left knee.

We pull over to a little lookout spot in the hills, a private little dirt lot on the top of the hilly road, which offers us a view of the ocean and the cliffs. The car faces the sunset directly, and neither of us gets out, settling on watching it from our little private space.

I sneak a look at him to see that he's already staring at me, his head tilting toward me, an unreadable expression on his face.

"Hi," I say.

"Hi," He breathes. "The sunset looks prettier with you here."

"Why aren't you looking at it then? It's about to disappear," I say.

"Because being with you is better than a thousand sunsets," He says.

"I didn't know you were so poetic," I challenge, my eyes locked on him, wondering what is going to happen next.

He scans my features. "Well, I have quite a beautiful muse, so I guess you just bring out that side of me,"

His words light me up inside and my entire face flushes at him calling me beautiful.

"Somehow, you've become my best friend in all of this," Hunter says, "And for that, I'll be so grateful, but I also just can't get over how unique and strong you are."

"You've become my best friend too," I say, "And, you're strong too."

He leans in a little closer. "I'm so proud of you for today. You have no idea, I wish I could show you,"

Only I have some ideas, some specific ways that I can show it.

"Thank you, I appreciate you," I respond.

My eyes are locked on his lips, but my hands are uncertain, as one is interlaced with his and the other one sits in my lap.

He slowly takes his seatbelt off, and I feel my heart race. The clicking sound only emphasizes the silence between us.

He's the first to speak. "Maybe we should get some air,"

"We don't have to," I say quietly.

Hunter's voice softens. "Trust me, Adele, I want to, but I want to wait until you're a hundred percent ready. I want this to move at your pace. Your pace is my pace,"

"I'm sorry, I guess you're right," I say, thinking back to what Selena's mom told me about not allowing myself to be so caught up in him. Only I know at this moment that it's too late because if I were to kiss Hunter right now, I don't think I'd be able to stop.

This is why I find myself unbuckling my seatbelt too, and being the boldest I have in a long time, if ever.

"Can we talk about the night of the party again?" I ask.

"Of course," Hunter replies.

"I appreciate you helping me, and for caring enough to want to make my first kiss special," I say, my leg bouncing up and down a little.

He gently squeezes my leg and I yelp, saying, "I guess what I'm trying to say is, thank you,"

"You're welcome, Adele. You deserve patience," he says.

Something about the way his eyes have darkened entrances me, and I just can't look away, feeling so many different emotions at once, so surprised to be able to experience these feelings after years of just feeling numb.

"Thank you," I reply.

"What are you thinking about, right this second?" he asks.

"I'm just surprised that I could feel these things. I feel like something in my heart was turned off until I met you," I say, twirling my hair with my fingers, nervous about sharing this much.

He faces me. "Adele, you've awakened something in me too. With the situation with my family, I stepped up because I had to. But lately, I've wanted to. You've made me want to be a better man,"

"You're an incredible man," I murmur.

He tenderly reaches behind my head and tilts my head to face him, looking at me with such adoration that I freeze.

"Did you do something different with your hair?" He asks.

"Yes, Selena gave me highlights," I say.

"Wow, Adele, you look stunning," he says.

I'm about to throw caution to the wind when his cell phone chimes. He looks at it then lets out an exasperated sigh.

"Is everything all right?" I ask.

He exhales a shaky breath. "Yes, I'm just overwhelmed. Things with my family are piling up, and I'm barely staying afloat,"

I squeeze his hand in mine and he squeezes mine back.

"Is there anything I can do to help?" I ask gently.

"Just you being here helps," he sighs, "I just, I wish I had more to give you,"

I want to tell him that he's already given me the world and then some.

"What do you mean?" I ask.

He looks uncertain, running a hand through his hair as he says, "I just wish I didn't bring all of this excess pain into our relationship, like my parents' mistakes shouldn't define us. You already have more than enough to worry about with the whole medical school thing, I don't need to burden you. I just wish I could be someone who makes life easier for you, not harder,"

"Hunter, look at me," I say softly, leaning into him and putting my hands around his neck as I close the space between us, "I want to be with you. I'm proud of the man you are and the way you've responded to your situation, especially of the way you stepped up when you could have easily just ignored it and chosen to go on with your life," I pause. "That's who you are, someone who shows up for people. But you are not your circumstances, and someday, you will be able to look back on all of this and see how it shaped you, but that stress and pain won't be there anymore. It'll be replaced by the good life you've built."

His face is mere centimeters from mine. "I never thought of it that way,"

I want to brush my lips against his. "Well, that's what I'm here for, I guess,"

We're still idling in my dad's car, watching the sky darken. "Things will get better, I promise," I tell him.

"How do you know that, though? What if my family is always struggling to stay afloat emotionally?" he asks, his eyes wary.

This man, beyond exhausted from football practice and work and trying to help run a household, looks like he's about to fall asleep.

"I want to tell you, but I'd rather show you instead," I reply, "But I know things will get easier."

"Okay," he says, still not changing the space between us,

neither closing the gap and kissing me or pulling away.

But I know that it's not the time for kissing; it'd feel too intimate right now. Now's the time to be a friend to him.

"Let's head back to my house, I have an idea," I say.

Back at my house, I encourage him to take a hot shower and I lay out some blankets for him on the couch. Meanwhile, I make him some lasagna and brownies, excited to help him relax after a long day.

I'm closing the oven door when I feel a pair of arms wrap around my waist.

"Hi," Hunter says, his voice as smooth as honey as he smells like woodsy pine.

"Hi," I say.

"What's this material? I like it," he asks, fiddling with the waistline of the skirt I'm wearing. The gesture sends shivers down my spine, and I realize this is the first time I've been held like this before.

"It's satin," I say matter-of-factly.

His voice is as smooth as honey. "I like it on you,"

"Thank you," I say, turning around to face him, but staying just as close.

"Wait, is all this for me?" he asks, his face lighting up.

"Yes, I may have gotten a little carried away, but the idea was you could bring some home to your siblings so you will all have dinner tomorrow. I made a second pan of lasagna for tomorrow's dinner for your family," I say.

"Wow, Adele, I don't even know what to say," His eyes meet mine. "Thank you so much."

The intensity of his stare has me stumbling back, nearly topping over myself.

"You don't have to say anything, just enjoy it," I say.

"I will," he says, serving me first, and then himself.

He even goes as far as opening my chair for me, which is a cute gesture. He tells me funny stories while we eat together, and I laugh more than I've ever laughed in my life about how goofy he was growing up.

"I needed this," he says, reaching for my hand to gently squeeze it.

"Hunter, you're going to get through this," I say, "but you need to reach out and ask for help when you need it. Even if it's not from me."

"I think I prefer to ask you though. You do look pretty beautiful in the kitchen," he says, earning a laugh from me.

"Well, you are always welcome here," I reply.

CHAPTER 20

Tonight is the big Homecoming game, and I'm even more nervous than Hunter is. He adjusts his jersey for the fourth time, tugging on the bottom of the jersey fabric, until I assure him, "You're going to do amazing out there. Just keep doing what you always do. And no matter the outcome of the game, it is going to be okay,"

"Thank you," he whispers into my hair.

He kisses my forehead before leaving to join the guys in the huddle. I watch in awe as his tall frame fades into the crowded field as he takes the center position in the group.

It's the final game of the season before playoffs begin, so everyone is here to watch. The bleachers are jam-packed with people from my school, all of their younger siblings and parents, and people from the community. I even see a few teachers I recognize in the crowd, which looks like one big blur of people.

I almost sigh with relief when I see Selena and Mario in the back of the stands, where they've saved me a spot.

Selena smiles sheepishly at me and holds the glittery blue sign that we made that says, "Go, Watts, 42! I believe in you!" I was too shy to bring it, but now that I've seen how nervous Hunter is about this game, I know I need to set my ego aside and offer him all the encouragement I can.

I silently thank Selena for bringing the sign with a smile since it's far too loud to hear me anyway.

I stand for the duration of the game, my eyes locked on Hunter, who plays the best game of his life. He leads the team with a humble confidence I've never seen before, making sure that all of the guys have the chance to participate in the plays. He hurls the ball across the field, and the crowd erupts into cheer as the game progresses in our favor. I'm so shaky and nervous that I nearly fall off the bleachers from cheering so enthusiastically; Selena and Mario have to catch me.

The end of the game goes by in the blink of an eye as one of the guys on our team scores the touchdown that gives us the victory. As the clock buzzes to signify our win, my heart somersaults inside of my chest as Hunter takes off his helmet and blows me a kiss. To the rest of the people here, it may look like a gesture of solidarity with our school, but the way he looks for me in the crowd makes me think it's something more. Like maybe, just maybe, it's for me.

As the people in the bleachers start making their way onto the field, I hang back, still trying to see where Hunter went. I shakily grab the handrail as I walk down, still uncertain about what to do. Perhaps he's just enjoying the win with his teammates, as he should.

With the sign still rolled up in my hand, I hug Selena and Mario goodbye as they head toward a celebratory dinner together. They invite me to join them, but I decline, hoping that I'll be seeing Hunter tonight. I know that even if I don't though, I'll be all right.

Our eyes meet from across the field, where he's hugging one of his teammates. I hold back a smile as he begins making his way toward me, his eyes on mine every step of the way. I want to meet him in the middle, but something about his intention has me frozen in place, uncertain of what to do with myself. So, I just stand and clutch my homemade sign for him, waiting for him with the cheesiest grin on my face.

"You did incredible out there, I'm so proud of you," I muse.

"Thank you," he says, "What is this?"

I look down at the ground, too shy to tell him, so I slowly unravel it.

He reads, "Watts 42, I believe in you!"

I blush furiously, hoping it wasn't too foolish of an idea.

"Wow, this is so sweet. Did you make this?" he asks.

I just nod.

To my surprise, he wraps his arms around me and lifts me as if I weigh nothing, giving me a sweet embrace and planting kisses on my cheeks.

"How did I get the sweetest girl?" he asks.

"I'm the lucky one," I say, smiling as he sets me down.

He leans in. "I have something to show you,"

"You do?" I ask.

"Yes, follow me," he says, a mischievous glint in his eyes as he takes my hand.

And I do because I'd gladly follow him anywhere.

He leads me to the car, and then says, "It's actually at your house,"

"Okay," I say, wondering what could make this day better.

He has me close my eyes when we get to my house, and I hold onto him for dear life as he leads us inside. Just his voice alone calms the storm in my head, a mixture of nerves and excitement, as we walk inside, me with my eyes closed. Once inside, he tells me that I can open my eyes.

I gasp when I see my dining room covered in red rose petals, arranged to say: Homecoming?

I turn to look at him when he pulls a bouquet of red roses out from behind his back.

"How did you do that?" I ask and he chuckles, his voice echoing throughout the house.

I embrace him once I see the dining room table set up with a white silk tablecloth and lit candles.

"Thanks for your patience, I know I'm a little late and all at asking you, especially since it's tomorrow," he says, hugging me back tightly now.

"I'd love to go with you," I assure him. "Trust me, you're worth any wait."

He reaches for a chair for me and instructs me to sit down as he goes to bring out the dinner.

"This is the first course of three," His cheeks are pink as he smiles at me.

Is he as nervous as I am around him? Because I'm certainly

feeling all kinds of fluttery things right now; it feels like my heart is dancing and he's a song I just can't get enough of. To know, based on his smile, that he feels at least a fraction of what I feel, is a thought that brings me the comfort I've been needing.

"Hunter, you are quite the cook," I say.

When he shoots me a disbelieving smile, I say, "I mean it," His eyes meet mine. "Thank you, I think I learned a thing or two from you the last time we cooked together,"

"This is delicious. Thank you," I say before digging into another bite of his homemade chicken pesto pasta.

"Thanks for being my Homecoming date,"

As we talk and enjoy one another's company, I relax, the way I always do around him. He reaches for my hand as we finish dessert together. The sensation of his hand clasping mine is unlike anything I've experienced. I feel safe with him, like I can fully rest in each moment and be present instead of being so wrapped up in fear all the time. Someway, somehow, his even-keeled, old-school country, straight-to-the-point ways have helped me fully be. It's as if he's replaced my insecurities and fears with confidence and peace.

"It would be an honor to be your Homecoming date," I respond.

We're settling on the couch when Hunter wraps his arm around my waist, accidentally brushing where my scar is, and the strangest thing happens: I flinch, not because it hurts or because I'm scared, but because my body just reacts weirdly, like it's out of my control. I immediately tense up and hear him whisper in my ear, "Are you okay? I'm sorry for moving too quickly,"

"I'm fine, I promise it's not that," I whisper.

His voice softens. "What is it then? I'm here if you want to talk about it," My heart stills as his eyes meet mine.

"Do you remember when I would wear sweatpants to PE even though it was scorching hot outside?" I ask.

"Yes," His hand is still hesitant, wanting to respect my space. He gestures to my back and I nod to let him know that it's okay.

After he puts his arm around my shoulders, I look at him and say, "Well, I guess me being bad at sports wasn't the only reason I put off taking PE for so long,"

He gazes intently at me, his eyes laced with concern, and says, "Do you feel comfortable sharing with me? Take all the time you need,"

"Well," I say, clearing my throat since it feels like there is a lump in my chest, "I avoided PE because I didn't want to change in front of anyone in the locker rooms. When I got into that, umm, car accident with my mom, it left me with a gash going down my stomach. It's kind of faded out now, but I don't know, I guess it sometimes feels like my body still hasn't bounced back there, like the nerves haven't recovered or something. And I try to be confident in myself, and I finally do feel that way, but my body hasn't gotten the memo with how I'm supposed to respond."

Hunter says nothing, just gently holding me instead. And I feel grateful that he just gives me the space to expose something so hard for me to open up about, even to acknowledge myself.

"So, I guess the whole taking things slow with you thing is a mixture of me being shy, and of me not being sure of how my body is going to react," I explain.

"Thank you for trusting me," His breath tickles my neck and sends shivers down my spine. "It's nice being the safe place you can land."

We're silent for a few minutes as he rubs my back, and I feel myself relax into him.

"Can I ask you something?" He gently combs through my waves.

I glance up at him. "Of course,"

"What is it about this that you're the most afraid of?" Time stills as his eyes meet mine.

"A lot of things," My voice is shaky. "The fear that you'll see my scar, or that I won't measure up. The fear that I'll never be normal and always feel this way." I gesture to myself.

"Adele," he says, taking my hand in his, "I'm with you for you, who you are on the inside. Do I think you're beautiful? Of course I do. I was speechless around you, even when you were wearing those sweatpants. I thought you were so adorable. But who you are as a person? The way you've stepped out and started letting people in more, using your life to make the lives of those around you better? That's the most beautiful. So, whatever this scar looks like, it's a part of you, and I'm going to believe that it's beautiful too. It's a sign of your strength, and it's a part of your story,"

I'm taken aback by the genuine compassion in his words, although I shouldn't be. Through his actions, he's continuously shown me that he cares about me.

My voice is breathy. "Thank you,"

"And Adele, that experience shaped you into who you are today. You don't need to try to get back to the old you, you just need to embrace and appreciate the woman you are today," he encourages me.

"Thank you for listening," I say, "I appreciate you."

"Always, it's what I'm here for," he says.

And I know in my heart that the best way to do that is to make it a point to enjoy every second with him at Homecoming tomorrow night.

CHAPTER 21

"I still can't believe it, both of us are going with our dream men to Homecoming," Selena says, having to scream over the country music we're listening to.

Mario is taking her out to dinner before, so she and I are doing each other's makeup before we go our separate ways with our dates.

Something is different with Hunter now. After our conversation last night, there's a newfound sense of trust there, and I'm even more looking forward to Homecoming as a result.

I've been a jittery, excited spazz all day, but I just can't help it. This is my first time going to a dance with a date, and I'm very grateful that it's with Hunter of all people. He's come to mean so much to me, and I'm eager to show him tonight.

It'll be our first appearance as a couple, since aside from the Shut-In, we haven't openly shown our relationship. But it's time, I can feel it.

The doorbell chimes, letting me know that Hunter is here to pick me up. We decided to go to his house before the dance, so this way, we could get some photos before.

My stomach is in knots as I walk to open the door, both excited and terrified for him to see my dress. I nearly trip over the form-fitting satin, which catches on my heel. Luckily, I caught myself as I let him in the house. There's no holding back the smile that breaks out on my face as I take in the sight of him in a dark navy suit that brings out his eyes and hugs his athletic frame, drawing attention to his broad shoulders. His smile though stands out as his gaze trails over my dress. I'm swimming in his eyes, unable to look away. We matched our outfits without even realizing it.

He's the first to speak. "You look stunning, Adele,"

"Thank you," My lips tilt up. "You look very handsome yourself."

He looks happier than I've ever seen him; he looks right at home, here with me, and I love it.

"I love how confident you look right now," he says, leaning down to kiss my cheek.

"Thank you," I say, knowing every potential insecurity I had in this dress faded away the second he laid eyes on me.

With my hand in his, I follow him to his truck, noticing how familiar his touch has become. My leg bounces up and down as we ride to his house. I gasp when I see my dad's car parked outside Hunter's house.

"Is that?" I ask, not finishing the thought, knowing Hunter can practically read my mind at this point.

"Yes," he says, "He wanted to be a part of your special day."

"Our special day," I say, smiling at him.

Once inside the house, I see my dad laughing with Hunter's dad, and something about the sight of the two of them talking so naturally makes me smile. Maybe because it gives me a glimmer of hope for a future with Hunter, especially knowing that our lives mesh so well together. Things do feel effortless with him.

My dad beams with pride as he sees us both. Even Hunter's dad smiles and gives me a big hug.

Dad's eyes are misty. "Wow, you're all grown up now,"

"Couldn't have said it better myself," Hunter's dad chimes in. "I'm proud of you two kids."

Both of our dads take pictures of us in the silliest, old-school poses, as my dad instructs us to "stare longingly into each other's eyes,"

At the dance, my hands shake as we walk in together, but no one says anything. Everyone is too busy dancing with one another, focused on their dates, to pay us any mind. Hunter picks up on my initial apprehension though, and leans in to whisper, "It's you and me, remember that. We're in this together," His words serve as a reminder of the way that what he and I have is something lasting; all of the temporary things of high school, like other people's opinions, are not. Just his acknowledgment, that reassurance of us, grounds me.

As we pass Jackie, she leans in and hugs me. "You look so pretty!"

The small gesture means so much to me because it feels incredible to have another friendly face around school.

I take in her beautiful dress and return the hug. "You too!"

After Hunter greets the guy that Jackie is dancing with, he leads me to the center of the dance floor. He slowly moves his arm around my waist, the other one around the back of my neck. Without thinking about it, I lean into him and close the space between us. The loud music seems to fade away as I embrace his touch, what it feels like to be held by him like this. Known. Cherished.

And one glance at Hunter as he cups my face leaves me feeling off-kilter, as if the room around us has faded away. I'm drowning in the passion in his eyes again, and the room spins as he twirls me to a soulful song about young love.

Selena and I make eye contact from across the room and she gives me a small thumbs-up and a smile.

The fluttery feeling in my chest grows stronger the more Hunter and I dance chest to chest, even during the fast pop songs where we scream along to the lyrics. As the dance comes to a close, Hunter says, "Would you like to go somewhere with me after the dance?"

"I'd love to," I reply.

As the dance comes to a close, I realize once I see the duffel bag in his trunk that he's participating in the Senior Swim. It's a tradition for Seniors to go for a late-night swim following the Homecoming dance. I'd never once considered participating since I wasn't even sure if it was just a myth or not.

"Tonight is all your choice, Adele," he says quietly, "but if you did want to swim, I know a place where we can go, just the two of us."

Just the two of us.

The words give me nervous goosebumps.

"I'd like that," I lower my voice a little, "although, I'm still not the best at swimming."

As handsome as Hunter looks tonight, though, I'm not sure how much I want to swim. I think I'd rather get lost in him instead.

Hunter's voice softens. "I'll keep you safe. I know a spot where the waves don't get too rough,"

My tone is playful. "How convenient,"

His laughter, a mix of flirtatious and nervous, fills the car. "I like to be prepared," He pauses. "Are you sure about this though? Because we could also cuddle and watch a movie together. I know how much you like being cozy, and it is a little chilly tonight."

He's giving me another chance to change my mind, and the thoughtful gesture only adds fuel to the fire I have for him right now. Because the way he's been so understanding from the start is making me wild with desire for him right now. Of course, I don't even know where to start with any of the things I want to do, but at least it's there. It's something I thought I was incapable of feeling until him.

He makes me want to explore all of the things I was afraid of. And it's all because with him, I know I have nothing to fear.

After he scans my facial expression for several moments to confirm that I am one hundred percent in for a swim with him, he pulls over to a small rocky clearing.

He closes his eyes while I change in the dark car, fumbling around with my dress. It takes me several minutes to shimmy out of it, but he's patient.

"How did you know my swimsuit size?" I ask quietly, keenly aware that I'm exposed to him a mere few inches away from me.

"I had some help from Selena." His eyes are still clamped shut, but he gives me a cheeky smile and shrugs.

The car begins to feel a lot smaller as it sinks in that he's put a lot of thought into this. He wanted to make every detail special for me.

No wonder Selena was acting so peppy earlier today. I appreciate that she cared enough to plan something sweet for me.

I stifle a laugh as soon as I see the thin, stringy bikini. Of course, Selena would pick something way out of my comfort zone. It is pretty dark outside, and it is Hunter. I trust him. If I'm going to do this, I might as well go all out.

It takes me a few seconds to shimmy into the swimsuit that barely covers anything. I exhale a shaky breath as I smooth down the minimal fabric before finally settling into my seat again.

"I'm ready," I whisper, keenly aware of how his car engine is now off, only emphasizing that it's just the two of us.

His voice is husky as he asks, "Want to go for a swim?"

"Yes," I say breathily.

He helps me out of the door as I climb out with shaky legs. It feels like my entire body is buzzing with anticipation. Is this happening? Then I think back to just how many times he's been intentional and realize that it makes sense that tonight would be no different. It's simply another way for me to express the way I feel about him, just in a deeper way.

His gaze is locked on my own eyes as he reaches toward me and helps me out of the truck. My legs tremble as I step down, reality settling in that we're doing this.

He takes my hand in his, and we walk, our steps in sync, toward a small bay. The peaceful hissing of the waves softly crashing over the sand draws me toward the water. I let out a yelp as my ankles made contact with the freezing water as we slowly wade into our knees. The soft glow of the moonlight exposes me to the outline of his swim trunks. I reach for his chest and my fingers come into contact with his bare skin. Seeing as we are swimming, it shouldn't surprise me, but this is all a first for me. My fingers linger on his heart, aware of the rhythm of his pulse. I can't seem to meet his gaze yet, so I focus on admiring him first.

He's the first to speak. "I was thinking about our conversation last night," His eyes meet mine, and heat is pooled in them. "And I thought this might be a good way to break the ice and make you more comfortable."

"Comfortable with what?" I ask in a teasing tone.

"With being vulnerable," Hunter's voice is gentle. "With letting me show you how I accept you."

"Can I?" he asks, gesturing to my torso.

I nod, but he waits for my audible, "Yes,"

His fingers gently trace my exposed abdomen, running along the line of my scar, moving with it. In response to the tenderness of his touch, my body is electrified. Blood rushes through my head as goosebumps tickle my stomach in a tingling sensation following his every move. He caresses the skin like it's a work of art instead of a scar. And maybe it is because it's a part of my story. His fingers linger at the point where my skin meets my bathing suit. Heat courses through me like a wildfire. It feels like all of my cells are activated as he brushes against my hip. And it takes all my willpower not to wrap my arms around him and pull him in close, closing the space between us.

"You. are. So. beautiful," he says, lightly caressing me with each word, treating me delicately.

I light up under his touch. "Thank you,"

I'm thrown for a loop when he takes my hands, gently maneuvering them over my scar, and placing his hands on top. The heat from his hands, and the intensity of his touch, have my heart tumbling. It feels like the words in my head are jumbled up, and I'm just trying not to explode with desire.

"What's on your mind?" he asks.

My voice is breathy. "I think my mind, heart, and body are all finally on the same page,"

"Is that so?" His eyes tilt up as he chuckles.

I wish I could capture how blissful he looks right now.

I lean into him. "Yes, every part of me is a hundred percent in agreement with kissing you,"

"Well, in that case," He lowers his voice a little. "I'm ready too. But I want you to know though, if it's too much, we'll take a step back and try again another time when you're ready."

"Thank you," I assure him, "but I know I'm ready. Somehow, you giving me the space to let down my walls like this, was what I needed."

My breath hitches as he steps closer to me. If I wait any longer, I might explode from anticipation.

His fingers palm the crevice at the back of my neck and it takes me a moment to catch my breath. A second to remember that it's all real. He looks at me like I'm some kind of gift before he closes his eyes. The moment our lips meet, the strangest euphoric heat flows from the top of my head to my toes. I gingerly reach for his hair, pulling him in as close as I can, feeling the sturdiness of his build. I could spend all night exploring his sculpted edges.

Even flushed against each other doesn't feel quite close enough. One of his hands finds my waist, and I nearly faint from the sensation of so much bliss at once. Kissing him is both a rollercoaster ride and a safe space to land at the same time; he's gentle in all the right ways, waiting for me to respond, but so intentional about the way he leads us.

As we explore each other's mouths, the way we move together feels as natural as breathing. The world stills as I melt into him, rhythmically moving and allowing myself to experience the extent of being caressed by him. His kisses consume me, and I find myself deepening them, drawing him closer until we're pressed against one another as I arch my back and stand on my tippy toes.

This connection to him pulses through me in waves, so quickly that it's almost dizzying, especially since I've never felt this way before. It's both exhilarating and peaceful at the same time.

I'm so caught up in kissing him that I have no concept of time; I have no idea if minutes or hours have passed. It isn't until we're both shivering that we pull ourselves away from each other, albeit begrudgingly. We both chuckle as our teeth chatter in the cold.

Hunter offers me a shy smile, looking equally as out of sorts from the kiss as I am as he takes my hand in his. "I still can't believe how lucky I am to have met you,"

My voice is bright. "Me too,"

"Let's get you warm and home safe," Hunter leads us back to his truck. And instead of staring out the window at the glow of the moon, I keep looking at the man with flushing cheeks and a big smile as he drives a little slower than usual.

When we get home, he gives me my favorite hoodie, packed courtesy of Selena. He plants a delicate kiss on my forehead as he walks me to my door. Our eyes meet, and he gives me a small, hidden smile as if to reinforce that what we shared tonight was just as special to him too. We pause before I head inside, neither of us saying anything else. Everything to be said has already been shared tonight, expressed in unspoken harmony. I beam at him, glowing differently now, just wanting to fully savor this moment.

When my dad asks me about the dance, I try to emphasize the dancing part, but I don't think he fails to notice the extra pep in my step and the flush that is probably still on my neck and face. Sleep comes easily as the joy of tonight washes over me like waves, shaping the dreams I have, which are filled with reminders of him.

CHAPTER 22

"Adele, what a nice surprise!" Shelby says, hugging me as she opens the door.

It's bright and early, and Hunter is at work at the auto shop, which is exactly why I'm doing this now.

"Hi! I hope it's okay I stopped by unannounced," I start glancing back toward my parked car.

"Of course! Hunter is at the shop though, but you probably already know that" Shelby offers me a kind smile.

"I was hoping to surprise him," I hold out the two small bags in my hand. "I brought him a gift, but I don't want him to know it's from me." I've never done anything sentimental like this before, so it feels strange.

"Your secret's safe with me," she replies, pretending to zip her lips with her finger over her mouth.

"Thank you." I pull the picture frame, a black-rimmed frame with the photo I took of him and Shelby before her dance, out of the bag.

"Wow, Adele. This is sweet, thank you!" She grins. "I'll put it in the living room, on our table next to the couch. We'll see how long it takes him to notice. I know he'll appreciate it though. This is our first picture in a long time."

"You're welcome," I hold out the second bag to her. "I got you something too."

She gives me another hug as I hand her the bag. It's something small, just a little set of lotion and lip gloss, but I know she'll appreciate it.

"Do you want to come inside? We could have breakfast together or something," She kicks back the rusty screen door with her foot.

"I can't, but I would love to do that another time," I tell her. "I'm taking my driver's license test today!"

"That's great, Adele! Does Hunter know?" she asks.

I shake my head, trying to contain my excitement. "No, I'm going to surprise him,"

"Good luck, you're going to do amazing," she says.

The smile she has as I walk away is so rewarding.

My dad, who was waiting for me in the car, said, "Are you ready?"

I shrug. "As ready as I'll ever be, I guess,"

"You're going to do great," he tells me.

And I surprisingly do. Aside from my hands trembling during the entire test, and taking forever to take the parking portion, I pass the driver's license test. I am so overwhelmed with gratitude that I cry when I find out.

Dad mistakes my tears for sad ones and offers to take me to lunch.

"I passed!" I explain, "these are happy tears."

"Even better! I'm so proud of you," Dad exclaims. "Let's go out to celebrate!"

We settled on eating at the Coffee Shack because I love people-watching on Main Street, especially now that the leaves are finally changing colors.

"Have you told Hunter yet?" Dad asks.

"How could I have told him? I haven't seen him yet today," I say.

Dad grins. "I guess I thought you text him a lot,"

"Oh, I guess I wanted to wait to tell him in person," My voice goes up an octave just thinking about how excited I am to tell Hunter.

"Good idea, I know he'll be so proud," my dad says.

As I'm about to take a sip of my drink, my dad asks, "So, did you have fun last night? I guess I never got to hear much about the dance,"

I gulp, glad he asked me before I could spit out my drink.

"Yes, it was really fun," I say, searching my brain for a part of the dance to focus on, "it was nice going with Hunter."

"That's good," My dad eyes me from across the table, and his expression is pensive as he arches a brow. "You know, I was talking to his dad for quite a while. Hunter's pretty serious about you."

"Is that something you're okay with?" I ask him, chugging my coffee at this point.

It feels like my throat is closing in. Conversations like this with Dad are still new to me. I'm glad that we're both trying, though, as awkward as it can be at times.

"Yes," Dad pauses thoughtfully. "I never thought I would be, but he's a stand-up guy. And you're all grown up at this point too. I couldn't be prouder of you, you have a really good head on your shoulders."

"Thanks, Dad," I say, squeezing his hand across the table, "I'm happy with him, and I'm serious about him too. That being said, I still am living my life and working toward my goals. Now we're just doing it together."

"What are his goals?" Dad asks.

"He plans on taking over his dad's auto shop," I say.

Dad pauses. "I guess that works out well since you'll be staying nearby too, in Meadowbrook,"

"It does," I say, "but I want you to know, Dad, I'm going to Meadowbrook for me, not for him. It's my dream."

"Trust me, I know," Dad chuckles. "You're one of the most headstrong people I know."

"What does that mean?" I ask, laughing.

"When you were younger, and you didn't want to go somewhere, it was near impossible trying to convince you otherwise. Once you had your mind set on something, there was no changing it," Dad explains.

He notices my silence, and then says, "It's a good thing, Adele,"

I think back to the way that Hunter has become such a huge part of my life in such a short span of time.

"You don't think I'm too set on Hunter, though? You'd tell

me if it was a bad idea?" I ask.

"Not at all," Dad shakes his head. "You've gotten to know him as friends first, so you've seen who he is. And he's not the charming type. He's a good one."

He is a good one.

"How did you know that you and Mom were a good match?" I ask him.

He takes a sip of his coffee, then says, "Because she brought out good parts of me that I didn't even know existed. She inspired me because of the way she treated others, especially how kind she was. And being around her made me that way too. Being with her and doing life with her came as naturally as breathing. Life is hard, Adele, but love shouldn't make it any more difficult. The fight and makeup cycles and up and down drama aren't true love. True love is the kind when you're best friends first."

His words linger in my thoughts for the rest of the afternoon.

~

"I hope it's all right, me dropping by unannounced," Hunter wears a sheepish smile. His eyes gleam with excitement. "I wanted to surprise you."

The worn-out blue jeans he's wearing go perfectly with the cowboy hat he has on.

"You're always welcome to come by," I can't keep my eyes off him as I stand by the door. Realizing I've just been standing still, I say, "Come on in."

"I was hoping to take you to the Drive-In theater tonight," he says, "they're playing a romance movie."

"I'd love that," I look down at my outfit, suddenly feeling underdressed. "Do I have time to change?"

"Yes, of course, I'll just wait in the kitchen," He follows me into the kitchen, making himself right at home, which I love.

The table is scattered with mail, from college promotional letters to bills to documents for my dad's work.

"Sorry, it's so messy in here," I gesture to the pile of papers.

"Adele, you have seen my house, right?" he asks and we share a smile.

I kiss him on the cheek before I go to my room to change.

I flush when I look in the mirror in my room, my thoughts going back to last night.

As we're starting to leave, his truck's engine sputters for several moments, failing to come to life. Hunter mutters an apology under his breath, shaking his head.

Once he sees the concern written on my arching brow, he gives me an embarrassed smile. "Sometimes my car takes a moment to get started,"

"I'm in no rush," I offer him a reassuring grin. "Just enjoying your company."

That seems to calm his nerves a little, as the flush in his face fades and he begins to relax a little. After several minutes, his car does start.

On the drive to the theater, he tells me all about the new romance movie that's playing and I listen intently, touched that he cares enough to plan something special like this for me, especially knowing that romance movies aren't his genre of choice.

He pulls into a space at the back of the lot, giving us the perfect view as well as our own privacy. I nestle next to him in the bed of his truck, wrapping a blanket around myself. I snuggle into his shoulder, and he drapes his arm around me, pulling me closer to him. I do my best to concentrate on the movie, but it's hard to follow the plot when I can't stop thinking about how at home I feel in the embrace of Hunter. Neither of us moves, even as the credits of the movie start playing.

The rumble of the other cars' engines coming to life as they pull away still does nothing to draw either of us out of the perfect little ambiance we've created. After the last car leaves, I find myself humming to fill the silence.

A gust of wind sends shivers down my spine, and I wrap the blanket closer around myself to ward off the chilly air.

"Adele," Hunter begins, giving me a warm look as our eyes

meet.

"Yes?" I ask, feeling a flush creep up my neck.

"Could you sing for me?"

I glance up at him, surprised to find the way his lips tilt up as I nod my head shyly.

"Yes," I murmur, "I sing better when I'm standing though."

He pulls me to him as he helps me stand. I get up a little too quickly and almost bump into his chest.

He chuckles as he steadies me. "I've got you, Anderson. I won't let you go,"

I move my hands from his sturdy chest to his back as I work up the courage to sing.

I haven't sung before for anyone other than my parents; even Selena hasn't heard me sing for her.

I let my eyelids flutter shut as I begin vocalizing the lyrics that I've written about him.

I start singing cautiously and quietly, feeling my voice quiver as the words I've been unable to express in speaking tumble out. I think back to the way I felt so much safer blending into the background until Hunter patiently gave me the space to open up more. The song I'm singing to him is an expression of the fears that initially held me back. That trepidation sometimes still does. But, I'm here now.

My eyes being closed increases my awareness of my other senses, like the comfort of Hunter's touch as he delicately traces little circles in my palm with his thumb. As I open myself in this new manner, I just hope he knows how much he means to me. Maybe this song will change that.

My voice becomes smoother and richer as I become more comfortable, allowing myself to use my entire range to sing my heart out. I increase the volume of my singing until I'm belting the way my mom used to. I cautiously open my eyes, surprised to find the way his irises light up as our eyes connect.

Wandering in the dark
Can't see where to start

Cuz this is my first time
It feels like in a long time
That I've tried
And I don't wanna lose sight
Of why I made these changes
And one mistake could erase it

One step in front of the other
I can't get too close to another
After what I've been through
It feels like it's no use

Expanding my world
One step at a time
Taking back memories
That should have been mine

I'm scared to fall again
And Cuz I know that I'd shatter
And I used to be fearless
But this is me after

I can't take a chance
When everything's tainted
So why chase romance
When we might not make it

One step in front of the other
I can't get too close to another
After what I've been through
It feels like it's no use

Expanding my world
One step at a time
Taking back memories
That should have been mine

I'm scared to fall again
And Cuz I know that I'd shatter

And I used to be fearless
But this is me after

I lean into you
But never too close
Can't tell you the truth
That's just how it goes

It feels like the breath has left my lungs as I finish the song, and I'm unsure if it's because of how wholeheartedly I sang or because of the way Hunter is looking at me as if I was made just for him.

"Wow," he whispers, "I love that song. I don't think I've heard it before."

I glance down. "That's because I wrote it,"

He cups my cheek with his hand, tilting my chin up. "You wrote that?"

I nod my head. "Yes,"

"Wow, Adele," He gently tugs me a little closer until we're flush against one another. I can feel the way his heart is pounding a little, and I wish I knew what was going through his head right now. Does he also feel the way this connection between us is growing stronger? It feels like we're on the same wavelength right now.

He leans down so that he's at eye level with me, giving me a front-row seat to the emotion written all over his face: adoration. "How did I get so lucky?" He tenderly outlines my features with his hand. "I can't believe you're real."

I can't believe he's real.

I tighten my hold on him and goosebumps form all over my body. "I'm the lucky one,"

I take a little shaky breath, for courage, and then I lean in until my lips lightly brush against his. Joy floods my body as I gently kiss him. After we break apart, I tilt my head back and let a smile take over my face. I haven't felt this weightless in years.

CHAPTER 23

Hunter's shoulders sag as the blaring loud scoreboard dings to confirm that it's too late. Harmony Falls lost the championship in a split-second play. Although Hunter threw the ball across the field to one of his teammates, a guy from the opposing school jumped in front of our player and caught the ball, ruining our chance at a victory in the first playoff game.

It feels like time stills as our usually peppy student body of fans becomes eerily silent as well as processes the outcome of the game. We lost at home, which makes it feel even more discouraging.

The bleachers are uncharacteristically quiet, with all of the dejected classmates still letting the news sink in. My heart feels heavy in my chest at the thought of what Hunter has been working so hard toward not coming to fruition.

I want to rush toward Hunter but I don't even know what to say. How can I comfort him with the right words when this is something that he's been striving toward for years? I don't even know much about sports, but even I know the significance of winning a championship as a Senior, which makes this loss even more devastating.

As I begin making my way toward the field, I feel my heart start doing somersaults in my chest as he stops the other team from walking away, insisting on giving each guy a handshake. Slowly, the rest of our players follow suit, hesitantly offering their congratulations to the winning school. The tension subsides as the response shifts from sorrow to peace.

Hunter's smile lifts a little as soon as he sees me. I can feel him holding back a little, probably because of the small moisture

I see in his eyes. He's distraught, and rightfully so.

I settle on saying nothing, instead pulling him in for a close hug. His body melts into mine as I support him this time, allowing him to relax as the weight of the loss settles in for him. I rub small circles on his back.

His whisper tickles my neck, "Can we go somewhere? It hurts being here,"

I nod, keeping my arm around him as I walk with him toward his car.

Once we're inside, he lets out a shaky breath. "I still can't believe it,"

I scooch closer to him, nearly resting on the small drink holder that separates our seats.

"Come here," I breathe.

I give him the space to just be, even if it's only for a moment, knowing that reality will sink in.

His eyes glisten with unshed tears as he whispers, "Football was the only thing I was good at, and I even screwed that up. If I would have just thrown a better pass..."

I gently press a finger to his lips. "Yes, you're talented at football, but you know what else you're incredible at?" I pause, "being an amazing man."

His lips part and tickle my finger as he says, "You're not disappointed in me?"

I shake my head and murmur, "Never. I'm so proud of you for showing up to the game and doing your best. Mostly, though, I'm proud of the person you are,"

I see the wheels turning in his brain, doubt forming for him as his eyes tilt down, so I plant a delicate kiss on his lips

Once we break apart, he murmurs, "Thank you," Just his tone sounds lighter. "Just for being you, Anderson. It's nice having you in my corner."

"There's nowhere I'd rather be than by your side,"

I throw myself into showing him: lightly tracing circles on his back, pressing my lips against his until we need to come up for air.

His lips flushed against my neck. His hands tangled up in my hair.

The unspoken words of dreams lost are somehow brought together by a courage I didn't know I could have but letting down my guard comes easier when it comes to him. I completely come undone in the hopes that I can show him just how much he means to me.

"I," I plant a kiss on his cheek. "Am," I pull him closer to me, till we're nearly at the threshold that can't be crossed in a car. It reminds me of the night we went swimming, only this somehow feels more intimate, despite both of us being fully clothed right now. "Proud of you."

As much as I want to spend the rest of the night in Hunter's car, we decide that it'd be best for us to go somewhere together so that we don't get carried away.

Hunter's eyes are far away as he drives us to a party that his team is throwing. It feels weird to go to a party after the game but it must have been planned before the loss.

I can see the wheels turning in his mind as his doubt settles in. My words might not have been enough.

He offers me a convincing smile, and I decide to keep quiet. Maybe all he needs is some company.

I shudder at the location of the party, as the events from last time come racing back to me at record speed. All of the cruel remarks and the way I felt so frozen, completely powerless under Mitch's hostile touch until Hunter stepped in.

Hunter turns toward me and gently whispers. "We don't have to go in, Adele. I didn't realize it was at Sean's house,"

I see the empty expression in his eyes and feel my heart restrict, wishing that I could be better at expressing words that could comfort him after tonight. "It's okay," I reassure him, "I know I'm safe with you."

He reaches for my hand, sending trickles of waves up my forearm. "I'll always keep you safe, Adele,"

Once we're inside the party, Hunter stays by my side, his arm wrapped around me. His eyes scan the party as if looking for a threat, and I can't help but feel guilty. This party is for him and his teammates to come together after a loss; it's not about me.

"I'm going to use the restroom," I lie, "why don't you go catch up with your teammates?"

His shoulders tense a little. "Are you sure?"

I nod, searching his eyes. "Yes,"

His tone softens a little. "Okay," His irises meet mine, still containing the same intensity as earlier. "Please text me if you need anything, and I'll be right there."

I gently squeeze his shoulder. "Thank you, I will,"

Panic rises in my chest as I walk toward the restroom. Now that I'm further into the house, I need a moment to myself to calm down as the awful way I felt the last time I was here all comes back to me.

After a couple of grounding breaths, I remind myself that I'm safe. I'm okay now. It still fails to soothe the knot forming in my stomach.

The walls become a little blurry as I make my way back to the living room, where Hunter is talking to Sean.

I feel a lump in the back of my throat once I see the way Hunter's shoulders are tense as he waves his hands around.

His back is to me.

As far as I know, Hunter and Sean tolerate each other, but they're not buds.

I step a little closer, blending into the background so well that no one notices me.

Only when I hear what Hunter's saying, do I wish I had waited another moment to come back.

"I'm just checking," Hunter barks, "that he is not here tonight."

Nausea rises in my body because I know exactly who Hunter is talking about. Mitch.

Sean tries to keep his voice level, but I can tell from his body language that he's frustrated with Hunter for making a scene. Sean is way too concerned with his image and puts that first and foremost, which is why he failed to do or say anything when Mitch put his hands on me. Sean clears his throat. "Come on, just enjoy the party. He's not coming until later. You'll already be long gone,"

"That's not good enough," Hunter spits out, "we're supposed to be a team."

Sean lowers his voice a little. "Look, dude, I see where you're coming from, but I can't light myself on fire for you. You know Mitch would freak out if he wasn't invited tonight,"

Hunter's voice becomes gruff, almost like his dad's as he quips, "I still can't believe this. I thought you were better than this, Sean."

Sean hangs his head down. "Yeah, well, I thought we were going to win tonight, but we can't always get what we want,"

This seems to be the breaking point for Hunter, who raises his voice a little. "Screw this. I'm done with this,"

Sean puts his hands up and takes a step back. "Go home and get yourself together, man."

Hunter looks like he's going to lunge forward, so I step forward, lightly grabbing his hand.

I clear my throat, not even bothering to look at Sean, knowing my anger at him will be evident in my gaze. I make it known in my tone instead. "Let's go, Hunter. Anywhere but here,"

Hunter's expression softens a little when he sees me. "Sounds like a plan,"

I gently squeeze his palm in mine as we make our way out of the party, practically having to push past people because it's so crowded. It makes me want to go home even more.

Once we're inside Hunter's car, he pulls off by the little lookout area near the hills. Neither of us says anything, not in the mood to get out of the car and see the view. We've both got too much swimming in our minds right now.

Hunter is filled with rage and disappointment, and I'm filled with anxiety right now. Quite a pair we make.

Hunter finally speaks up. "I'm done with this town,"

I glance toward the sparkling water, illuminated by the

moon, just outside of the hills. "This town, or certain people?" I prompt him gently.

His eyes soften a little. "Some people," He sighs. "Mainly, though, I'm just sick of screwing things up."

I want to reach for his hand, but I don't, too afraid to ruin this chance for him to open up. "What do you mean?"

He pauses. "I know I got a little carried away in there with Sean. I was a little too protective of you. I think I just get a little too invested sometimes," He gingerly clasps my hand in his.

I'm aware of the heat reverberating throughout my body in response to his touch. I need to get inside before I find myself crossing any lines in an attempt to comfort him. "I know, and I love that about you,"

I pause, and my heart stops in my chest.

Did I just say that out loud?

The horrified look on Hunter's face tells me I did.

Now was probably not the best time to realize that I am in love with Hunter.

His hand goes limp in mine, and his lips tilt down into a frown. "Let's get you home,"

The words echo in my head: no 'I love you; back.

The blast of the heater is the only sound for several moments until Hunter takes an audible deep breath.

"I've loved getting to know you," Hunter pauses. "But I think we should break up."

He says it so matter-of-factly like it's some kind of business deal he's changed his mind about. Like I haven't spent hours kissing his face off. As if we haven't shared secrets and formed a deep friendship.

He speaks so certain of it that I realize I do have no choice in the matter. There's no need to beg, negotiate, or plead with him.

He's done with us. I can see it in his eyes, in the blank stare he gives me; the abrupt way he lets us go, without a reason why. It feels like the air is sucked out of my lungs.

"Did I do something wrong?" My voice is shaking, on the

verge of tears.

It feels like this is a bad dream, but the hot air blowing my waves in every direction, and his silence, are both tangible reminders that it's not. Because if this was a dream, I could change the ending.

His voice is harsh and emotionless. "No, it's just better to do this now,"

His eyes look hazy and distant.

The entire car becomes blurry as my eyes tear up. I try to hold my tears in, telling myself I can cry all I want later, but not in front of him. I want to reach out to him to feel his hand in mine, but he has a tight grip on the steering wheel. The blasting heat adds salt to the wound because I feel all sweaty and flustered.

"You're not going to say anything?" he asks.

"It sounds like you're already set on throwing us away," My voice wavers. "What did I do wrong? I don't understand."

My eyes betray me as tears come flooding out. My throat feels scratchy from trying to hold my sobs in.

"Your fire is one of my favorite things about you," He turns toward me. "Please don't lose that in some attempt to be what you think I want, because you are what I want. You, being yourself. I want the best for you, Adele, even if that's not with me."

Doesn't he know that his breaking up with me doesn't feel like he's letting me go? It feels like I've been completely blindsided here, fumbling around in the dark."

I can't even meet his eyes. "Was I just too much? Because that's what it feels like,"

He softly drums his fingers on the steering wheel. "Not at all, Adele. I loved being with you. I'm a better man with you,"

His use of the past tense almost shatters me.

"What is it then?" I ask in a soft voice, holding back the wretched sobs I know I'll be crying the second I'm alone after he officially tells me that this is it. The end I finally stopped dreading, stopped predicting, has finally come, way earlier than

I thought it ever would.

"We're just going two completely separate directions. I refuse to be the man to hold you back from what you want," Hunter's words sound rehearsed as if this is some kind of script he's memorized. Why would he even think that?

"That's not what I want," I plead. "It's never been what I wanted."

"I'd rather be the boy who broke your heart than the man who kept you from a better life," His eyes darken when he sees me.

"If that's what you believe, then you don't know me at all," I spit out, "I thought what we had was real."

I fight the urge to slam the car door as I get out, mustering all my self-control to keep it together.

This is my first breakup but there's something about being broken up with at such a vulnerable moment that makes it sting more.

It feels like my heart has just been ripped out of my chest.

Hunter pulls up to my house, and I won't turn back, but I know he's going to wait until I'm safely inside to drive off. The gesture makes him throw us away even more because it makes it so confusing.

The rain is pounding down and I don't even bother covering my head as I walk inside my house, storming through until I get to my backyard, where I allow the rain to melt into the tears streaming down my face. I cry until I'm shivering, soaking wet, and defeated beyond repair. The guy who helped me shine brighter took all the light inside of me until I had nothing left.

CHAPTER 24

"You need to go to school today," Dad says, referring to me skipping school yesterday.

All of my mail is still spread out on the kitchen table, and I groan when I push it aside, attempting to eat some toast. My first "real" meal since the breakup. I haven't even told Selena about it yet, because I know she's going to chew him out. I'd rather just keep the last of the dignity I have left.

"Please, Dad? My grades are good," I plead.

"This isn't about grades," His voice softens. "It's about you ensuring that you don't let him take away your joy. You have a life to live."

"I just feel so humiliated," I sigh in frustration. "You don't even understand; I have no closure: no explanation, nothing."

"I know you're hurting, Adele," He gives me a pointed look. "But you can't allow it to cause you to go backward."

"Fine," I know he's right. "Since you're off today, could I please borrow the car? I think driving myself to school will help clear my head."

"Of course," he says, "Now go. You're already late!"

At school, my head is still pounding from crying all day yesterday. I stop in the musty, dim bathroom on the way to the first period for a quick appearance check. The puffiness of my eyes and the frizzy state of my hair confirm that I do look like someone who got dumped. At least I fit the role. I try to put a little lip gloss on, but it doesn't help. Even my skin looks lifeless today.

"You look awful," Selena says at lunch. "Are you okay?"

"Thanks," I say, my voice sharp as I push around the food on my plate.

"What happened?" she asks.

We're eating lunch on a bench outside because I couldn't face the idea of having to see Hunter today, especially not like this. However, I will have to see him in AP Chem, which I am strongly considering skipping.

"Hunter broke up with me," Even saying the words out loud makes my heart drop. It feels like I'm reliving the way he just cut the cord so easily as I broke down. Was it that easy for him to just walk away, after everything?

She leans in and nearly knocks her water bottle over as she shakes her hands around.

"He what?" she asks, her voice lowering into an angry whisper.

That makes two of us.

"He dumped me," I recall, "right after I told him I loved him and kissed his face off."

"Oh my gosh, Adele, I'm so sorry," Her eyes search mine. "Why did you wait this long to tell me?"

"I was embarrassed," I say, "especially since you were so nice about making Homecoming special, which somehow made getting dumped worse."

My eyes sting with tears again, and I frantically wave at my eyes, trying to fan away the incoming tears.

"Adele, I just can't believe this. He's so into you," she murmurs

"I thought so too," I let out a shallow breath. "And I want to show up and be confident, but it's just driving me nuts how he completely shut me out. I don't even know how to move past this."

"We'll get through this together," She tries to sound convincing, but I know she knows this will take me out for a while.

I offer her a half-smile. "Thank you,"

Her tone is gentle. "Did he say why?"

"Nope, it was sudden," I explain, "something confusing about him not wanting to hold me back."

"Maybe he just needs some time," Selena assures me, "if I were to guess, something bigger is going on."

I set my food down, still too upset to finish it. "I just wish he hadn't cut me out,"

"Give him some time, Adele," Selena meets my gaze. "And if he doesn't offer you an explanation, then you'll know that it was for the best."

My chest feels hollow as I go through the motions for the rest of the day, especially when there's no sign of Hunter at AP Chem or PE.

I'm driving home when I get a phone call from an unfamiliar phone number. I slow down as it connects to my Bluetooth. The sound is muffled.

"Hello?" I ask, assuming it's from Meadowbrook University.

"Adele? It's me, Shelby," Her voice sounds so broken that my heart sinks.

"Is everything all right?" I ask.

"I don't know," Shelby sighs. "Hunter gave me your phone number a couple of weeks ago, in case of emergencies. I hope it's okay I'm calling you; I'm just stuck at a friend's house, and Hunter hasn't been picking up his phone."

"You're always welcome to call me," I reassure her, "Where are you?"

She gives me her address and I rush over as quickly as I can. My tires creak as I press on the gas, fearing the worst.

Shelby comes running over to my car, her eyes misty and puffy. Her breathing comes out in the labored breaths I know all too well, panic.

"Are you all right?" I gently ask as she climbs in my car.

"I will be." She offers me a hesitant smile.

"Breathe," I instruct her, softly counting to four, and having her follow along.

Inhale. Exhale.

Somehow helping her do it helps me to calm down too.

I stay quiet as I drive us to her house, realizing it's the

furthest I've ever driven. I keep my eyes locked on the road as we ride in silence.

"Thanks for the ride," Her voice is still quiet. I want to hug her, but I've got both hands on the wheel, so I just nod and smile.

"Anytime," The tires of my car creak as we pull up to her house. "I'm here if you want to talk about what happened."

"Thank you," Shelby replies. "Hunter was supposed to pick me up, and I guess I just started freaking out when he didn't show. I started getting all shaky."

"Hey hey, it's okay. I'm sure he has a reason for being late," I assure her.

"He's been acting weird lately," Her voice is laced with concern.

I offer her a reassuring smile. "Let's get you home safe, and then we'll figure out what happened to him,"

"Thank you,"

Once we're at her house, I see his truck parked out front, serving as a painful reminder of the last place I saw him before we ended. My heart sinks when I think back to the breakup.

Shelby sighs and visibly relaxes. "He's okay,"

My breathing slows as it sets in that he's all right.

I offer her a small smile. "See? Everyone's home safe,"

"Thanks, Adele. I just thought the worst when he didn't show," Shelby smiles shyly. With her hair in braided pigtails, it strikes me how the few years that separate us should be a big gap, but I feel so close to her.

"That's a completely normal response," I reassure her, "Thanks for trusting me."

"For what it's worth," Shelby faces me. "I think he made a huge mistake letting you go."

Tears sting my eyes, so I just glance down. "I'm sure he had his reasons,"

"Well, I look up to you," Shelby's bright eyes meet mine. "Even more so now that you helped me, especially when you had no reason to."

"I'll always help you, Shelby. Regardless of what happened

between your brother and me, your family will have a special place in my heart. I'm always here if you ever need anything," I respond.

"Thank you," she says.

She gives me a quick hug and my throat constricts as she walks inside, likely to come face to face with the man I'm lovesick over.

My knuckles turn pale as I squeeze the steering wheel for dear life, overwhelmed by the realization that I am not familiar with driving this far.

It's only a fifteen-minute drive, but every second goes by agonizingly slowly. I pull over to the side of the road, my hands trembling as the cars whiz past me, disappearing far ahead of me in a flash. With a shaky breath, I pull myself together and attempt to make it home in one piece. Numbness replaces fear as I begin to pull into my driveway, and I wish it hadn't.

"It's going to get easier, kiddo," Dad remarks when he sees me and takes in my disheveled state.

"I sure hope so," I mutter, "remind me to never fall in love again."

"If you're hurting," he pauses, "I know he's hurting too, kicking himself for letting you go."

"I want him to be happy though," I say, "even if it's not with me, I guess."

Once I'm in my room, I pick up a romance book for the first time in weeks. Once Hunter was in my life, I didn't feel the need to escape anymore. I already had everything I could have ever dreamed of. I scroll through a few pages and my legs start bouncing up and down as I become restless, because even the most thoughtful remarks, the most passionate kisses, and the craziest romantic gestures could never live up to Hunter. I like the fact that what he and I shared was down to earth. It makes losing it harder though.

Even humming one of the songs I wrote does nothing to soothe my sorrows like it usually does, because it just takes me back to the night I sang for him.

My dad calls my name for dinner, and I freeze because all I want to do is sulk in my room, but I pick myself up and drag myself into the dining room.

My dad insists we say grace, which is something we haven't done in years, and I don't feel like I'm going through the motions when we do it. It feels like something is changing.

"Look, Adele," My dad clears his throat. "I know you don't want to hear this, but I need to say it."

"Go right ahead, I'm listening," I sigh. "It's only been a couple of days and I'm already driving myself up the wall. I'll take any unsolicited advice at this point."

Dad softly clears his throat. "I know this is hard, especially since it's so unexpected," Dad begins.

"But?" I ask, waiting for this part of his speech.

"But," he says, earning a smile from me, "I think you need to think about how you are going to respond to this. How are you going to grow as a person from this? In case it isn't already clear, Hunter is not going to be a guaranteed part of your life anymore."

I exhale a shaky breath. "Geeze, dad,"

He's right though. I can see now that maybe, just maybe, I was leaning on Hunter a little too much.

"How are you going to move forward in your own life?" he asks, "because this could be some setback, the reason why you spend the next couple of months sitting in your room in sweatpants, or it could be a new opportunity for you to keep the momentum you've had going in living your own life."

I see what he's saying now: keep going.

My tone sounds as exasperated as I feel. "I guess I've just lost my way, and I don't know how to get back,"

"I have some ideas," Dad remarks.

When I arch my brow at him, he chuckles and says, "I was off today, so it gave me some time to think about this,"

"Well, I hope you're not worried," I respond. "I'll get my fire back."

"That's the spirit," my dad says.

As soon as I'm pulling onto the highway, I turn to my dad and ask, "Remind me why we're doing this again?"

I squint my eyes to try to see the hilly mountain road. My foot feels as heavy as a lead weight as I keep it pressed on the gas. I shake as I try to keep up with the surrounding traffic. I'm driving to Meadowbrook, the furthest I'll have ever driven.

According to him, this is the best way to take my life back.

"Take the next exit," Dad instructs, "and turn right away."

I sigh with glee as I pull out and see a flashing neon sign called "The Cafe", which contrasts the small dark parking lot.

Dad and I snake through a small dark opening in the hole in the wall building. Loud music rings in my ears as we make our way through. On the small stage, the singer's soulful voice fills the entire space. Sharpie lines of different colors, sizes, and fonts cover the walls in sad poems and lyrics.

"How did you know about this place?" I whisper yell to my dad as we settle into a small leather couch in the corner.

"Your mom took me here when I first met her," He looks around the space. "It was the cool hangout spot for our college. It looks like it still is. I just thought it'd get your mind off of things."

I just smile at Dad, completely unable to picture my dad coming here during college. The people around us are all hunched over notebooks, typing away on their laptops, or softly strumming on various guitars and ukuleles.

As I sip on my hot chocolate, Dad points to something behind me. "Maybe writing something on the wall will help,"

I look over to where he's referring, and see a black Sharpie hanging from a string on a wall with lots of quotes and poems on it. A small sign says, "Fill the blank space and let your heart speak,"

On shaky legs, I walk over and think about what to say.

My handwriting is jagged and uncertain as I write,
I've held on for so long
It feels like I belong
As the girl who's
Got it all under control

My hands are tired
And my soul's weary
But I'm scared to leave behind
The things that make me

It's not my role
I'm releasing control
And starting this moment
I'm letting it go

I love Hunter, I'm certain of that, but I'm not going to lose myself in the process of losing him. And for the first time since the breakup, I feel a little more like myself again.

CHAPTER 25

After Coach Z called me into his office to "check in", I walk toward my car, both frustrated at getting out of school late and at how heavy my backpack was today. Mainly though, I'm just distraught over Hunter.

Coach Z pulled me aside and asked me about the breakup, remarking that both Hunter and I have been off for the last couple of days. I told him that things didn't work out, but that I was capable of being an adult about it, so long as I am far away from Hunter. Coach Z did not appreciate that comment and lectured me for ten minutes about the importance of being amicable. The way the conversation ended, though, really threw me for a loop.

"Don't take it out on yourself, Adele. You owe yourself that much,"

Coach Z's words echo in my head as I storm toward my dad's car. If only he knew how hard it is. The first guy I've ever kissed, someone who's spent time getting to know me and who I've given my heart to, dropped me without good reason. Of course, I'm back to wearing sweats and keeping my head down at school. And yes, it has gone through my head at least ten times today that if I looked like some of the cheerleaders at school, this might not have happened, but at least I showed up to my classes today. And I drove myself. So at least I'm trying.

I halt when I hear Hunter's voice behind me. I nearly trip over my backpack and it takes me a moment to steady myself.

"Adele, wait,"

I almost gasp when I come face to face with him. If I thought I looked down, Hunter looks like he's been hit by a bus.

"Why would you do all that if you were planning on

leaving?" he asks me, his voice broken. "I just don't understand." His eyes are weary, rimmed with dark circles, and I feel an overwhelming urge to hug him and not let go. But he broke my heart with a haphazard explanation for ending things between us, so I just stood with my arms by my side.

The nearly empty parking lot reflects how I feel inside today, completely lifeless. After a long day of going through the motions after our breakup, the last thing I want is to be confronted by the man who dropped my heart.

He takes a hesitant step toward me. His uncertainty shows how we're just strangers now. "The picture frame. Why'd you give it to me if you planned on heading out of state?"

I freeze, startled by him being so direct about something that has no relevance whatsoever to our breakup.

His tone is a little more mellow now. "I found it this morning. I didn't put the pieces together until now that it was from you,"

"I wanted you to see the support you have with your family, for it to feel cozy for you when you're at home. I just thought it'd be a nice reminder." My voice is barely above a whisper.

His shoulders deflate. "I don't understand,"

"Me neither. You're the one who broke up with me, so I have no idea what you meant by me leaving. If I had planned on leaving, I most definitely would not have gone to Homecoming with you," I reply, tears threatening to break loose.

Homecoming. Everything we shared together feels fraudulent after the way he swept everything from under me. I notice his eyes narrow at my mention of Homecoming and I can't help but wonder why. Why is he hurting when he chose this? Why couldn't he choose us?

"Look, Hunter, it's cool. We can still see each other around and stuff," I wave between us, "I get it. Football season is over, and you were having second thoughts. It's okay, I won't act all crazy about it."

"That's not it at all. I just, I wish things were different,

Adele," he says, his eyes downcast. "You have no idea."

"Could you be more specific please?" I ask, my voice strained.

Seeing him all distraught like this, over something he initiated, is indeed going to drive me to start acting crazy.

His shoulders slump as he murmurs, "I just wish you were staying,"

"I never left!" I say, exasperated. "You left me! And I still don't know why. Imagine how I'm feeling, because last time I checked, I was kissing your face off, half-naked, and then you leave me days later with some lame excuse of not wanting to hold me back when I have never once done anything to make you feel that way. I just wish you would have communicated with me if you do feel like I think I'm better than you or whatever."

The gusts of wind begin picking up as the clouds darken around us.

My eyes water because of the breeze.

"That's not it, not at all." He takes a hesitant step closer to me.

"Can you please share what's been going on?" I ignore the anticipation in my body, especially the heaviness of my chest.

"When we were at your house, I saw all of the letters," he murmurs.

"What letters?" I ask, giving him a blank stare.

I'm shivering under the frigid breeze, so he puts his jacket around me in a stiff motion. He pulls away from me as he lets go of the jacket, acting as if I'm some kind of object that will explode if he comes too close.

My body doesn't match his energy; instead, my body wants to melt into him. I pull the jacket tighter around myself.

"The ones from all of the out-of-state colleges," he explains, "It made me realize that we don't belong together. It wasn't going to work out anyway, so why not just end things now? I can't be the guy that keeps you in this town, especially if it's not what you want. I'd rather you be happy."

"Then why didn't you ask me?" I ask.

He pushes his hair out of his eyes. "About what? I already knew you were going to medical school,"

I regret not telling him about my plans to teach, wondering why I thought it was a good idea to surprise him. It hurts that he didn't give us a chance.

"About the letters," I lower my voice a little. "Why didn't you ask me about what I want instead of just assuming?"

His words stir something in me. "What is it you want?"

Our eyes meet, and I look into his soul, knowing this will be the last time I see him for a while, at least in the sense of being on speaking terms. The thought makes my stomach clench.

"Those letters were just promotions, I'm not even applying to any of those schools," I sigh. "I already planned on going to Meadowbrook University to study Elementary Education."

"What?" His face falls. "Why didn't you tell me?"

He shuffles back and forth, putting his hands in his pockets.

"Because I didn't want you to think I was making that choice for you, but I'm doing it for myself, Hunter. And, I thought you'd know that I wouldn't lead you on. I've been in this since the start," I pause. "If I was dead set on going to a school across the country, I would have communicated that to you because we're in this together. I wouldn't just give up on us." The bitterness is evident in my sharp tone but I want him to know how I feel.

Just the look he gives me lets me know that the trust between us has collapsed. "Well, I wish you would have told me about the teaching and Meadowbrook."

"You're right," I meet his gaze. "I'm sorry for not telling you. You deserved to know."

He looks completely unrecognizable with his baggy hoodie and his deflated posture.

"Hunter, let someone in, please," I plead, "it doesn't have to be me."

"I'm so sorry, Adele," His voice cracks. "I messed up."

He fidgets with his hands in his pockets and I feel myself choke up as I reply, "I'm sorry too, I thought we were building something amazing, but maybe we just weren't ready,"

"Do you think that we could start over?" he asks.

Memories from a couple of nights ago flood my head, specifically the difference between his voice, his gaze, and his touch in comparison to today, as he currently stands three feet away from me.

"I'm sorry. I don't think we can. I think that trust is gone, especially since you broke up with me immediately after we got...involved," I say, my face heating up. "I wish you the best though and I hope you reach out to someone because you need to be reminded that there's way more to who you are than football. I know the season is over, and it sucks to think about what's next when there are so many unknowns, but I can't be with you when you don't recognize all of the amazing reasons why I was so sad to lose you. For me, it was never about football or popularity, or any of that shallow stuff," I wave my hands around as my emotions get the best of me. "It wasn't even about tutoring you or my stupid list. It was about us coming together and building a friendship based on trust, but we can't do that if you don't trust me when I say that I'm fully in this. You need to look at yourself first and figure some things out."

It feels like the air has deflated from my lungs, and I immediately regret my words, wishing I had been more gentle and less harsh about it, especially since he's hurting.

"I'm sorry, Adele. You're right." It takes him a moment to meet my gaze. When he does, I wish he hadn't. The broken smile he gives me nearly rips my heart to shreds.

"It's okay," I say, abruptly pulling the jacket off myself and offering it to him.

"Keep it," His eyes meet mine. "It looks better on you."

I look at it and realize it has his last name etched in white embroidered letters on the back. I take it anyway since it's a tangible reminder that I didn't imagine what happened between us. This way I'll have some confirmation that at one point in time, I meant as much to Hunter as he's come to mean to me.

"Take care, Hunter," I say, slowly backing away until I find my car, the last car in the parking lot.

He remains idling in his car, and I hear the faint sound of country music coming from his radio. He and I play a little waiting game, and I know he's waiting for me to leave, to make sure I get out of the parking lot safely, so I put my pride aside and finally slowly put my car in drive. My hands shake as I hold onto the steering wheel with all my strength, taking everything that I have not to pull over and break down.

I don't even know how to process everything going through my head right now: sadness, confusion, anger, and regret. My mind is spinning as questions and what-ifs spiral through my thoughts, which are centered on being hurt by him. I wait to fall apart until I'm in my driveway.

In the corner of my eye, I see his pickup truck. He slowly makes a U-turn when he sees I've made it safely home, and the gesture of him following me home to make sure I got there safely, even after I chewed him out like that, tugs on my heart. If only we could press rewind and try again. Everything feels so tainted though. I wish I knew what was running through his head and why he didn't just tell me how he felt.

Before I can stop myself, I'm sobbing in my car, hit with the realization that I don't just like him, I love this man. Hot tears sting my eyes and burn at my throat. I cry until I have nothing left to cry. But I have no idea where to go from here, because how can something so special have been ruined so quickly?

CHAPTER 26

Hunter hasn't been to school in two days, but who's counting? I haven't seen him since our hash-out in the parking lot. I've thrown myself into everything I can think of: running, studying, reading. And now, singing.

In a moment of pure desperation to do anything to get rid of the awful sinking feeling in my chest, which constantly feels like someone is sitting on it when I think about Hunter, I signed up for an open mic at the Java Shoppe. Which is why I'm currently tapping on the microphone to see if it's on.

Selena gives me a thumbs-up from the front row. I push my hair behind my ears since it's hanging in my eyes; no more hiding. I'm stepping out tonight.

"Thanks for coming," I announce, looking around the room.

Then, I close my eyes and let the music carry me to another place. My voice shifts from weak and nervous to impassioned and soulful. Everything fades away as I focus only on the soft strumming of Mario on the guitar, the lyrics I've written, and the intense need I have to give this all I have. I pour so much of myself into the song that my concept of time disappears. I don't even realize the song has ended until I hear the applause. My eyes slowly open and I become overwhelmed by the crowd in front of me.

I cautiously step down from the makeshift wooden stage and hug Selena, who cheers me on. "I can't believe you did that!" she says.

"Me neither!" I gesture around us. "I don't think I could've done that with my eyes open. I had no idea so many people came to this."

Since I was the last act, people began to start mingling with each other; huddling in groups. Braxton and Jackie run up to greet me, and it feels great to have made some new friends.

Braxton beams at me. "I told you that you could do it!"

"You did incredible, Adele," Jackie gushes.

"Thank you," I reply, pulling Jackie in for a quick hug. After introducing both of them to Selena and Mario, our little group disperses as the crowd thins out.

I'm talking to Mario and Selena when I see the smile on her face shift as she raises her eyebrows. I turn my head, and my heart drops when I see that she's staring at Hunter. He's standing with a group of guys from the football team, and his eyes meet mine immediately. He smiles for a second, then goes back to looking straight-faced, and my chest sinks. There's nothing that compares to that awful feeling of going back to strangers again.

I turn back to Selena, who tells me, "We can just go out the other exit, Adele,"

Her dark eyes mirror my own conflicted emotions.

I sigh. "I hate this,"

Knowing that he's here in this room, my stomach clenches as all I can focus on is the fact that he and I are no longer together. It's this icky feeling that takes over my head. Sweat forms on my forehead as I forget why I even came here tonight.

Selena has to repeat herself a couple of times, finally raising her voice a little as she says, "Let's get you home,"

"Thank you," I whisper.

I put my arm in hers and I don't look back as we walk out of the Java Shoppe. As we walk to our cars, Selena pauses outside of my car. "Text me when you get home okay?"

"I will, I promise I'll drive safe and slow," I assure her. "I think I'm just going to take a few minutes in my car, I might take a long way home."

"I'm incredibly proud of you," Selena gently squeezes my shoulder. "Don't let seeing him take that away." Her dark eyes are narrow as she mentions him.

"Thanks," I say.

She envelops me in a bear hug before she climbs into Mario's car, waving as he drives away. Then it's just me in the dark parking lot. Everyone has either left or is still inside.

I'm waiting at the curb, gathering myself before climbing into my car, when I hear the voices carry. I can make out a group of five or so guys in the dim parking lot as they walk toward the car. I freeze when I recognize the subject matter they're talking about.

"Your girl was amazing up there," one of the voices says. A couple of them chuckle.

"She's not my girl,"

The harshness of Hunter's voice stops me in my tracks, and I freeze where I'm sitting down by my car. I ignore the chill of the concrete as I try to determine my next steps. Do I hide? Confront him? Go back inside?

Wherever this conversation is headed, I'm not sure if I want to know if that's what he's starting with.

"She's more than that," Hunter continues.

"I still think it's stupid that you broke it off with her, who cares about what Mitch says," the same voice says.

I finally recognize the voice as Sean's. I shudder as the voices become closer.

"It's for the best," Hunter says.

"Is it really, though? Because you've been a wreck since you broke up with her," another voice says.

To my relief, they're all piling into a car as the conversation comes to a close.

"Pull yourself together, whatever you decide. This is a big year for you," Sean says, hugging Hunter as he climbs into the car. It's then that I realize that Hunter is not climbing into the car with them. Not wanting Hunter to see me, I take my chance while they're hugging and tiptoe back inside the Java Shoppe.

The bright and loud atmosphere of the Java Shoppe charges me with exhilaration since I know I need to wait it out until Hunter drives away.

I'm sipping a coffee by myself, waiting as the Java Shoppe

starts to slow down, when I see the last person that I'd expect to see here: Mitch.

Well, now or never, I guess.

His eyes roam over me as he smiles smugly at me.

"Anyone joining you tonight?" he asks snidely.

I stand a little taller. "Just me, but I'm perfectly fine with that," I reply.

"I guess you're not expecting Hunter," he says, "I heard about the breakup." His voice is dripping with conceit.

"What do you want, Mitch?" I ask.

I see other people beginning to leave, and I stand up and start packing up my things, gathering my trash into a pile.

Mitch says, "It's rude to leave a conversation before it's finished."

"I don't owe you anything, Mitch. I have nothing to say to you," I say.

He towers over me with his arms outstretched, blocking my path as I try to walk toward the garbage can. "Well, your Prince Charming isn't here to drive you home this time, I guess you'll have to drive yourself home tonight, Princess,"

His words cause my throat to become tight.

"I don't know what your problem with me has been, and frankly, I don't care." I maneuver around him as I throw my trash away, aware of the way he doesn't move. He towers over me and his lips twist into a menacing smile that gives me chills.

He eyes me once again. "You sure have quite a big mouth for someone so mousy,"

I raise my voice a little louder. "I'm not afraid of you, Mitch. You have ten seconds to leave me alone before I start screaming bloody murder. I don't care that we're in a public place. You need to get away from me,"

"Whatever, I'm leaving," He throws his hands up, nearly knocking me out of his way. "Just remember, Watts saw what a waste of time you are. What'd you do, Adele? Demand he slows down? Use that big mouth of yours to tell him off instead of kissing him?"

Blood pounds in my ears as I hear the ridiculous lies that he's spewing. I start walking out the door, taking big, angry strides.

To my horror, he follows me, and I realize my mistake. His thunderous footsteps are so close behind me that he nearly steps on my foot as he begins to overtake me.

My throat constricts as I think back to the last time that he was close to me, and I remember that that was in public. Who knows what he'll do now that he has the opportunity? I have my keys in my hand, but my car is at the edge of the lot, just out of view.

My heart stills as it sinks in that safety feels unattainable right now.

I think back to the advice my dad has given me and know that I need to get back inside ASAP, especially since the parking lot is nearly pitch black.

My steps pound on the pavement with increased intensity as I throw myself into hurling my body away from him.

Mitch is a few inches behind me, about to catch me once again. My car is still a good twenty feet away, just out of reach. I turn back toward him and see his tall, muscular frame, ready to pounce. My feet remain planted in the ground, feeling like dead weight. It feels like too much at once. My heart is nearly pounding out of my chest. I begin to fear for the worst as I remember the dare that I "owe" him.

"Ah, so you're back to being invisible again now that you and Hunter are over," Mitch snickers.

I know it's my last chance before I have to fight back, so I yell as loud as I can: "I love Hunter, I do, but I refuse to stop living my life just because he broke my heart,"

And then I let out a blood-curdling scream, using all of the breath in my lungs. Time stops as I scream and scream, my knees sinking below me as my fight or flight kicks in. I don't stop screaming and kicking until the flashing red and blue lights become a blur in the dark empty parking lot. The iridescent lights reflect off the concrete and remind me that this is real.

"Hey, I've got you. You're safe,"

I recognize Hunter's voice, whispering in my ear. Just his presence calms my racing pulse.

"I'm going to hold you now, okay? You're about to collapse. Is it okay if I touch you?" he asks.

"Yes," I whisper. My knees give out as I sink into his arms, which gently steady me.

I feel a soft sob escape as the numbness fades away to horror.

"Hey, you're okay, he didn't touch you. I promise," he whispers.

"How do you know that?" I ask him.

He clears his throat as he moves his hand in front of my eyes. I gasp when I see the purple bruises sprawled across his fingers.

"I...I already got suspended for beating him up once," Hunter lets out a shaky breath. "That's why I haven't been at school. I got grounded too, so that's why I haven't reached out."

"What happened?" I ask.

He's about to answer me when Dad comes rushing over. The color is completely drained from his face as he walks over toward me. The sight of my dad is the thing that sets me off and causes my entire body to become one big sob.

The rest of the night happens in slow motion as I answer countless questions from the cops, some of which make me roll my eyes, especially the, "What is your history with Mitch?"

Dad has my back the entire time though and completely chewed out the officer for that one. Needless to say, my dad earns countless brownie points. Although Dad drives me home, Hunter insists on following us in his truck. My eyes become heavy on the ride home as the stress and exhaustion from the day set in. Hunter's presence, though, brings me an overwhelming sense of peace. Dad helps me out of the car, letting me lean on his shoulder as we walk inside.

"I'm too tired to go to my bed, I'll just sleep on the couch tonight," I croak out.

Dad's voice is kind. "If you insist,"

I'm grateful he doesn't question me. Something just doesn't feel right about sleeping in my bed after such a shocking night, almost as if climbing into my bed in my current state would disrupt the comfort that I associate my room with.

I don't want any long-term reminders of tonight. I want to shower and have a clean slake tomorrow.

As I'm settling into the couch, Hunter plants a kiss on my forehead. "We'll talk tomorrow." The gesture almost feels as if I imagined it.

I just nod my head, too exhausted to respond. The faint whispers of my dad and Hunter are the last things I hear before sleep washes over me.

CHAPTER 27

As soon as I wake up, I notice the heaviness in my puffy eyes as I open them. The aching in my arms along with the dark bruises that lune them brings me back to last night.

"I already called your school and explained what happened," Dad says gently. Pink sleep lines frame his puffy eyes. Even his dress shirt is covered in wrinkles. He looks like he didn't sleep a wink last night.

Everything comes back into my mind at full force.

My voice wavers. "I was hoping it was just a scary dream,"

My dad steps across the room to sit next to me on the couch. "How long has that guy been harassing you?"

I'm still curled into a ball with my blanket wrapped snugly around me.

"He doesn't go to my school," I slouch as I think back to the party. "He harassed me over the summer, but Hunter stepped in. He actually kind of helped me before he even knew me well."

Dad's face falls. "Why didn't you tell me?"

"I didn't want to worry you, and besides, I thought it was over. I had no idea he was going to show up. If I had known, I would have," I say.

Anger flashes in Dad's eyes. "He won't be going anywhere near you,"

This doesn't feel real. None of it does.

"Dad, I have no idea what would have happened if...if Hunter hadn't helped me last night. I can't even imagine," I shudder.

"I know. I was up all night just thinking about it," Dad responds, "but, you had a guardian angel watching over you or something."

Maybe so.

"I'm so sorry, Dad. I should have told you," I reply.

"Adele, there's no reason to be sorry," His forehead furrows. "I'm just glad you're okay. I spoke with the front office of your school, and they've approved of you having a week off of school."

"Dad, I can't miss school," I beg, "I'll fail."

"We'll figure something out," he says, "but other things are more important right now, like making sure you're okay."

"I'm fine," I say, "A little shaken up, but fine. Go to work dad, I don't need you to babysit me."

My dad gives me a small smile, then says, "The only reason I'm going to work today is that I'm afraid I'm going to melt down if I don't."

"Dad. I'm fine," I gesture to the couch. "I'll just stay here and rest."

He leans in to hug me, then steps back, saying, "Are you feeling up for a hug?"

I reach out to hug him. "Always,"

As Dad's leaving for work, he reminds me to keep the door locked.

I reassure him, "Dad, I'm going to be fine. I'll bounce back from this. It's what we Andersons do,"

I'm halfway through a movie when I hear a soft tap at my door. I tiptoe to the peephole to see Hunter at the door. I run my hand through my hair, which is flying all over the place, and then decide that it doesn't matter what I look like. At this point, this man has already seen me fall apart anyway. There's no sense in pulling myself together.

"Hi," I whisper, letting him in as I retreat to my spot on the couch.

He stays quiet as he follows me and takes a seat a few feet away from me on the couch.

"Hi," His brows draw together as he looks behind me.

I follow his gaze to the television, where a scene of a girl holding a flashlight walking down a dark alley is playing.

I scramble for the remote and pause it, nearly tripping over myself.

"Are you sure this is what you should be watching, Anderson?" Hunter asks gently.

His use of my last name takes me back because it's been a while since he's called me that. Are we friends again at least? The thought gives me hope.

"It's Hallmark, so nothing bad ever happens," I finally meet his gaze, to find his eyes roaming over me, the worry etched on his face.

"I just wanted to come check on you," He stares intently at me. "But I know you're probably still processing everything. I know I am."

I wrap my blanket tighter around myself, wanting to disappear into the floor just because of how much better it feels having him here. I still care about him too much.

I remain poker-faced, though. The last time I opened myself up to him, he left unexpectedly. Why risk that now?

I simply nod my head, still peering at him.

He scooches closer to me. "Are you okay?"

I say nothing for a few moments and just shrug.

I try to sound less frightened than I feel. "I'm still startled, but I will be okay,"

Hunter's lips are pressed in a hard line. "It felt like my soul left my body when I saw him grab you," He shivers next to me on the couch, and I unwrap my blanket to share with him. Goosebumps cover my spine as we huddle together.

"Thanks again for saving me. I can't even think about what would have gone down if you weren't there," I shudder at the thought.

Hunter faces me. "I'll always protect you,"

I want to ask him why. Why he'd go as far as getting himself injured, but wouldn't fight for us.

"You saved my life," I whisper.

"Adele," He pauses and waits for me to look at him. The regret in his eyes surprises me. "Can we talk?"

"Of course," I take in my appearance. "Can I shower first?"

He flushes and then says, "Take all the time you need,"

"You can wait in my room if you want," I motion toward my bedroom.

I turn the shower to scalding hot, allowing the heat to wash away the icky feelings from last night. Every second helps as the grime is replaced by a silky floral aroma. I tilt my head back and run the smooth shampoo through my hair. The sensation of the water splashing me though reminds me of the night Hunter and I kissed. I try not to focus on it as I dry myself off. I comb through my hair and change into some jeans and a hoodie before joining Hunter in my room.

He's kneeling by my bed, looking at a picture of my dad and me. It's a recent one, of us cooking together and laughing. He's completely unaware that I'm here. I don't miss the way that Hunter's eyes also find the jacket he gave me folded on my bed. I guess I've just been having a hard time letting it go.

"Hi," I murmur.

He nearly topples my nightstand over when he hears me. He groans as he steadies himself. He looks larger than life in my room, hovering a few inches over me. I almost laugh at how out of place he looks next to my lavender walls and white lace bedding.

"Sorry, I didn't mean to startle you,"

"No, you're fine. I'm the one snooping around," Hunter chuckles, and the rich sound fills my entire room with a glimmer of joy.

I giggle. "I have nothing to hide. You're more than welcome to look," I gesture for him to keep exploring my room.

I kneel next to him and cup his chin with my hand. The scratchiness of his scruff tickles my fingers. A corner of his mouth lifts as he raises a brow. Am I really doing this? My pulse slows as the stress of last night leaves my body with just one touch. I could spend all day retracing all of the angles and edges of him. My finger pauses on his lips, and he finally reciprocates, lifting his hand.

221

Only I still as soon as I see it: the dark purple bruises that line his hand. With a shaky breath, I gently fold back his jacket, moving it further up his forearm. His arm goes limp in my hands.

His jaw locks. "Adele,"

My voice quivers. "Hunter," Tears shimmer in my eyes as I delicately caress the marks that line his skin. "What happened?"

"Mitch confronted me at the auto shop the same day you and I had that argument in the rain. He showed up with his fancy car and the biggest smirk on his face, ready to give me a hard time. He started spewing out all these disrespectful things and I just lost it on him," His eyes darken as he recounts losing his temper. "My dad grounded me until I explained what happened, and the school gave me a temporary suspension, which they took back after last night."

"What did he say?" I ask.

"Adele," He leans closer. It's taking all my self-control not to close the space between us. "He was just messing with me and I took the bait. What he said doesn't matter. The thing that matters is the way I focused on reacting to him when I should have been checking on you."

"Why didn't you just tell me what was going on?"

He tenses his arm. "I didn't want to cause you stress. You already had so many other things to worry about," Hurt clouds his features.

I begin putting the pieces together. "Was he giving you a hard time for a while then?"

He grimaces. "I thought it would have ended after we broke up,"

I wince. "I wish things were different,"

He closes his eyes. "Me too, Adele,"

His words linger in my mind as I climb into bed. I'm still processing the chaos of the last twenty-four hours.

Despite all of the craziness, my mind keeps going in a loop, circling back to one thing: I love Hunter.

CHAPTER 28

After spending all week on the couch, I'm anxious to leave the house now that fall break has begun. Dad wants me to rest after the incident at the Java Shoppe, but if I spend any more time stuck inside the house watching Hallmark, I'm going to lose it.

I've been struggling lately, stuck in my head again, replaying everything that happened with Hunter, wondering exactly why we got it wrong.

I need to distract myself. And I know the best way to feel better; help someone else.

"I'll see you in a couple of hours, kiddo." Dad adjusts his mesh hairnet, and I hold back a laugh because I know what's going through his head: his normally impeccably styled hair is going to be sticking out later. He's helping serve food at the Fall Festival at the Community Center while I help kids do fun crafts and games together.

I hug my dad, something we've slowly gotten better at lately. "See you soon,"

I walk into the cheery baby blue classroom where Sandra is already coloring with some of the first kids to arrive. I crouch down on my knees and dive into decorating little trees with them. The sticky glue gets all over my fingers as I help cut little leaves out magazine clippings and from photos. Some of them make family trees using family photos, while others make colorful collages that fill up the entire page.

We switch into a goofy game of freeze dance where the kids encourage me to join in. It isn't until I'm doing ridiculous disco dance moves that I begin to feel lighter. Like everything is going to be okay. I can't stop the laughter that erupts as the kids and I all get into the music. The kids are still giggling as they go to join their parents in the gymnasium, where a makeshift dance floor has been set up.

Sandra walks in as I'm cleaning the classroom. Sandra's eyes sparkle with enthusiasm as she waves me off. "I've got it from here, dear. You go enjoy the dance floor,"

"Are you sure?" I smile at her, looking down at my t-shirt and jeans. I didn't plan on dancing, but maybe it will lift my spirits.

She offers me a caring smile. "Yes,"

As I'm walking out, I turn to face her. "By the way, I'm going to be an elementary teacher. Science Day helped me to decide that,"

Sandra's eyes crinkle as her smile reaches them. "That's just wonderful,"

I look for Dad in the gymnasium but I can't find him anywhere. I turn around, glancing at all of the families gathered around the tables decorated with orange tablecloths and plastic pumpkins. My jaw almost drops when I see Hunter's entire family, including his dad, sitting together. Hunter's leaning into Shelby, who laughs beside him. I'd normally rush over and say hello, but I feel out of place now. I quickly turn toward the exit, deciding to see if my dad is in the hallway.

In the main hallway, I see my dad waving goodbye to Sandra. He frowns when he sees the inevitable blush and scowl on my face.

"You don't want to stay and dance?" His brow furrows.

I look down. "Not tonight," I don't want this to color the amazing experience I had tonight with those kids though, so I force a smile. "I loved tonight though."

"Me too." Dad's hazel eyes light up as he smiles. And I realize this is the happiest I've seen him since my mom passed away.

Dad's facial expression shifts from joy to curiosity as his eyes widen. A rush of warm air from the heated gymnasium behind me flows through my hair.

I turn around to see Hunter. I feel my shoulders tense because I'm not sure where I stand with him anymore. Are we friends again?

Seeing him in his worn blue jeans and a white t-shirt makes my heart pang. Because even him in his work outfit makes me fluttery. But the shy smile he wears, the one that doesn't quite reach his eyes, stirs something in me. It makes me realize that I want to see him look carelessly blissful again.

I'm the first one to speak. "Hi," I offer him a friendly grin, a peace offering of sorts. I want this to go well. I need this to go well. If he walked all the way over here, I need to meet him in the middle.

"I saw you leave, and I just wanted to say hi," Hunter's voice is softer than usual, probably because this is unfamiliar territory for us.

My shoulders slump. He's just being polite, just living out that small-town charm he was raised on. I wish I had the courage to tell him how much he means to me.

"I was hoping we could dance before you go," He's reading my features, but I know I'm expressionless, too afraid to let it show just how overjoyed I am about him being here.

I look over my shoulder at my dad, who gives me a smile and a wave as he begins walking toward the parking lot.

I turn to face Hunter again, taken aback by his invitation.

"I'd like that,"

He encloses my hand in his as we walk together, and I fight the urge to draw circles with my thumb across his hands that are callused from a hard day of work at the auto shop. For some reason, this takes me back to the way it felt to kiss him, so I push the thought aside, keeping my eyes and mind on the dance floor, which is now comprised of couples as a slow melody plays. I arch my brow because a peppy pop song was playing before I walked out.

Hunter picks up on my skepticism. "I might have made a song request," He gives me a sheepish smile.

I'm about to say something witty back when I recognize

the beat and lyrics of the song. It's the same song we slow danced to at Homecoming, there's no doubt about it. I ignore the tingling throughout my body as his hands hold my hips while we move in sync together.

Instead, I lay my head on his shoulder, letting my eyes flutter shut as I allow my instinct to guide my steps as we move together. I soak in the smooth vocals and the protective and caring embrace that Hunter holds me in. As the song fades out and transitions to a more upbeat, funky song, Hunter whispers in my ear. "I was hoping we could talk."

I nod and tilt my head to face him.

He drapes his arm around my shoulder and gives a quick wave to his family, who are dancing together across the dance floor. Shelby and Austin wave at me, and I hold back a smile as Colter gives us an encouraging thumbs-up while he jumps up and down with Hunter's siblings on the dance floor. It sinks in that Hunter's family has taken me in, too. He let me into every area of his life, even the not-so-pretty parts, like the pain he still carries every day.

That's when it hits me. But I need to hear it from him first. It's only fair that I allow him to tell me his side of the story.

I can see him about to speak, but he pauses when he sees the trembling in my arms as we enter the parking lot at the community center.

"I'm realizing that a parking lot isn't the best place for this conversation," Hunter's voice is gentle as his eyes scan my face for the fear that I know is still there.

I just nod and follow him to his truck. I hoist myself up into the passenger seat, acutely aware of his presence right behind me as he closes the door.

He sighs. "You know," His voice is so quiet that I have to slow my breathing to hear it. "I can't even describe the relief I feel every time I see you all buckled up safe and sound in my car."

I stay quiet as he begins driving us, and wonder what on earth he's talking about.

As soon as we pull into a gravel clearing, I speak up.

"What do you mean?" I ask.

"Let's talk outside,"

Once we're in the flower field he showed me weeks ago, he gestures for me to sit next to him on a picnic blanket he laid out in the grass. I want to tell him that I don't feel like sitting, that I'd rather just get this over with, but I hesitate.

I sink into the plush blanket and notice his intent gaze on me as he clears his throat softly. His lips part, and I think back to just how right it felt to have his lips on mine. "Before we dated, I never understood what it felt like to care about anyone outside of family so deeply," He starts, and my heart stills as his dirty blonde eyelashes are downcast as he taps his fingers together. "When my mom left us, I stepped into that role of making sure everyone was okay. Sure, I made that choice, but it didn't feel like it at the time. There's been a lot of moments where I've felt stuck in this town, trapped in a business I wasn't even sure about."

I suck in a breath as I reach for his hand.

It takes him a moment to wrap his hand around mine. The second our hands connect and intertwine, though, I see the specks of green in his captivating eyes as he leans in, and looks up at me for the first time since we've arrived at the field. "I was so caught up in everyone else, that I never checked to see if I was okay. But then, I fell for you, Adele. And, if I'm being honest, even over the summer at that party, I felt like this instinct to protect you, to reach for you. At first, I chalked it up to doing the right thing and making sure you were safe, but it was more than that. I'd always noticed you, even when you thought you were blending in."

My cheeks redden, and I inch closer to him. My thigh brushes against his, and the electricity pulsing through my entire body confirms the effect he has on me. It happened so gradually; I don't know how I couldn't see it. But now that I feel the subtle peace and inclination to connect with him, it's clear. I love this man. The one who puts everyone's needs above his own, who's been barely staying afloat, but has been putting on a convincing smile. The one who's experienced loss, but didn't let it harden his heart.

I need a moment to figure out how to vocalize my thoughts. I gently squeeze his hand, hoping he knows that I understand what he's saying. He's putting his heart on the line for me even though doing so has caused him pain in the past.

His words reiterate this. "I took a look at myself and I began to wonder how I'd be good enough for you. I looked at my beat-up pickup truck and the puzzle pieces I've been trying to put together in my broken family, and I got scared," His voice quivers, but he pushes forward. "But then I realized, you never gave me any reason to feel that way. You accepted me for who I am."

I let out a sad chuckle. "Hunter, I've felt the same way,"

"You have?" He leans in closer to me, turning his head so our faces are centimeters apart.

I nod. I focus on the dirty blonde lashes that frame his eyes and the angles of his jawline as I muster up the courage to be vulnerable. I owe him that much. "I was afraid that I was too weak for you. You seemed to take everything in stride, whereas I felt like I was struggling," A single tear spills out of my eye. "That's why I didn't tell you about Meadowbrook. I didn't want you to realize how behind I am at everything."

His eyes widen. "That's why?"

I nod, feeling exposed under his gaze as we stare at each other.

He beams at me. "But I'm so proud of you, Adele,"

My smile is shy, but joy radiates through me because of his encouragement. "Thank you, Hunter,"

"So," He bites his bottom lip and arches a brow. "It seems like both of us were doubting ourselves."

I shrug. "I guess so. It's probably why I was afraid to tell you that I got my license,"

He gasps, and a grin takes over his entire face. "You got your license?"

I gently nod my head, trying to keep the tears at bay. Because he understands. He knows how difficult this was for me, how big of a step it was for me to get my license, after witnessing the horrific aftermath of the car accident that took my mom from me forever. He saw the panic attacks and the way I couldn't even seem to get my head above water. But he never judged me; he gave me grace.

My eyes linger on his lips. He finally sees me, and that that knowledge has unleashed some new courage in me.

He ruffles my hair with his fingers, and unties it from its clasp in a clip, causing it to unravel into messy waves.

This moment wouldn't feel real to me if it weren't for the single raindrop that lands on my forehead, momentarily breaking up apart. I look up at the dark clouds that loom over us, then back at him.

He wears a flush on his cheeks that I'm certain mirrors my own. "You," His finger gingerly traces the small birthmark next to my eye. "Are," He wraps his arm around my waist. "Something else, Adele Anderson."

I lean on my tippy toes, inching closer to him.

To my surprise, he continues his speech. "You are breathtaking,"

I gasp as he runs a finger across my face and delicately wipes the single tear I just shed away.

He cups my chin and tilts my face to meet him. "I'm sorry it took me screwing up to realize it, Adele, but I love you,"

I lean in closer, basking in the feeling of our faces nearly touching. "I love you too,"

"I choose you," His finger grazes my cheek as he cups my face. "I choose us."

I close the space between us, and part my lips as I plant a kiss on his lips. His lips meet mine, and euphoria floods me. He feels the same

He reaches into his pocket. "I have something for you."

His hands brush against my hair as tousles it. Goosebumps form as he clasps a necklace around me, delicately caressing my skin.

I tilt my head down to see that it's a sterling silver key

necklace. "Wow, this is absolutely beautiful," I muse.

His breath connects with my neck as he whispers, "It was first supposed to be a gift for you taking back your life, but it's also now a reminder that you have the key to my heart."

I turn around and pull him in close. As my lips crash into his, I can't stop the fluttering in my chest as this man has come everything to me. What started as a simple agreement to help each other turned into something that I can see lasting a lifetime. Because now that I know all of the good that can come out of stepping out of my shell like this, there's no going back.

"You have the key to my heart too, Hunter."

ACKNOWLEDGEMENTS

Tremendous thank you to everyone who made this book possible! Thank you, Dad, for supporting me in my journey to drive again! A lot of the conversations we had sparked my interest in exploring the themes of this story. This book couldn't have been possible without your support. I am so grateful for your encouragement. To all of my loved ones, thank you for your enthusiasm about my writing!

And thank you, readers, for supporting my work! It truly means the world to me!

Love,

Elle DeMarco

BOOKS BY THIS AUTHOR

Starlit Chances

The man who broke her heart pushed her into the arms of her best friend, but their fake relationship is just that—fake—right? Lainey left heartbreak behind by moving back to her hometown. She never expected to bump into Jackson, the man who shattered her dreams of a happily-ever-after.

Of course, she didn't expect to start a fake relationship with Aaron, her best friend since childhood.

Aaron has always been there for her through every struggle. But when all she's ever known is heartbreak, Lainey isn't sure she can trust anyone with her fragile heart again. Besides, she doesn't want to risk their lifelong friendship for a relationship that could destroy everything between them.

But as their pretend love begins to feel more and more real, Lainey realizes that the move she made to protect her heart might lead to love. Does Aaron feel the same way; or is it still fake for him?

ABOUT THE AUTHOR

Elle DeMarco currently resides in a quaint coastal town where she dreams up her love stories. She is passionate about writing books that empower others. She especially loves writing romance books where people overcome setbacks associated with difficult circumstances. She enjoys singing, practicing yoga, and spending time with her loved ones.

Made in the USA
Columbia, SC
21 May 2024

35962709R00134